Praise for *Servants of*

"There is simply a sustained beauty of ph[ ] [ ]
to be said and the best way to say it, that [ ] [ ]
priateness that has always characterized the best prose, an atten[ ]
to the truth of human feeling that is in itself a supremely civilized value.
There is a strong and distinctive sensibility at work here, and a talent for
reaching to the essence of experience through scenes of fully imagined
physical description."

—Barry Unsworth, *New York Times Book Review*

"Mind-expanding stories refracted through the capacious imagination of
the author of *Ship Fever* and *Voyage of the Narwhal*."

—*O, The Oprah Magazine*

"Like fossil-hunters, most of [Andrea] Barrett's characters are looking for
a way to piece together fragments of the past; when, in the last story, a
cherished belonging of one character shows up in the life of another, we
feel rescued and redeemed."

—*The New Yorker*

"Barrett constructs out of these half-dozen long stories about scientists
and explorers a fictional archipelago that extends back in time as well as
space."

—Alan Cheuse, NPR

"Weaves a rich tapestry of science and history."

—Mel Gussow, *New York Times*

"A reader familiar with the immediate predecessors of *Servants of the
Map* gradually senses that Barrett is writing a huge serial novel, akin
to William Faulkner's Yoknapatawpha cycle or Louise Erdrich's inter-
connected Native American novels. . . . [B]lends exactitude and com-
passion, giving clarity and emotional force to Barrett's investigation of

people seeking to understand the laws that govern and trouble both the visible universe and their own invariably distinctive bodies and minds."

—Bruce Allen, *Atlantic*

"Ms. Barrett has made the waters that swirl between a love of science and the science of love her special domain."

—*Economist*

"Time and space course through these stories like a river slowly eroding its banks and altering the land upon which we stand."

—*Los Angeles Times Book Review*

"Barrett, wise and restrained, can say more about grief in one exchange than many authors can force into an entire book."

—*Entertainment Weekly*

"Just the usual brilliance."

—*Newsday*

"[Barrett] is surely among the very best writers writing in English today."

—*San Diego Union-Tribune*

"Six short stories that read like a novel. Prose so exquisite it reads like poetry. A natural order so awesome it puts science to shame."

—*Pittsburgh Post-Gazette*

"[Barrett] again explores complex scientific principles with ease and in a prose style saturated with poetic sentiment."

—*Time Out*

"Barrett is one of those rare authors who successfully blend literary finesse with sheer intelligence."

—*Denver Post*

"[These] six tales shimmer with intelligence. . . . A deeply satisfying book."   —*Indianapolis Star*

"Andrea Barrett's virtuosity is as unpredictable as it is compelling."
                                                                —*Tulsa World*

"Lovely, ruminative and mood-drenched. . . . One comes away from *Servants of the Map* with a fortified sense that the world is coordinated and meaningful, a foreign land whose secrets await discovery."
                                                —*Charleston Post & Courier*

"Andrea Barrett blends fact and fiction seamlessly in order to explore the human relationships that drive scientific discovery. For her characters, it's an eternally quixotic quest; for her readers, it's a consistently pleasant journey."   —*Ruminator Review*

"*Servants of the Map* is magical."   —*Nashville Tennessean*

"Another gem among Barrett's list of literary accomplishments."
                                                            —*Columbus Dispatch*

"Luminous. . . . Each [story] is rich and independent and beautiful and should draw Barrett many new admirers."
                                                —*Publishers Weekly*, starred review

"One understands how the intricacies of the complex phenomena Barrett has studied have possessed her imagination. . . . Gorgeous, illuminating, entrancing fiction."   —*Kirkus Reviews*, starred review

"Barrett's characters are deep and self-possessed, and their stories, so intelligently and delectably told, both romanticize and validate the quest for understanding life that drives scientists and artists alike."

—*Booklist*

"More of [Barrett's] unique melding of issues concerning scientific curiosity and featuring richly drawn, complex characters you won't soon forget." —*Book Sense*

ALSO BY ANDREA BARRETT

Natural History

Archangel

The Air We Breathe

The Voyage of the Narwhal

Ship Fever

The Forms of Water

The Middle Kingdom

Secret Harmonies

Lucid Stars

Servants of the Map

stories

Andrea Barrett

100
W. W. NORTON & COMPANY
Celebrating a Century of Independent Publishing

For information about permission to reproduce selections from this book, write to
Permissions, W. W. Norton & Company, Inc., 500 Fifth Avenue, New York, NY 10110

Composition by Sue Carlson
Manufacturing by LSC Harrisonburg
Book design by Antonina Krass
Production manager: Andrew Marasia

Library of Congress Cataloging-in-Publication Data

Barrett, Andrea.
Servants of the map / by Andrea Barrett.
p. cm.
ISBN 0-393-04348-7
I. Title.

PS3552.A7327 S47 2001
813'.54-dc21   2001044209
ISBN 978-1-324-06615-6 pbk.

W. W. Norton & Company, Inc., 500 Fifth Avenue, New York, N.Y. 10110
www.wwnorton.com

W. W. Norton & Company Ltd., 15 Carlisle Street, London W1D 3BS

1 2 3 4 5 6 7 8 9 0

Portions of this book have appeared previously—sometimes in substantially different form—in the following magazines: "Servants of the Map" in *Salmagundi*, "The Mysteries of Ubiquitin" in *Story*, "Theories of Rain" in *The Southern Review*, "Two Rivers" in *Triquarterly*, and "The Forest" in *Ploughshares*. "Servants of the Map" was also included in *The Best American Short Stories 2001* and in *Prize Stories 2001: The O. Henry Awards*; "Theories of Rain" was included in *Prize Stories 2000: The O. Henry Awards*; and "The Forest" in *The 1998 Pushcart Prize XXII*. My thanks to these publications and their editors.

For my Family

CONTENTS

What is life but a form of motion and a journey through a foreign world? Moreover locomotion—the privilege of animals—is perhaps the key to intelligence. The roots of vegetables (which Aristotle says are their mouths) attach them fatally to the ground, and they are condemned like leeches to suck up whatever sustenance may flow to them at the particular spot where they happen to be stuck. . . .

In animals the power of locomotion changes all this pale experience into a life of passion; and it is on passion, although we anaemic philosophers are apt to forget it, that intelligence is grafted.

—George Santayana
"The Philosophy of Travel"

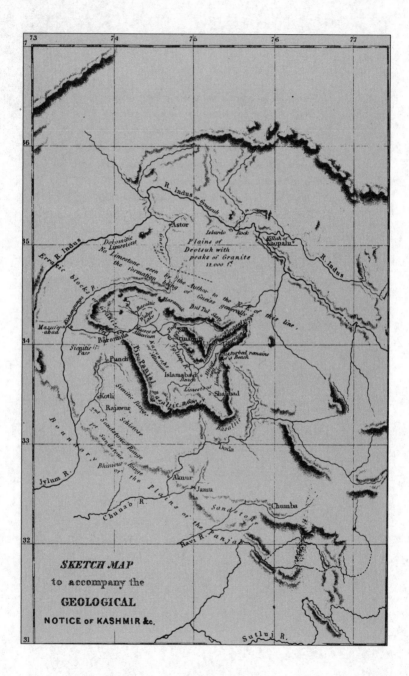

SKETCH MAP

to accompany the

GEOLOGICAL

NOTICE OF KASHMIR &c.

SERVANTS OF THE MAP

1

H E DOES NOT WRITE to his wife about the body found
on a mountain that is numbered but still to be named: not
about the bones, the shreds of tent, the fragile, browning
skull. He says nothing about the diary wedged beneath the rock, or about
how it felt to turn the rippled pages. Unlike himself, the surveyor thinks,
the lost man traveled alone. Not attached to a branch, however small and
insignificant, of the Grand Trigonometrical Survey of India. On this
twig charged to complete the Kashmir Series, he is nothing. A leaf, an
apricot, easily replaced; a Civil Junior Sub-Assistant in the Himalayan
Service.

The surveyor, whose name is Max Vigne, reads through the diary
before relinquishing it to his superiors. The handwriting trembled in the
final pages, the entries growing shorter and more confused. Hailstorms,
lightning storms, the loss of a little shaving mirror meant to send a

glinting signal from the summit to the admiring crowds below—after noting these, the lost man wrote:

> I have been fasting. Several weeks—the soul detaches from the flesh. The ills of spirit and body are washed away and here on the roof of the world, in the abode of snow, one becomes greatly strengthened yet as fresh as a child.

Although Max pauses in wonder over these lines, he still doesn't share them with his wife. Instead he writes:

April 13, 1863

Dear Clara—

I can hardly understand where I am myself; how shall I explain it to you? Try to imagine the whole chain of the Himalaya, as wide as England and four times its length. Then imagine our speck of a surveying party tucked in the northwest corner, where the Great Himalaya tangles into the Karakoram—or not quite there, but almost there. We are at the edge of the land called Baltistan, or Little Tibet: Ladakh and Greater Tibet lie to the east. And it is so much more astonishing than we imagined. The mountains I wrote you about earlier, which we crossed to enter the Vale of Kashmir—everything I said about them was true, they dwarf the highest peaks I saw at home. But the land I am headed toward dwarfs in turn the range that lies behind me. Last Wednesday, after breakfast, the low clouds lifted and the sun came out. To the north a huge white mass remained, stretching clear across the horizon. I was worried about an approaching storm. Then I realized those improbable masses were mountains, shimmering and seeming to float over the plains below.

How I wish you could see this for yourself. I have had no mail from you since Srinagar, but messengers do reach us despite our frequent moves and I am hopeful. This morning I opened an envelope from the little trunk you sent with me. Have any of my letters reached you yet? If they have, you will know how much your messages have cheered me. No one but you, my love, would have thought to do this. On the ship, then during our tedious journey across the plains to the Pir Panjal; and even more throughout the weeks of preparation and training in Srinagar, your words have been my great consolation. I wait like a child on Christmas Eve for the dates you have marked on each envelope to arrive: I obey you, you see; I have not cheated. Now that the surveying season has finally begun and we're on the move, I treasure these even more. I wish I had thought to leave behind a similar gift for you. The letters I wrote you from Srinagar—I know the details about my work could not have been of much interest to you. But I mean to do better, now that we're entering this astonishing range. If I share with you what I see, what I feel: will that be a kind of gift?

Yours marked to be opened today, the anniversary of that wonderful walk along the Ouse when I asked you to marry me and, against a background of spinning windmills and little boys searching for eels, you stood so sleek and beautiful and you said "yes"—it made me remember the feel of your hand in mine, it was like holding you. I am glad you plan to continue with your German. By now you must have opened the birthday gifts I left for you. Did you like the dictionary? And the necklace?

I should try to catch you up on our journeys of these last few weeks. From Srinagar we labored over the Gurais pass, still knee-deep in snow: my four fellow plane-tablers, the six Indian chainmen, a crowd of Kashmiri and Balti porters, and Michaels, who has charge of us for the summer. Captain Montgomerie of the Bengal Engineers, head of the entire Kashmir Series, we have not seen since leaving Srinagar. I am told it is his habit to tour the mountains from April until October, inspecting the many small parties of triangulators and plane-tablers, of which we are only one. The complexities of the Survey's organization are beyond explaining: a confusion of military men and civilians, Scots and Irish and English; and then the assistants and porters, all races and castes. All I can tell you is that, although we civilians may rise in the ranks of the Survey, even the most senior of us may never have charge of the military officers. And I am the most junior of all.

From the top of the pass I saw the mountain called Nanga Parbat, monstrous and beautiful, forty miles away. Then we were in the village of Gurais, where we gathered more provisions and porters to replace those returning to Srinagar. Over the Burzil pass and across the Deosai plateau—it is from here that I write to you, a grassy land populated by chattering rodents called marmots. The air is clear beyond clearness today and to the north rises that wall of snowy summits I first mistook for a cloud: the Karakoram range, which we are to map. Even this far away I can see the massive glaciers explored by Godfrey Vigne, to whom I am so tangentially related.

I wonder what he would have thought of me ending up here? Often people ask if I'm related to that famous man but I deny it; it would be wrong of me, even now that he's dead, to claim such a distant connection. My eccentric, sometimes malicious supervisor, Michaels (an Irishman and former soldier of the Indian army), persists in calling me "Mr. Vaahn-ya," in an atrocious French accent. This although I have reminded him repeatedly that ours is a good East Anglian family, even if we do have Huguenot ancestors, and that we say the name "Vine."

All the men who've explored these mountains—what a secret, isolated world this is! A kind of archipelago, sparsely populated, visited now and again by passing strangers; each hidden valley an island unto itself, inhabited by small groups of people wildly distinct from each other—it is as if, at home, a day's journey in one direction brought us to Germany, another's to Africa. As if, in the distance between the fens and the moors, there were twenty separate kingdoms. I have more to tell you, so much more, but it is late and I must sleep.

What doesn't he tell Clara? So much, so much. The constant discomforts of the body, the hardships of the daily climbs, the exhaustion, the loneliness: he won't reveal the things that would worry her. He restrains himself, a constant battle; the battle itself another thing he doesn't write about. He hasn't said a word about the way his fellow surveyors tease him. His youth, his chunky, short-legged frame and terribly white skin; the mop of bright yellow hair on his head and the paucity of it elsewhere: although he keeps up with the best of them, and is often the last to tire, he is ashamed each time they strip their clothes to bathe in a freezing stream or a glacial tarn. His British companions are tall and hairy, browning in the sun; the Indians and Kashmiris and Baltis smoother and slighter but dark; he alone looks like a figure made from snow. The skin peels off his nose until he bleeds. When he extends his hat brim with strips of bark, in an effort to fend off the burning rays, Michaels asks him why he doesn't simply use a parasol.

Michaels himself is thickly pelted, fleshy and sweaty, strong-smelling and apparently impervious to the sun. They have all grown beards, shaving is impossible; only Max's is blond and sparse. He gets teased for this and sometimes, more cruelly, for the golden curls around his genitals. Not since he was fourteen, when he first left school and began his apprenticeship on the railway survey, has he been so mocked. Then he had his older brother, Laurence, to protect him. But here he is on his own.

The men are amused not only by his looks, but by his box of books and by the pretty, brass-bound trunk that holds Clara's precious gift to him: a long series of letters, some written by her and others begged from their family and friends. The first is dated the week after he left home, the last more than a year hence; all are marked to be opened on certain dates and anniversaries. Who but Clara would have thought of this? Who else would have had the imagination to project herself into the future, sensing what he might feel like a week, a month, a year from leaving home and writing what might comfort him then?

His companions have not been so lucky. Some are single; others married but to wives they seem not to miss or perhaps are even relieved to have left behind. A Yorkshireman named Wyatt stole one of Clara's missives from Max's camp stool, where he'd left it while fetching a cup of tea. "Listen to this," Wyatt said: laughing, holding the letter above Max's head and reading aloud to the entire party. "Max, you must wear your woolly vest, you know how cold you get." Now the men ask tauntingly, every day, what he's read from the trunk. He comforts himself by believing that they're jealous.

A more reliable comfort is his box of books. In it, beyond the mathematical and cartographical texts he needs for his work, are three other gifts. With money she'd saved from the household accounts, Clara bought him a copy of Joseph Hooker's *Himalayan Journals*. This Max cherishes for the thought behind it, never correcting her misapprehension that Sikkim, where Hooker traveled in 1848, is only a stone's throw from where Max is traveling now. At home, with a map, he might have put his left thumb on the Karakoram range and his right, many inches away to the east, on the lands that Hooker explored: both almost equally far from England, yet still far apart themselves. Clara might have smiled—despite her interest in Max's work, geography sometimes eludes her—but that last evening passed in such a flurry that all he managed to do was to thank her. For his brother Laurence, who gave him a copy of Charles Darwin's *Origin of Species,* he'd had only the same hurried thanks. On the flyleaf, Laurence had written: "New ideas, for your new life. Think of me as you read this; I will be reading my own copy in your absence and we can write to each other about what we learn."

Repeatedly Max has tried to keep up his end of this joint endeavor, only to be frustrated by the book's difficulty. For now he has set it aside in favor of a more unexpectedly useful gift. Clara's brother, far away in the city of New York, works as an assistant librarian and sometimes sends extra copies of the books he receives to catalog. "Not of much interest to me," he wrote to Max, forwarding Asa Gray's *Lessons in Botany and Veg-*

etable Physiology. "But I know you and Clara like to garden, and to look at flowers in the woods—and I thought perhaps you would enjoy this."

At first, finding his companions uncongenial, Max read out of bore-dom and loneliness. Later Gray's manual captured him. The drawings at the back, the ferns and grasses and seedpods and spore capsules: how lovely these are! As familiar as his mother's eyes; as distant as the fossil-ized ferns recently found in the Arctic. As a boy he'd had a passion for botany: a charmed few years of learning plants and their names before the shock of his mother's death, his father's long decline, the necessity of going out, so young, to earn a living and help care for his family. Now he has a family of his own. Work of his own, as well, which he is proud of. But the illustrations draw him back to a time when the differences between a hawkweed and a dandelion could fascinate him for hours.

Charmed by the grasses of the Deosai plateau, he begins to dip into Dr. Hooker's book as well. Here too he finds much of interest. When he feels lost, when all he's forgotten or never knew about simple botany impedes his understanding, he marks his place with a leaf or a stem and turns back to Gray's manual. At home, he thinks, after he's safely returned, he and Clara can wander the fields as they did in the days of their courtship, this time understanding more clearly what they see and teaching these pleasures to their children. He copies passages into his notebook, meaning to share them with her:

Lesson I. Botany as a Branch of Natural History

The Organic World, is the world of organized beings. These consist of *organs*; of parts which go to make up an *individual,* a *being.* And each indi-vidual owes its existence to a preceding one like itself, that is, to a parent. It was not merely formed, but *produced.* At first small and imperfect, it grows and develops by powers of its own; it attains maturity, becomes old, and finally dies. It was formed of inorganic or mineral matter, that is, of earth and air, indeed; but only of this matter under the influence of life; and after life departs, sooner or later, it is decomposed into earth and air again.

He reads, and makes notes, and reads some more. The *Himalayan Journals,* he has noticed, are "Dedicated to Charles Darwin by his affectionate friend, Joseph Dalton Hooker." What lives those men lead: far-flung, yet always writing to each other and discussing their ideas. Something else he hasn't told Clara is this: before leaving Srinagar, in a shop he entered meaning only to buy a new spirit level, he made an uncharacteristically impulsive purchase. A botanical collecting outfit, charming and neat; he could not resist it although he wasn't sure, then, what use he'd make of it. But on the Deosai plateau he found, after a windstorm, an unusual primrose flowering next to a field of snow. He pressed it, mounted it— not very well, he's still getting the hang of this—and drew it; then, in a fit of boldness, wrote about it to Dr. Hooker, care of his publisher in England. "The willows and stonecrops are remarkable," he added. "And I am headed higher still; might the lichens and mosses here be of some interest to you?" He doesn't expect that Dr. Hooker will write him back.

In his tent made from blankets, with a candle casting yellow light on the pages, Max pauses over a drawing of a mallow. About his mother, who died when he was nine, he remembers little. In a coffin she lay, hands folded over her black bombazine dress, face swollen and unrecognizable. When he was five or six, still in petticoats, she guided him through the marshes. Her pale hands, so soon to be stilled, plucked reeds and weeds and flowers. *Remember these,* she said. *You must learn the names of the wonderful things surrounding us.* Horsetails in her hands, and then in his; the ribbed walls and the satisfying way the segments popped apart at the plump joints. Pickerel rush and mallow and cattail and reed; then she got sick, and then she died. After that, for so many years, there was never time for anything but work.

2

May 1, 1863

Dearest Clara—

A great day: as I was coming down an almost vertical cliff, on my way back to camp, a Balti coming up from the river met me and handed me a greasy, dirty packet. Letters from you, Laurence, and Zoe—yours were marked "Packet 12," which I had thought lost after receiving 13 and 14 back in Srinagar. From those earlier letters I knew you had been delivered safely of our beloved Gillian, and that Elizabeth had welcomed her new sister and all three of you were well: but I had no details, and to have missed not only this great event but your account of it made me melancholy. How wonderful then, after five long months, to have your description of the birth. All our family around you, the dawn just breaking as Gillian arrived, and Elizabeth toddling in, later, to peer at the infant in your arms: how I wish I had been with you, my love.

And how I wish I knew what that long night and its aftermath had really been like; you spare my feelings, I know. You say not a word about your pains and trials. In Packet 13 you mentioned recovering completely from the milk fever, but in 12 you did not tell me you had it, though you must have been suffering even then. Did we understand, when I took this position, how hard it would be? So many months elapse between one of us speaking, the other hearing; so many more before a response arrives. Our emotions lag so far behind the events. For me, it was as if Gillian had been born today. Yet she is five months old, and I have no idea of what those months have brought. Zoe says Elizabeth is growing like a cabbage, and Laurence says he heard from your brother in New York and that the family is thriving; how fortunate that the wound to his foot, which we once so regretted, has saved him from conscription.

I am well too, though terribly busy. But what I want, even more than sleep, is to talk to you. Everything I am seeing and doing is so new—it is nothing, really, like the work I did in England—so much is rushing into me all at once—I get confused. When I lie down to sleep everything spins in my brain. I can only make sense of my new life the way I have made sense of everything, since we first met: by describing it to you. That great gift you have always had of listening, asking such excellent questions— when I tell you enough to let you imagine me clearly, then I can imagine myself.

So, my dearest: imagine this. If this were an army (it almost is; three of Montgomerie's assistants are military officers, while others, like Michaels and his friends, served in the military forces of the East India Company until the Mutiny, then took their discharge rather than accept transfer to the British Army), I'd be a foot-soldier, far behind the dashing scouts of the triangulating parties who precede us up the summits. It is they who measure, with the utmost accuracy, the baseline between two vantage points, which becomes the first side of a triangle. They who with their theodolites measure the angles between each end of that line and a third high point in the distance: and they who calculate by trigonometry the two other sides of the triangle, thus fixing the distance to the far point and the point's exact position. One of the sides of that triangle then becomes the base for a new triangle—and so the chain slowly grows, easy enough to see on paper but dearly won in life. In the plains these triangles are small and neat. Out here the sides of a triangle may be a hundred miles or more.

Is this hard to follow? Try to imagine how many peaks must be climbed. And how high they are: 15,000 and 17,000 and 19,000 feet. My companions and I see the results of the triangulators' hard work when we follow them to the level platforms they've exposed by digging through feet of snow, and the supporting pillars they've constructed from rocks. Imagine a cold, weary man on the top of a mountain, bent over his theodolite and waiting for a splash of light. Far from him, on another peak, a sig-

nal squad manipulates a heliotrope (which is a circular mirror, my dear, mounted on a staff so it may be turned in any direction). On a clear day it flashes bright with reflected sunlight. At night it beams back the rays of a blue-burning lamp.

The triangulators leap from peak to peak; if they are the grasshoppers, we plane-tablers are the ants. At their abandoned stations we camp for days, collecting topographical details and filling in their sketchy outline maps. You might imagine us as putting muscle and sinew on the bare bones they have made. Up through the snow we go, a little file of men; and then at the station I draw and draw until I've replicated all I see. I have a new plane-table, handsome and strong. The drawing-board swivels on its tripod, the spirit level guides my position; I set the table directly over the point corresponding to the plotted site of my rough map. Then I rotate the board with the sheet of paper pinned to it until the other main landscape features I can see—those the triangulators have already plotted—are positioned correctly relative to the map.

As I fill in the blank spaces with the bends and curves of a river valley, the dips and rises of a range, the drawing begins to resemble a map of home. For company I have the handful of porters who've carried the equipment, and one or two of the Indian chainmen who assist us—intelligent men, trained at Dehra Dun in the basics of mapping and observation. Some know almost as much as I do, and have the additional advantage of speaking the local languages as well as some English. When we meet to exchange results with those who work on the nearby peaks and form the rest of our group, the chainmen gather on one side of the fire, sharing food and stories. In their conversations a great idea called "The Survey" looms like a disembodied god to whom they—we—are all devoted. Proudly, they refer to both themselves and us as "Servants of the Map."

I will tell you what your very own Servant of the Map saw a few days ago. On the edge of the Deosai plateau, overlooking Skardu, I saw two far-away peaks towering above the rest of the Karakoram, the higher gleaming brilliant blue and the lower yellow. These are the mountains which Mont-gomerie, seven years ago, designated K1 and K2. K2 the triangulators have calculated at over 28,000 feet: imagine, the second highest mountain in the world, and I have seen it! The sky was the deepest blue, indescribable, sparkling with the signals which the heliotropes of the triangulating parties twinkled at one another. Do you remember our visit to Ely Cathedral? The way the stone rose up so sharply from the flat plain, an explosion of height—it was like our first glimpse of that, magnified beyond reason and dotted with candles.

We have thunderstorms almost every day, they are always terrifying; the one that shook us the afternoon I saw K2 brought hail, and lightning so close that sparks leapt about the rocks at my feet and my hair bristled and crackled. The wind tore my map from the drawing board and sent it spin-ning over the edge of the plain, a white bird flying into the Indus valley below. But I do not mean to frighten you. I take care of myself, I am as safe as it is possible to be in such a place, I think of you constantly. Even the things I read remind me of you.

In Asa Gray's manual, I read this today, from

Lesson VII: Morphology of Leaves—

We may call foliage the *natural form* of leaves, and look upon the other sorts as *special* forms,—as *transformed* leaves . . . the Great Author of Nature, having designed plants upon one simple plan, just adapts this plan to all cases. So, whenever any special purpose is to be accomplished, no new instruments or organs are created for it, but one of the three general organs of the vegetable, *root, stem,* or *leaf,* is made to serve the purpose, and is adapted by taking some peculiar form.

Have I told you I have been working my way through this manual, lesson by lesson? I forget sometimes what I have written to you and what I have not. But I study whenever I can and use what I learn to help make

sense both of my surroundings and of what I read in the Himalayan Journals: *which I treasure, because it's from you. As the book Laurence gave me
requires more concentration than I can summon, I've set it aside for now
(my guilty secret; don't tell him this): but Dr. Hooker I think even more
highly of since my arrival here. The rhododendron that Zoe, my thoughtful
sister, gave us as a wedding present—do you remember how, when it first
flowered, we marveled at the fragrant, snowy blossoms with their secret
gold insides? It was raised in a greenhouse in St. John's Wood, from seeds
sent back by Dr. Hooker. I wish I could have been with you this spring to
watch it bloom.*

    I am drifting from my point, I see. Forgive me. The point, *the reason I*

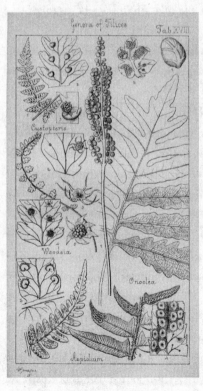

*copy this passage, is not to teach
you about leaves but to say these
words brought tears to my eyes;
they made me think of our marriage. When we were together our
lives were shaped like our neighbors', as simple as the open leaves
of the maple. Now we are apart,
trying to maintain our connection over this immense distance.
Trying to stay in touch without
touch; how that effort changes us.
Perhaps even deforms us.*

    *To an outsider we might now
look like the thick seed leaves of
the almond or the bean, or the
scales of buds or bulbs; like spines
or tendrils, sepals or petals, which
are also altered leaves. Do you*

know that, in certain willows, pistils and stamens can sometimes change into each other? Or that pistils often turn into petals in cultivated flowers? Only now do I begin to grasp the principles of growth and change in the plants I learned to name in the woods, those we have grown at home—there is a science to this. Something that transcends mere identification.

I wander, I know. Try to follow me. The point, dear heart, is that through all these transformations one can still discern the original mor- phology; the original character is altered yet not lost. In our separation our lives are changing, our bond to each other is changing. Yet still we are essentially the same.

I love you. So much. Do you know this?

It is raining again, we are damp and cold. I miss you. All the time.

Max regards the last page of his letter doubtfully. That business about the alteration of leaves; before he sends it, he scratches out the line about the effects of his and Clara's separation. *Deform*: such a frightening word.

His days pass in promiscuous chatter, men eating and drinking and working and snoring, men sick and wounded and snow-blind and wheez- ing; always worries about supplies and medicines and deadlines. He is never alone. He has never felt lonelier. There are quarrels everywhere: among the Indian chainmen, between the chainmen and the porters, the porters and his fellow plane-tablers; between the plane-tablers and the triangulators; even, within his own group, among the parties squatting on the separate peaks. Michaels, their leader, appears to enjoy setting one team against another. Michaels takes the youngest of the porters into his tent at night; Michaels has made advances toward Max and, since Max rebuffed him, startled and furious, has ceased speaking with him directly and communicates by sarcastic notes.

Wyatt has approached Max as well; and a man from another party— the only one as young as Max—with a shock of red hair as obtrusive as a kingfisher's crest. Now all three are aligned against him. When the whole group meets he has seen, in the shadows just beyond the ring of light sent out by the campfire, men kneeling across from each other, britches unbuttoned, hands on each other. . . . He closed his eyes and turned his back and blocked his ears to the roar of laughter following his hasty departure. Yet who is he to judge them? So starved for love and touch is he that he has, at different times, found himself attracted to the middle-aged, stiff-necked wife of an English official in Srinagar, a Kashmiri flower-seller, a Tibetan herdsman, the herdsman's dog. He has felt such lust that his teeth throb, and the roots of his hair; the skin of his whole body itching as if about to explode in a giant sneeze.

In the act of writing to Clara, Max makes for himself the solitude he so desperately needs. He holds two strands of her life: one the set of letters she writes to him now—or not *now*, but as close to now as they can get, four months earlier, five, six—and the other the set of letters she wrote secretly in the months before he left, trying to imagine what he might need to hear. Occasionally he has allowed himself the strange pleasure of opening one letter from each set on the same day. A rounded image of Clara appears when he reads them side by side: she is *with* him. And this fills him with a desire to offer back to her, in his letters, his truest self. He wants to give her everything: what he is seeing, thinking, feeling; who he truly is. Yet these days he scarcely recognizes himself. How can he offer these aberrant knots of his character to Clara?

He tries to imagine himself into the last days of her pregnancy, into the events of Gillian's birth, the fever after that. He tries to imagine his family's daily life, moving on without him. Clara is nursing Gillian, teaching Elizabeth how to talk, tending the garden, watching the flowers unfold; at night, if she is not too weary, she is bending over her dictionary and her German texts, and then . . . He wonders what would happen if he wrote, *Tell me what it feels like to lie in our bed, in the early morning light, naked and without me. Tell me what you do when you think of me. What your hands do, what you imagine me doing.*

He doesn't write that; he doesn't write about what he does to himself on a narrow cot, in a tent made from a blanket strung over a tree limb, the wind whistling as he stifles his groans with a handkerchief. Even then he doesn't feel alone. Close by, so near, his companions stifle noises of their own. His only truly private moments are these: bent over a blank page, dreaming with his pen.

3
—————————

June 11, 1863

Dearest, dearest Clara:

The packet containing this letter will follow a very zigzag course on its way to you; a miracle that my words reach you at all. Or that yours reach me—how long it has been since the last! A ship that sailed from Bordeaux in March is rumored to have arrived at Bombay and will, I hope, have letters from you. Others from England have reached me—yet none from you—which is why I worry so. But already I hear your voice, reminding me that the fate of mail consigned to one ship may differ so from that consigned to another. I know you and the girls are well.

I am well too, although worried about you. I do what I can to keep busy. Did I tell you that I received, in response to some modest botanical observations I had sent to Dr. Hooker, a brief reply? He corrected my amateur mistakes, suggested I gather some specimens for him, and told me his great love of mosses dated from the time he was five or six. His mother claims that when he was very tiny he was found grubbing in a wall, and that when she asked what he was doing, he cried that he had found Bryam argenteum *(not true, he notes now), a pretty moss he'd admired in his father's collection. At any age, he says—even mine—the passion for botany may manifest itself.*

I found this touching and thought you would too. And I'm honored that he would answer me at all. In the hope of being of further use to him, I

plan to continue my observations. Where I am now—deep in the heart
of the Karakoram—nothing grows but the tiny lichens and mosses that
are Dr. Hooker's greatest love. I can classify hardly any of them, they're
extremely difficult. Except for them the landscape is barren. No one lives
here: how would they live? Yet people do pass through from the neighboring
valleys, the glaciers serving as highways through the mountains: I have met
Hunzakuts, Baltis, Ladakhis and Nagiris and Turkis. But so far no travelers from home, although I hear rumors of solitary wanderers, English and
German and French. One elderly adventurer has apparently haunted these
mountains for decades, staying at times in Askole and Skardu; traveling
even on the Baltoro Glacier and its branches—can this be true? If he exists,
no one will tell me his name.

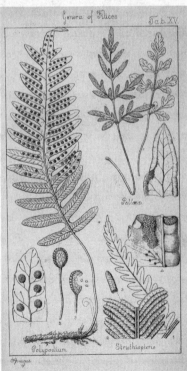

Around me is a confused mass
of rock and glacier and mist,
peaks appearing then disappearing beyond the curtains of clouds.
The glaciers, covered with rocks
and striated like frozen rivers, you
would never mistake for snowfields
or for anything else; the porters
fear them and have their own
names for them, while the chainmen claim that, deep within them,
are the bodies of men who died in
the mountains and are now being
slowly carried down the stream of
ice. Some decades from now, at the
foot of the glacier, a glove or a couple of bones may be spit out.

I have seen wild sheep the size
of ponies. I have slept ten nights at

a stretch above 15,000 feet; I have woken buried in snow, lost in clouds; days have passed when I could make no sightings and sketch no maps, when we have nothing to eat and huddle together forlornly, watching avalanches peel down the side of the peaks. The weather here is beastly. At the snout of the Baltoro we were nearly swept away by a river leaping from an ice cave. There are no vistas when one travels the glaciers, more a sense of walking along a deep corridor, framed by perpendicular walls. I have a headache nearly all the time, and my neck aches from always gazing upward. The mornings are quiet, everything frozen in place by the frosts of the night. By afternoon the landscape has come alive, moving and shifting as rocks fall, walls of mud slide down, hidden streams dammed by the ice break free with a shout. No place for men.

I travel now in a party of six. Me in charge, the sole Englishman (the others lead similar parties, on other glaciers, on their way to other peaks); two Indian assistants who aid me with the measurements and mapping; three porters. We are on the Baltoro itself as I write. So frequent are the crevasses, and so deceitfully covered with snow, that we tie ourselves together with ropes and move like a single long caterpillar. Yesterday we stopped by the edge of a huge open fissure and, while the other men rested, I tied all our ropes together and sounded the depth; 170 feet of rope failed to reach bottom. Framing us, on both sides of the glacier, are some of the world's highest peaks.

My task has been to map where Montgomerie's K2 lies in relation to the Karakoram watershed. And this I have done, though there is no clear sight of it from the glacier itself. With my men I climbed the flank of an enormous mountain called Masherbrum. My men—I ought to try and tell you what it's like to live in such enforced companionship. They . . . I will save this for another letter. You know how awkward I have always been. With my own family, with you, I can be myself but here, with strangers—it is terrible, the old shyness seizes me. Without you by my side, to start the conversation and set everyone at ease, I am so clumsy. I do try, but it does no good. Especially with the porters and the chainmen I am at a loss. The barriers of language and our very different circumstances and habits and religions—I ought to be able to break through these, given the bonds of our shared work. Somewhere they too have wives and children, families and homes but I can't imagine them, I can't see these men in any other setting and I think they can't see me any more clearly. For them, I am simply the person who gives orders. In my early days surveying seemed like a perfect career for such a solitary creature as myself. I didn't understand that, out here, I would be accompanied ceaselessly by strangers.

Yet one does not need to talk all the time. And some things are beyond conversation—several thousand feet up the flank of Masherbrum, as we were perched on a sharp bleak shoulder, there it suddenly rose: K2, sixteen or seventeen miles away, separating one system of glaciers from another. We believe the reason it has no local name is that it isn't visible from any inhabited place; the nearest village is six days' march away and the peak is hidden by others, almost as large. I cannot tell you how it felt to see it clearly. I have spent two days here, mapping all the visible peaks and their relationships to each other and the glaciers.

I will entrust this to the herdsman I met, who is on his way to Skardu; may it find its way to you. One of our porters speaks a language somewhat familiar to this herdsman. The pair had a discussion involving much pointing at Masherbrum, an insistent tone on the part of the porter, violent head-shakings from the herdsman. Later I asked the porter what they'd been talking about. The herdsman had asked where we'd been; the porter had shown him the shoulder from which we saw K2. "You have never been there," the herdsman apparently said. "No one can go there. It is not for men."

He does not write to Clara about his glacial misadventures. Walking along on a hazy day with his party strung out behind him, he had seen what resembled a small round rock perched on the ice in the distance. Fresh snow had fallen the night before and the glare was terrible; over his eyes he'd drawn a piece of white muslin, like a beekeeper's veil, which cut the worst of the blinding light but dimmed the outlines of everything. One of his companions had bound a sheet of slit paper over his eyes, while others had woven shades from the hair of yaks' tails or had unbound their own hair and combed it forward until it screened their eyes. Max was nearly upon the round rock before he recognized it as a head.

A narrow crevasse, its opening covered by drifted snow; a wedge-shaped crack the width of a man at the top, tapering swiftly to a crease: inspecting it, with his veil raised, Max could imagine what had happened. The testing step forward, the confident placement of the second foot; and then one last second of everyday life before the deceitful bridge crumbled and the man plunged down, leaving his head and neck above the surface. The slit would have fit as intimately as a shroud, trapping the man's feet with his toes pointed down. No room to flex his knees or elbows and gain some purchase—but his head was free, he was breathing, he wasn't that cold, and surely—surely?—he could pull himself out.

The man had a name, although it would take a while to determine it: Bancroft, whom Max had met only once, a member of one of the triangulating parties, disappeared three days before Max arrived. The ice inside the crevasse, warmed by the heat it stole from Bancroft's body, would have melted and pulled him inch by inch farther down, chilling him and slowing his blood, stealing his breath as fluid pooled in his feet and legs and his heart struggled to push it back up. By nightfall, with the cold pouring down from the stars, the cold wind pouring down from the peaks, the slit which had parted and shaped itself to Bancroft's body would have frozen solid around him. After hours of fruitless work, Max and his companions had reluctantly left Bancroft in the ice.

Max had not told Clara any of this: it would have frightened her. It frightened him. And yet despite that he went walking alone, ten days later. The sun was out, the sky was clear; the men had stopped in the middle of the afternoon, refused to go farther without a rest, and set up camp against his wishes. Irritated, he'd refused to waste the day. He'd mapped this section already, but wanted more detail for his sketches: how the ice curved and cracked as it ground past the embracing wall of the mountain. In Wales, when he was being trained, he and Laurence had seen erratic boulders and mountains with deeply scored flanks which were caused, said the bookish young man who led them, by a glacial period that covered all Europe with ice. Now it was as if he'd walked backward into that earlier time.

He fell into a fissure, forty feet deep. A thick tongue of ice, like the recalcitrant piece of heartwood bridging two halves of a split log, stretched between the uphill and downhill walls of the crevasse and broke his fall. He landed face down, draped around a narrow slab, arms and legs dangling into empty space. Feebly he said his own name, calling himself back to life. Then Clara's, and his daughters', his sister's, and his mother's. Above him he found a ceiling of snow, with a narrow slit of blue sky where his body had broken through. He could move his feet, his hands, his shoulders; apparently nothing was broken. Slowly, hugging the ice with his thighs, he sat upright. Before him the uphill wall of the crevasse glimmered smooth in the blue shadows. Slim ribs of ice, bulges and swellings reminiscent of Clara's back and belly. Behind him the downhill wall was jagged and white and torn. To his right the crevasse stretched without end, parallel faces disappearing into darkness. But to his left the walls appeared to taper together.

He might make of himself a bridge, he thought. A bridge of flesh, like the bridge of ice. With his back pressed against the wet uphill wall, his legs extended and his hobnailed boots pressed into the crunching, jagged downhill wall, he suspended himself. He moved his right foot a few inches, then his left; sent all his strength into the soles of his feet and then slid his back a few inches, ignoring the icy stream that chattered so far below. Again and again, right foot, left foot, heave. Time stopped, thinking stopped, everything stopped but these small painful motions. The walls drew closer together and he folded with them, his legs bending at the knees, then doubled, until finally he hung in a sideways crouch.

He reached the corner without knowing what he'd do when he got there. The crevasse was shaped like a smile; where the two lips met, the bottom also curved up. He released his right leg and let it slide down, touching some rubble on which he might balance. He stood, he straightened partway. Soaked, scared, exhausted, and so cold. Above him was not the sky, but a roof of snow. Like a mole he scratched at the bottom surface. He tore his fingernails and ripped his hands. When he realized what was happening he stopped digging with his right hand and dug only with his left.

He dug himself out. He hauled himself up. How many hours did this take? His left hand was bloody and blue, his right torn but still working; how lucky he had been. On the surface of the glacier, under the setting sun, he closed his eyes and fixed in his mind the dim, shadowed, silent grave he'd known for a few hours. Among the things he would not write Clara—he would never write a word of this—was how seductive he'd found the cold and quiet. How easy he would have found it to sleep on the leaf of ice, his head pillowed on his arm while snow drifted over the broken roof, sealing him in silent darkness. Nothing would have been left of him but his books and maps, and the trunk with Clara's letters. So many still unopened, dated months in the future, a year in the future. It was the thought of not getting to read them that made him wake up.

4
———————

July 21, 1863

Dear heart—

    This week I received your Packet 15, from March; you cannot know what a relief it is to hear from you. But why do I say that when I know you suffer the same torments? It is very upsetting to hear that none of my letters have reached you, and that you have as yet no news of my travels across the country to Kashmir, never mind news of my journeys in the mountains. Although perhaps by now you do: it was still March, *I remind myself, when you hadn't heard from me. It may be September or December before you receive this, and you will be in possession of all my other letters by then, smiling to see me worry in this.*

We heard a ship leaving Calcutta was burnt down to the waterline just after it embarked; all the passengers were saved but everything else on board was lost and I wonder if some of my letters were on it, now bits of ash on the sea. When I think about the hands through which these must pass, to find their way to you: a passing herdsman to another party of the Survey, to another messenger, to some official in Srinagar; perhaps to Calcutta, perhaps to Bombay; through a merchant's hands, or a branch of the military: hand to hand to hand, to a ship, or several ships, and the hazards of weather and human carelessness every inch of the way. . . . My dear, you must keep these accidents in mind, when you worry about me. It grieves me to think of your suffering. Remember the promise we made to each other, to consider not just the accidents that might happen to us, but to our correspondence. Remember how tough I am. How prudent.

Thank you for the story about Elizabeth and the garden. I love to think about the three of you, bundled up and watching the birds as they flick within the branches of the hedgerow. Gillian in your arms, Elizabeth darting along the hawthorns, pursuing the sparrows: these glimpses of your life together keep me going. If you knew how much I miss you . . . but I have promised myself I will write sensibly. *I want you to think of me as I am, as you have always known me, and not as a stranger perpetually complaining. I'm glad Mrs. Moore's nephew—Gideon?—has been so helpful during his stay with his aunt and has been able to solve the problem with the drains. When next you see him, please tell him I am grateful. Do you see him often?*

I received with the letters from you and our family two more letters from Dr. Hooker. He has received mail from me, from as late as April; how is it my letters are reaching him but not you? When I get home I will let you read what he writes, you will find it fascinating. He is in touch with botanists and collectors all over the world; involved with so many projects and yet still he takes the time to encourage an amateur such as myself. On his own journey, he said, as he climbed from the terai to the snowline he traversed virtually the entire spectrum of the world's flora, from the leech-infested, dripping jungle to the tiny lichens of the Tibetan plateau. I have a similar opportunity, he says. If I am wise enough to take it. I copy for you here a little paragraph, which he included with questions about what is growing where, and requests for a series of measurements of temperature and altitude.

"When still a child," he writes, "my father used to take me on excursions in the Highlands, where I fished a good deal, but also botanized; and well I remember on one occasion, that, after returning home, I built up by a heap of stones a representation of one of the mountains I had ascended, and stuck upon it specimens of the mosses I had collected, at heights relative to those at which I had gathered them. This was the dawn of my love for geographical botany. It pleases me greatly that, though you have started your botanizing as a grown man, you may come to share a similar passion."

Is that not a lovely tale? The mountain was small, by our standards here, less than 4,000 feet. He has been very encouraging of my efforts and with his help I have set myself a study plan, as if I'm at university. I would like to make myself worthy; worthy to write to such a man as Dr. Hooker, and receive a response. Worthy of seeking an answer to the question that now occupies everyone: how the different forms of life have reached their present habitats. When else will I have a chance like this?

What draws me to these men and their writings is not simply their ideas but the way they defend each other so vigorously and are so firmly bound. Hooker, standing up for Darwin at Oxford and defending his dear friend passionately. Gray, in America, championing Darwin in a series of public debates and converting the world of American science one resistant mind at a time. Our group here is very different. Although the work gets done—the work always gets done, the maps accumulate—I have found little but division and quarrels and bad behavior.

You may find my handwriting difficult to decipher; I have suffered much from snow-blindness. And a kind of generalized mountain sickness as well. We are so high, almost all the time; the smallest effort brings on fatigue and nausea and the most piercing of headaches. I sleep only with difficulty; it is cold at night, and damp. Our fires will not stay lit. But every day brings new additions to our map, and new sketches of the topography: you will be proud of me, I am becoming quite the draughtsman. And I manage to continue with my other work as well. I keep in mind Hooker's travails in Nepal and Sikkim: how, in the most difficult of circumstances, he made excellent and detailed observations of his surroundings. I keep in mind Godfrey Vigne, and all he managed to note. Also a man I did not tell you about before, whose diary passed through my hands: how clearly he described his travels, despite his difficulties! By this discipline, and by my work, I hold myself together.

This week my party climbed a peak some 21,000 feet high. We were not the first ones here: awaiting us was the station the strongest and most cunning of the triangulators built last season. I have not met him, he remains an almost mythical creature. But I occupied his heap of stones with pride. He triangulated all the high peaks visible from here and the map I have made from this outline, the curves of the glaciers and the jagged valleys, the passes and the glacial lakes—Clara, how I wish you could see it! It is the best thing I have ever done and the pains of my body are nothing.

I have learned something, these past few months. Something important.

On the descent from such a peak, I have learned, I can see almost nothing: by then I am so worn and battered that my eyes and mind no longer work correctly; often I have a fever, I can maintain no useful train of thought, I might as well be blind.

On my first ascents, before I grasped this, I would make some notes on the way up but often I would skip things, thinking I would observe more closely on the way down. Now I note everything on the way up. As we climbed this giant peak I kept a note-book and pencil tied to my jacket pocket and most of the time had them right in my hand: I made note of every geological feature, every bit of vegetation or sign of a passing animal; I noted the weather as it changed over the climb, the depth of the snow, the movements of the clouds. This record—these records, I do this now with every ascent—will I think be invaluable to subsequent travelers. When I return I plan to share them with Dr. Hooker and whoever else is interested.

It's an odd thing, though, that there is not much pleasure in the actual recording. Although I am aware, distantly, that I often move through scenes of great beauty, I can't feel that as I climb; all is lost in giddiness and headache and the pain of moving my limbs and drawing breath. But a few days after I descend to a lower altitude, when my body has begun to repair itself—then I look at the notes I made during my hours of misery and find great pleasure in them. It is odd, isn't it? That all one's pleasures here are retrospective; in the moment itself, there is only the moment, and the pain.

I must go. A messenger from Michaels came by the camp this morning with new instructions and leaves soon to contact three other parties; if I put this into his hands it will find its way down the glacier, out of the mountains, over the passes. To you.

After relinquishing the letter to Michaels's messenger, he thinks: *What use was that?* For all those words about his work, he has said little of what he really meant. How will Clara know who he is these days, if he hides both his worries and his guilty pleasures? He still hasn't told her about the gift he bought for himself. A collecting box, like a candle box only flatter, in which to place fresh specimens. A botanical press, with a heap of soft drying paper, to prepare the best of his specimens for an herbarium; and a portfolio in which to lay them out, twenty inches by twelve, closed with a sturdy leather strap and filled with sheets of thin, smooth, unsized paper. Always he has been a man of endless small economies, saving every penny of his pay, after the barest necessities, for Clara in England. He has denied himself warm clothes, extra blankets, the little treats of food and drink on which the other surveyors squandered their money in Srinagar, and before. But this one extravagance he couldn't resist: not a dancing girl, not a drunken evening's carouse, but still he is ashamed.

A different kind of shame has kept him from writing about the doubts that plague his sleepless nights. He knows so little, really—why does he think his observations might be useful? He ought to be content with the knowledge that the work he does each day is solid, practical, strong; these maps will stand for years. In Dehra Dun, and in Calcutta and back in England, copyists and engravers will render from his soiled rough maps clean and permanent versions. In a year the Series will be complete: Jammu and Kashmir, Ladakh and Baltistan, caught in a net of lines; a topographical triumph. Still he longs to make some contribution more purely his.

He dreams of a different kind of map, in shades of misty green. Where the heads of the Survey see the boundaries of states and tribes, here the watershed between India and China, there a plausible boundary for Kashmir, he sees plants, each kind in a range bounded by soil and rainfall and altitude and temperature. And it is this—the careful delineation of the boundaries of those ranges, the subtle links between them—that has begun to interest him more than anything else. *Geographical botany,* Dr. Hooker said. What grows where. Primulas up to this level, no higher; deodar here, stonecrops and rock jasmines giving way to lichens. Why do rhododendrons grow in Sikkim and not here? He might spend his life in the search for an answer.

When he and his crew gather with the other small parties, he's reminded that no one shares his interests—at night his companions argue about the ebb and flow of politics, not plant life. The Sikh Wars and the annexation of the Punjab, the administration of Lord Dalhousie, the transfer of power from the East India Company to the Crown, the decisions of the regional revenue officers—it is embarrassing, how little all this interests him. Among the surveyors are military men who have served in the Burmese War, or in Peshawar; who survived the Mutiny or, in various mountains, that stormy year when supplies to the Survey were interrupted and bands of rebels entered Kashmir. He ought to find their stories fascinating. Germans and Russians and Turks and Chinese, empires clashing; Dogras and Sikhs, spies and informants—currents no one understands, secrets it might take a lifetime to unravel. Yet of all this, two stories only have stayed with him.

The first he heard on a snow bench carved in a drift on a ridge, from an Indian chainman who'd served for a while in the Bengal army, and who worked as Max's assistant for two weeks, and then disappeared. They were resting. The chainman was brewing tea. At Lahore, he said, his regiment had been on the verge of mutiny. On a June night in 1857, one of the spies the suspicious British officers had planted within the regiment reported to the brigadier that the sepoys planned an uprising the following day. That night, when the officers ordered a regimental inspection, they found two sepoys with loaded muskets.

There was a court-martial, the chainman said. He told the story quietly, as if he'd played no part in it; he had been loyal, he said. Simply an observer. Indian officers had convicted the two sepoys and sentenced them to death. "There was a parade," the chainman said. His English was very good, the light lilting accent at odds with the tale he told. "A formal parade. We stood lined up on three sides of a square. On the fourth side were two cannon. The sepoys—"

"Did you know them?" Max had asked.

"I knew both of them, I had tried to talk them out of their plan. They were . . . The officers lashed those two men over the muzzles of the cannons. Then they fired."

Below them the mountains shone jagged and white, clean and untenanted. Nearby were other Englishmen, and other Indians, working in apparent harmony in this landscape belonging to neither. Yet all this had happened only six years ago.

"There was nothing left of them," the chainman said. He rose and kicked snow into the fire; the kettle he emptied and packed tidily away. "Parts of them came down like rain, bits of bone and flesh, shreds of uniforms. Some of us were sprinkled with their blood."

"I . . ." Max had murmured. What could he say? "A terrible thing." The chainman returned to work, leaving Max haunted and uneasy.

The other story was this, which Michaels encouraged a triangulator to tell one night when three different surveying teams gathered in a valley to plan their tasks for the next few weeks. An Indian atrocity to match the British one: Cawnpore, a month after the incident reported by the chainman. Of course Max had heard of the massacre of women and children there. No one in England had escaped that news, nor the public frenzy that followed. But Michaels's gruff, hard-drinking companion, who in 1857 had been with a unit of the Highlanders, told with relish certain details the newspaper hadn't printed.

"If you had seen the huts," said Michaels's friend: Archdale, Max thought his name was. Or maybe Archvale. "A hundred and twenty women and children escaped the first massacre on the riverboats—the mutineers rounded them up and kept them in huts. We arrived not long after they were butchered. I saw those huts, they looked like cages where a pack of wild animals had been set loose among their prey."

"Tell about the shoes," Michaels had called from the other side of the fire. All the men were drinking; Michaels had had a case of brandy carried in from Srinagar. His face was dark red, sweating, fierce. That night, as always, he ignored Max almost completely.

"The shoes," Archdale said. He emptied his glass and leaned forward, face shining in the firelight. "Picture this," he said. "I go into one hut and the walls are dripping with blood, the floor smeared, the smell unthinkable. Flies buzzing so loudly I thought I'd go mad. Against one wall is a row of women's shoes, running with blood, draped with bits of clothing." The Indian chainmen and the Balti porters were gathered around their separate fires, not far away. Could they hear Archdale? Max wondered. Was it possible Archdale would say these things within earshot of them? "Against the other wall, a row of children's shoes, so small, just like those our children wear at home. And"—he leaned farther forward here— "do you know what was in them?"

No one answered. Was Gillian wearing shoes yet? "What?" Max said, unable to stop himself.

"Feet!" Archdale roared. "*Feet!* Those filthy animals, those swine, they had lopped off the children's feet. We found the bodies in the well."

That terrible story had set off others; the night had been like a night in hell; Max had fled the campfire soon after Archdale's tirade and rolled himself in a blanket in a hollow, far from everyone, carved into the rocky cliffs. When he woke he'd been surprised not to find the campground littered with bodies.

Since hearing those tales he has wondered how there could be so much violence on both sides; and how, after that, Englishmen and Indians could be up in these mountains working so calmly together. How can he make sense of an empire founded on such things? *Nothing,* he thought after hearing those stories. And still thinks. *I understand nothing.*

Dr. Hooker wrote at great length, in a letter Max didn't mention to Clara, about the problems of packing botanical collections for the journey home: the weight, the costs; the necessity of using Ward's cases; the crating of tree ferns and the boats to be hired. How kind he was, to take such trouble in writing Max, and to warn him of these potential hazards!

And yet how little Dr. Hooker understands Max's own situation. There is no possibility of paying for such things without depriving Clara and his daughters. His collections are limited to the scraps he can dry and preserve in his small press—bad enough he spent money on that; the herbarium sheets he can carry; the sketches and observations in his notebook. He can offer Dr. Hooker only these, but they are not nothing and he hopes his gifts will be received without disappointment.

The lost man whose skull he found—the first one, when he'd just entered these mountains—had at least left behind a record of the movements of his soul. What is he doing, himself? Supporting his family, advancing his career; when he returns to England, he'll have no trouble finding a good position. But he would like also to feel that he has *broadened* himself. Hunched over his plane-table, his temples pounding as he draws the lateral moraines of the glacier below him, he hears his mother's voice.

Look. Remember this. The ribbon of ice below him turns into a snow-covered path that curves through the reeds along the river and vanishes at the horizon; across it a rabbit is moving and his mother stands, her hand in his, quietly keeping him company. They watch, and watch, until the path seems not to be moving away from them, but toward them; the stillness of the afternoon pouring into their clasped hands. *There is something special in you,* she said. *In the way you see.*

A few days ago, on his twenty-eighth birthday, he opened the birthday greeting Clara had tucked in his trunk. She had written about the earlier birthdays they'd shared. And about this one, as she imagined it: *Your companions, I know, will have made you a special birthday meal. Perhaps you'll all share a bottle of brandy, or whatever you drink there. I am thinking of you, and of the birthdays in the future we will once more spend together.*

Reading this, he'd felt for the first time that Clara's project might fail. He is no longer the person she wrote to, almost a year ago now. She may have turned into someone else as well. That Gideon she mentions, that nice young man who prunes the trees and brings her wood and does the tasks Max ought to be doing himself: what other parts of Max's life is he usurping? Max conjures up someone broad-shouldered, very tall—Max and Clara are almost the same height—unbuttoning his shirt and reaching out for Clara. . . . Impossible, it makes him want to howl. Surely she wouldn't have mentioned him if their friendship was anything but innocent. Yet even if it is, it will have changed her.

He himself has changed so much, he grows further daily from her picture of him. There was no birthday celebration; he told no one of this occasion. If he had, there would have been no response. It is his mother, dead so many years, who seems to speak most truly to the new person he is becoming. As if the years between her death and now were only a detour, his childhood self emerging from a long uneasy sleep. Beyond his work, beyond the mapping and recording, he is *seeing*; and this—it is terrifying—is becoming more important to him than anything.

5

October 1, 1863

Dearest Clara—

Forgive me for not writing in so long. Until I received your Packets 17, 18, and 19, all in a wonderful clump last week (16, though, has gone astray), I had almost given up hope of us being in touch before winter. I should have realized your letters couldn't find me while we were among the glaciers. We are in the valley of the Shighar now, and from here will make our way back to Srinagar. I don't yet know what my winter assignment will be. The triangulating parties will winter at the headquarters in Dehra Dun, recalibrating the instruments and checking their calculations and training new assistants. There is talk of leaving a small group of plane-tablers in Srinagar, to complete topographical maps of the city and the outlying areas and lakes. I will let you know my orders as soon as I get them.

At least you know I am alive now. Though how can you make sense of my life here on the evidence of one letter from when I first arrived in Kashmir, and one from deep in the mountains? The others—I must have faith they will find their way to you. Your description of your journey to London, trudging through those government offices as you tried to get some word of me—this filled me with sadness, and with shame. You are generous to say it is not my fault that you went so long without word of me, that you blame a careless ship's captain, clumsy clerks, and accidents: but it is my fault, still. I am the one who left home. And that I have not written these last weeks—can you forgive me? I console myself with the thought that, since my earlier letters were so delayed, perhaps a trickle of them will continue to reach you during the gap between then and now. But really my only excuse is the hardships of these last weeks. I am so weary; the cold and the altitude make it hard to sleep. And when I do catch a few brief hours I am plagued by nightmares. The men I work with tell me stories, things I would never repeat to you; and though I try not to think about them they haunt me at night.

The season in the mountains is already over; we stayed too long. We crossed one high pass after another during our retreat. And Clara, you can't imagine the weather. I couldn't work on my maps, or keep up my notes, or even—my most cherished task—write to you; when I heated the inkpot, the ink still froze on its short journey to the paper. My hands were frozen, my beard a mass of icicles. I wore everything you packed for me, all at once, and still couldn't stay warm. Lambs' wool vest and drawers, heavy flannel shirt and lined chamois vest, wool trousers and shirt, three pairs of stockings and my fur-lined boots, thick woolen hat, flannel-lined kidskin jacket, over that my big sheepskin coat, and then a Kashmir shawl wrapped twice about me, binding the whole mass together—I sweated under the weight of all this, yet grew chilled the instant we stopped moving. Nights were the worst, there is no firewood in the mountains and we had already used up all we'd carried. Food was short as well.

I shouldn't tell you these things; never mind. Now that we are down in the valleys things are easier. And I am fine. Soon enough we'll reach Srinagar, and whether I stay there or move on to Dehra Dun I am look-

ing forward to the winter. Long quiet months of cleaning up my sketch maps, improving my drawings, fitting together the sections into the larger picture of the Himalayan system. From either place I may write to you often, knowing the chances of you getting my letters in just a few months are good: and I may look forward to receiving yours with some regularity. Still I have some of the letters in your trunk to look forward to, as well: I ration these now, I open one only every few weeks, sometimes ignoring the dates with which you marked them. Forgive me, I save them for when I most need them. This evening, before I began to write to you, I opened one intended for Elizabeth's birthday. How lovely to be reminded of that happy time when you leaned on my arm, plump and happy as we walked in the garden and waited for her birth. The lock of Elizabeth's hair you enclosed I have sewn into a pouch, which I wear under my vest.

What else do I have to tell you? So much has happened these last weeks that I don't know how to describe it all; and perhaps it wouldn't interest you, it is just my daily work. Yesterday I had a strange encounter, though. Camped by the edge of a river, trying to restore some order to my papers while my companions were off in search of fuel, I looked up to see a stranger approaching; clearly a European although he wore clothes of Kashmiri cut. When I invited him to take tea with me he made himself comfortable and told me about himself. A doctor and an explorer, elderly; he calls himself Dr. Chouteau and says he is of French birth, though his English is indistinguishable from mine. This he explains by claiming to have left home as a boy of fourteen; claiming also to have been exploring in these mountains for over forty years. We did not meet in Srinagar, he told me, because he lives in a native quarter there. I think he may be the solitary traveler of whom I heard such odd rumors earlier in the season, though when I asked him this he shrugged and said, "There are a few of us."

We passed together the most interesting afternoon I've had in weeks. My own companions and I have grown weary of each other, we seldom speak at all; but Dr. Chouteau talked without stopping for several hours. A great liar, I would have to say. Even within those hours he began to contradict himself. But how intriguing he was. He is very tall, thin and hawk-nosed, with a skin burnt dark brown by years in the sun and deeply lined. His ragtag outfit he tops with a large turban, from which sprout the plumes of some unidentifiable bird. He showed me his scars: a round one, like a coin, on the back of one hand, and another to match on the front—here a bullet passed through, he said, when he was fighting in Afghanistan. A hollow in his right calf, where, in Kabul, a bandit hacked at him with a sword as he escaped by horse. For some time he lived among a Kafir tribe, with a beautiful black-eyed mistress; the seam running from eyebrow to cheekbone to chin he earned, he says, in a fight to win her. He has been in Jalalabad and the Kabul river basin; in the Pamirs among the Kirghiz nomads; in Yarkand and Leh, Chitral and Gilgit.

Or so he says. Myself, I cannot quite credit this; he is elusive regarding his travel routes, and about dates and seasons and companions. But perhaps he truly did all these things, at one time or another, and erases the details and connections out of necessity: I think perhaps he has been a spy. For whom?

I try to forget what you have said about the way you gather with our families and friends and pass these letters around, or read them out loud; if I thought of that I would grow too self-conscious to write to you at all. But I will tell you one peculiar thing about Dr. Chouteau if you promise to keep this to yourself. He has lived to such a robust old age, he swears, by the most meticulous attention to personal hygiene. And how has he avoided the gastric complaints that afflict almost all of us when we eat the local foods? A daily clyster, he says. The cleansing enema he administers to himself, with a special syringe. I have seen this object with my own eyes, he carries it with him and showed it to me. It looked rather like a hookah. Far better this, he said, looking at my bewildered countenance, than the calomel and other purgatives on which less wise travelers rely.

Some of the other things he told me I can't repeat, even to you: they have to do with princes and dancing-girls, seraglios and such-like: when I am home again I will share these with you, in the privacy of our own bed.

Clara, I am so confused. Meeting this stranger made me realize with more than usual sharpness how lonely I am, how cut off I feel from all that is important to me. My past life seems to be disappearing, my memories grow jumbled. Who was the Max Vigne who went here or there, did this or that? It's as if I am dissolving and reforming; I am turning into someone I don't recognize. If I believed in the doctrine of the transmigration of souls, I might suspect that the wind is blowing someone else's soul in through my nostrils, while my old soul flies out my ears. In the mountains I lay awake in the cold, frozen despite my blankets, and my life in England—my boyhood, even my life with you—passed by my eyes as if it had been lived by someone else. Forgive these wanderings. The household details of which you wrote, the problems with the roof, the chimney, the apple trees—I know I should offer some answers in response to your questions but it feels pointless. You will have long since had to resolve these things before you receive my advice. I trust your judgment completely.

Good night; the wind is blowing hard. What a fine thing a house is. In my tent I think of you and the girls, snug inside the walls.

After that, he does not write to Clara for a while.

The river valleys, the high plains, the dirt and crowds and smells and noise of Srinagar, where the surveying parties are reshuffled and he finds himself, with three other plane-tablers, left behind in makeshift quarters, with preliminary maps of the city and the valley and vague instructions to fill in the details while everyone else (Michaels too; at least he is finally free of Michaels!) moves on to Dehra Dun, not to return until spring: and still he does not write Clara. He does not write to anyone, he does not keep up his botanical notes, he makes no sketches other than those required for the maps. He does his work, because he must. But he does no more. He cannot remember ever feeling like this.

6

If he could make himself write, he might say this:

Dearest Clara—

Who am I? Who am I meant to be? I imagine a different life for myself, but how can I know, how can anyone know, if this is a foolish dream, or a sensible goal? Have I any scientific talent at all? Dr. Hooker says I do, he has been most encouraging. If he is right, then my separation from you means something, and the isolation I've imposed on myself, and the long hours of extra work. But if I have no real gift, if I am only deluding myself . . . then I am wasting everything.

There is something noble, surely, in following the path of one's gifts; don't we have a duty to use our talents to the utmost? Isn't any sacrifice, in the pursuit of that, worthwhile? In these past months I have often felt that the current which is most truly me, laid aside when I was still a boy and had to face the responsibilities of family life, has all this time continued to flow the way water moves unseen beneath the glaciers. When I am alone, with my notes and plants and the correlations of weather and geology and flora springing clear before me, I feel: This is who I am. This is what I was born to do. But if in fact I have no real capacity for this work, if it is only my vanity leading me down this path—what then?

He has grown morose, he knows. Worse than morose. Maudlin, self-pitying. And self-deluding: not just about his possible talents, but in the very language with which he now contemplates writing Clara. Nobility, duty, sacrifice—whose words are those? Not his. He is using them to screen himself from the knowledge of whatever is shifting in him.

On the journey back to Srinagar, among the triangulators and plane-tablers led by Michaels and eventually joined by Captain Montgomerie himself, Max was silent, sullen, distant. If he could, he would have talked to no one. In Srinagar, once the crowd of officers and triangulators left for Dehra Dun, he felt still worse. Investigating the streets and alleys, the outlying villages and the limestone springs, he was charmed by what he saw and wished it would stay the same. But meanwhile he couldn't help hearing talk of his government annexing Kashmir and turning the valley into another Simla: a retreat for soldiers and government officials, people he would prefer to avoid.

When he returns at night to the room he shares with three other plane-tablers, he flops on his cot and can't understand why he feels so trapped. Didn't he miss having walls and a roof? Perhaps it isn't the dark planks and the stingy windows that make him grind his teeth, but his companions' self-important chatter about measurements and calculations, possibilities for promotion. He shuts his ears to them and imagines, instead, talking with the vainglorious old explorer whose tales left him feeling lost, and full of questions.

The stories he wrote to Clara were the least of what happened that afternoon. Dr. Chouteau had been everywhere, Max learned. Without a map; maps meant nothing to him. Max's work he'd regarded with detached interest, almost amusement. Looking down at the sheets of paper, the carefully drawn cliffs and rivers and glaciers, Dr. Chouteau had said, *I have been here. And here. Here. And so many other places.* He spoke of the gravestone, seen in Kabul, that marked the resting place of an Englishman who'd passed through there a century and a half ago. Of wandering Russians, Austrians, Chinese, Turks, the twists and turns of the Great Game, the nasty little wars. Godfrey Vigne, he'd said—*Isn't it odd, that you share that last name?*—had been no simple traveler, but a British spy. Those forays into Baltistan a way of gathering information; and his attempts to reach Central Asia a way of determining that the only routes by which the Russians might enter India lay west of the Karakoram. *I knew him,* Dr. Chouteau said. *We were in Afghanistan together. He was the one who determined that Baltistan has no strategic importance to the British plans for India.*

More than anyone else, Dr. Chouteau made Max understand the purpose of his work. *I never make maps,* Dr. Chouteau said. *Or not maps anyone else could read. They might fall into the wrong hands.* Max's maps, he pointed out, would be printed, distributed to governments, passed on to armies and merchants and travelers. Someone, someday, would study them as they planned an invasion, or planned to stop one. What can Max's insignificant hardships matter, when compared to the adventures of such solitary travelers as Dr. Chouteau, or the lost man he saw when he first arrived in the mountains; of Godfrey Vigne or of Dr. Hooker? In Srinagar, Max understands that his journeys have been only the palest imitations of theirs.

He hasn't heard from Dr. Hooker in months. And although he knows he ought to understand, from Clara's trials, that accident may have been at work, he interprets this as pure rejection. The observations he sent weren't worthy; Hooker has ceased to reply because Max's work is of no interest. All he will leave behind are maps, which will be merged with all the other maps, on which he will be nameless: small contributions to the great Atlas of India, which has been growing for almost forty years. In London a faceless man collates the results of the triangulations into huge unwieldy sheets, engraved on copper or lithographed: two miles to an inch, four miles to an inch—what will become of them? He knows, or thinks he knows, though his imagination is colored by despair: they will burn or be eaten by rats and cockroaches, obliterated by fungus, sold as waste paper. Those that survive will be shared with allies, or hidden from enemies.

Max might write to Dr. Hooker about this; in Sikkim, he knows, Dr. Hooker and a companion had been seized while botanizing and held as political hostages. That event had served as excuse for an invasion by the British army and the annexation of southern Sikkim. Although Dr. Hooker refused to accompany the troops, he gave the general in charge of the invasion the topographical map he'd drawn. That map was copied at the surveyor general's office; another map, of the Khasia Hills, made its way into the Atlas of India, complimented by all for its geological, botanical, and meteorological notes. Max has seen this one himself, though its import escaped him at the time. Dr. Hooker did it in his spare time, tossing off what cost Max so much labor.

But what is the point of tormenting himself? In the increasing cold he reads over Dr. Hooker's letters to him, looking for the first signs of disfavor. The letters are imperturbably kind, he can find no hint of where he failed. For comfort he turns, not to the remaining letters in Clara's trunk—those forward-casting, hopeful exercises make him feel too sad—but instead to the first of her letters to reach him. From those, still brave and cheerful, he works his way into the later ones. A line about Gillian's colic, and how it lingered; a line about the bugs in the rhubarb: unsaid, all the difficulties that must have surrounded each event. *The roof is leaking, the sink is broken, Elizabeth has chicken pox,* Clara wrote. *Zoe is bearing bravely her broken engagement, but we are all worried about her.* What she means is: *Where are you, where are you? Why have you left me to face this all alone?*

Her packet 16, which failed to reach him in October with the rest of that batch, has finally arrived along with other, more recent letters. In early April she described the gardens, the plague of slugs, the foundling sparrow Elizabeth had adopted, and Gillian's avid, crawling explorations; the death of a neighbor and the funeral, which she attended with Gideon. Gideon, again. Then something broke through and she wrote what she'd never permitted herself before:

Terrible scenes rise up before my eyes and they are as real as the rest of my life. I look out the window and I see a carriage pull up to the door, a man steps out, he is bearing a black-bordered envelope; I know what is in it, I know. He walks up to the door and I am already crying. He looks down at his shoes. I take the letter from him, I open it; it is come from the government offices in London and I skip over the sentences which attempt to prepare me for the news. I skip to the part in which it says you have died. In the mountains, of an accident. In the plains, of some terrible fever. On a ship which has sunk—I read the sentences again and again—they confirm my worst fears and I grow faint—hope expires in me and yet I will not believe. In the envelope, too, another sheet: The words of someone I have never met, who witnessed your last days. *Though I am a stranger to you, it is my sad duty to inform you of a most terrible event.* And then a description of whatever befell you; and one more sheet, which is your last letter to me.

You see how I torment myself. I imagine all the things you might write. I imagine, on some days, that you tell me the truth; on others that you lie, to spare my feelings. I imagine you writing, *Do not grieve too long, dearest Clara. The cruelest thing, when we think of our loved ones dying in distant lands, is the thought of them dying alone and abandoned, uncared for— but throughout my illness I have had the attentions of kind men.* I imagine, I imagine . . . how can I imagine you alive and well, when I have not heard from you for so long?

I am ashamed of myself for writing this. All over Britain other women wait, patiently, for soldiers and sailors and explorers and merchants—why can't I? I will try to be stronger. When you read this page, know that it was written by Clara who loves you, in a moment of weakness and despair.

At least that is past now, for her; from her other letters he knows she was finally reassured. But that she suffered like this; that he is only hearing about it now . . . To whom is she turning for consolation?

Winter drags on. Meetings and work; official appearances and work; squabbles and work. Work. He does what he can, what he must. Part of him wants to rush home to Clara. To give up this job, this place, these ambitions; to sail home at the earliest opportunity and never to travel again. It has all been too much: the complexities and politics, the secrets underlying everything. Until he left England, he thinks now, he had lived in a state of remarkable innocence. Never, not even as a boy, had he been able to fit himself into the world. But he had thought, until recently, that he might turn his back on what he didn't understand and make his own solitary path. Have his own heroes, pursue his own goals. But if his heroes are spies; if his work is in service of men whose goals led to bloodstained rooms and raining flesh—nothing is left of the world as he once envisioned it.

He wanders the city and its outskirts, keeping an eye out, as he walks, for Dr. Chouteau. He must be here; where else would he spend the winter? Stories of that irascible old man, or of someone like him, surface now and then; often Max has a sense that Dr. Chouteau hides down the next alley, across the next bridge. He hears tales of other travelers as well—Jacquemont and Moorcroft, the Schlagintweit brothers, Thomas Thomson, and the Baron von Hugel. The tales contradict each other, as do those about Dr. Chouteau himself. In one story he is said to be an Irish mercenary, in another an American businessman. Through these distorted lenses Max sees himself as if for the first time, and something happens to him.

That lost man, whose skull he found when he first arrived in the mountains—is this what befell him? As an experiment, Max stops eating. He fasts for three days and confirms what the lost man wrote in his diary: his spirit soars free, everything looks different. His mother is with him often, during that airy, delirious time. Dr. Chouteau strolls through his imagination as well. In a brief break in the flow of Dr. Chouteau's endless, self-regarding narrative, Max had offered an account of his own experiences up on the glacier. His cold entombment, his lucky escape; he'd been humiliated when Dr. Chouteau laughed and patted his shoulder. *A few hours,* he said. *You barely tasted the truth. I was caught for a week on the Siachen Glacier, in a giant blizzard. There is no harsher place on this earth; it belongs to no one. Which won't keep people from squabbling over it someday. The men I traveled with died.*

When Max hallucinates Dr. Chouteau's voice emerging from the mouth of a boatwoman arguing with her neighbor, he starts eating again, moving again. The old maps he's been asked to revise are astonishingly inaccurate. He wanders through narrow lanes overhung by balconies, in and out of a maze of courtyards. The air smells of stale cooking oil, burning charcoal, human excrement. He makes his way back and forth across the seven bridges of Srinagar so often he might be weaving a web. Temples, mosques, the churches of the missionaries; women carrying earthenware pots on their heads; barges and bakeshops and markets piled with rock salt and lentils, bottles of ghee—his wanderings he justifies as being in service to the map, although he also understands that part of what drives him into the biting air is a search for Dr. Chouteau. If Max could find him, if he could ask him some questions, perhaps this unease that has settled over him might lift.

As winter turns into early spring, as he does what he can with his map of the valley and, in response to letters from Dehra Dun, begins preparations for another season up in the mountains, his life spirals within him like the tendril of a climbing plant. One day he sits down, finally, with Laurence's gift to him and begins working slowly through the lines of Mr. Darwin's argument. The ideas aren't unfamiliar to him; as with the news of Cawnpore and the Mutiny, he has heard them summarized, read accounts in the newspapers, discussed the outlines of the theory of descent with modification with Laurence and others. But when he confronts the details and grasps all the strands of the theory, it hits him like the knowledge of the use made of Dr. Hooker's maps, or the uses that will be made of his own. He scribbles all over the margins. At first he writes Laurence simply to say: *I am reading it. Have you read it? It is marvelous. The world is other than we thought.* But a different, more complicated letter begins to unfurl in his mind.

A mountain, he reads, *is an island on the land. The identity of many plants and animals, on mountain-summits, separated from each other by hundreds of miles of lowlands, where the alpine species could not possibly exist, is one of the most striking cases known of the same species living at distant points, without the apparent possibility of their having migrated from one to another . . . the glacial period affords a simple explanation of these facts.*

He closes his eyes and sees the cold sweeping south and covering the land with snow and ice, arctic plants and animals migrating into the temperate regions. Then, centuries later, the warmth returning and the arctic forms retreating northward with the glaciers, leaving isolated representatives stranded on the icy summits. *Along the Himalaya,* Mr. Darwin writes, *at points 900 miles apart, glaciers have left the marks of their former low descent; and in Sikkim, Dr. Hooker saw maize growing on gigantic ancient moraines.* The point of Dr. Hooker's work, Max sees, is not just to map the geographical distribution of plants but to use that map in service of a broader theory. Not just, *The same genus of lichen appears in Baltistan and in Sikkim.* But, *The lichens of the far ends of the Himalaya are related, descending from a common ancestor.*

It is while his head is spinning with these notions that, on the far side of the great lake called the Dal, near a place where, if it was summer, the lotus flowers would be nodding their heads above their enormous circular leaves, by a chenar tree in which herons have nested for generations, he meets at last not Dr. Chouteau, but a woman. Dark-haired, dark-eyed: Dima. At first he speaks to her simply to be polite, and to conceal his surprise that she'd address him without being introduced. Then he notices, in her capable hands, a sheaf of reeds someone else might not consider handsome, but which she praises for the symmetry of their softly drooping heads. Although she wears no wedding ring, she is here by the lake without a chaperone.

The afternoon passes swiftly as they examine other reeds, the withered remains of ferns, lichens clustered on the rocks. Her education has come, Max learns, from a series of tutors and travelers and missionaries; botanizing is her favorite diversion. He eyes her dress, which is well cut although not elaborate; her boots, which are sturdy and look expensive. From what is she seeking diversion? She speaks of plants and trees and gardens, a stream of conversation that feels intimate yet reveals nothing personal. In return he tells her a bit about his work. When they part, and she invites him to call on her a few days later, he accepts. Such a long time since he has spoken with anyone congenial.

Within the week, she lets him know that he'd be welcome in her bed; and, gently, that he'd be a fool to refuse her. Max doesn't hide from her the fact that he's married, nor that he must leave this place soon. But the relief he finds with her—not just her body, the comforts of her bed, but her intelligence, her hands on his neck, the sympathy with which she listens to his hopes and longings—the relief is so great that sometimes, after she falls asleep, he weeps.

"I have been lonely," she tells him. "I have been without company for a while." She strokes his thighs and his sturdy smooth chest and slips down the sheets until their hipbones are aligned. Compactly built, she is several inches shorter than him but points out that their legs are the same length; his extra height is in his torso. Swiftly he pushes away a memory of his wedding night with long-waisted Clara. The silvery filaments etched across Dima's stomach he tries not to recognize as being like those that appeared on Clara, after Elizabeth's birth.

He doesn't insult her by paying her for their time together; she isn't a prostitute, simply a woman grown used, of necessity, to being kept by men. Each time he arrives at her bungalow he brings gifts: little carved boxes and bangles and lengths of cloth; for her daughter, who is nearly Elizabeth's age, toy elephants and camels. Otherwise he tries to ignore the little girl. Who is her father, what is her name? He can't think about that, he can't look at her. Dima, seeming somehow to understand, sends her daughter off to play with the children of her servants when he arrives. Through the open window over her bed he sometimes hears them laughing.

Dima has lived with her father in Leh and Gilgit and here, in a quarter of Srinagar seldom visited by Europeans; she claims to be the daughter of a Russian explorer and a woman, now dead, from Skardu. For some years she was the mistress of a Scotsman who fled his job with the East India

Company, explored in Ladakh, and ended up in Kashmir; later she lived with a German geologist. Or so she says. In bed she tells Max tales of her lovers, their friends, her father's friends—a secret band of wanderers, each with a story as complicated as Dr. Chouteau's. Which one taught her botany? In those stories, and the way that she appears to omit at least as much as she reveals, she resembles Dr. Chouteau himself, whom she claims to know. A friend of her father's, she says. A cartographer (but didn't he tell Max he never made maps?) and advisor to obscure princes; a spendthrift and an amateur geologist. Bad with his servants but excellent with animals; once he kept falcons. She knows a good deal about him but not, she claims, where he is now.

One night, walking back from her bungalow, a shadowy figure resembling Dr. Chouteau appears on the street before Max and then disappears into an alley. Although the night is dark, Max follows. The men crouched around charcoal braziers and leaning in doorways regard him quietly. Not just Kashmiris: Tibetans and Ladakhis, Yarkandis, Gujars, Dards—are those Dards?—and Baltis and fair-haired men who might be Kafirs. During this last year, he has learned to recognize such men by their size and coloring and the shape of their eyes, their dress and weapons and bearing. As they have no doubt learned to recognize Englishmen. If Dr. Chouteau is among them, he hides himself. For a moment, as Max backs away with his hands held open and empty before him, he realizes that anything might happen to him. He is no one here. No one knows where he is. In the Yasin valley, Dr. Chouteau said, he once stumbled across a pile of stones crowned by a pair of hands. The hands were white, desiccated, bound together at the wrists. Below the stones was the remainder of the body.

When he leaves the alley, all Max can see for a while are the stars and the looming blackness of the mountains. How clear the sky is! His mind feels equally clear, washed out by that moment of darkness.

During his next weeks with Dima, Clara recedes—a voice in his ear, words on paper; mysterious, as she was when he first knew her. Only when Dima catches a cold and he has to tend her, bringing basins and handkerchiefs and cups of tea, does he recollect what living with Clara was really like. Not the ardent, long-distance exchange of words on which they've survived for more than a year, but the grit and weariness of everyday life. Household chores and worries over money, a crying child, a smoking stove; relatives coming and going, all needing things, and both of them stretched so thin; none of it Clara's fault, it is only life. Now it is Dima who is sick, and who can no longer maintain her enchanting deceits. The carefully placed candles, the painted screen behind which she undoes her ribbons and laces to emerge in a state of artful undress, the daughter disposed of so she may listen with utmost attention to him, concentrate on him completely—all that breaks down. One day there is a problem with her well, which he must tend to. On another her daughter—her name is Kate—comes into Dima's bedroom in tears, her dress torn by some children who've been teasing her. He has to take Kate's hand. He has to find the other children and scold them and convince them all to play nicely together, then report back to Dima how this has been settled. He is falling, he thinks. Headfirst, into another crevasse.

During Dima's illness it is with some relief—he knows it is shameful—that he returns at night to his spartan quarters. Through the gossip that flies so swiftly among the British community, the three other surveyors have heard about Dima. Twice Max was spotted with her, and this was all it took; shunned alike by Hindus and Moslems, Christians and Sikhs, she has a reputation. That it is Max she's taken up with, Max she's chosen; to Max's amazement and chagrin, his companions find this glamorous. They themselves have found solace in the brothels; Srinagar is filled with women and they no longer turn to each other for physical relief. But to them, unaware of Dima's illness and her precarious household, Max's situation seems exotic. The knowledge that he shares their weaknesses, despite the way he has kept to himself—this, finally, is what makes Max's companions accept him.

They stop teasing him. They ask him to drink with them, to dine with them; which, on occasion, he does. They ask for details, which he refuses. But despite his reticence, his connection to Dima has made his own reputation. When the rest of the surveyors return from Dehra Dun and they all head back to the mountains, Max knows he will occupy a different position among them. Because of her, everything will be different, and easier, than during the last season. It is this knowledge that breaks the last piece of his heart.

April arrives; the deep snow mantling the Pir Panjal begins to shrink from the black rock. Max writes long letters to Laurence, saying nothing about Dima but musing about what he reads. Into Srinagar march triangulators in fresh tidy clothes, newly trained Indian assistants, new crowds of porters bearing glittering instruments, and the officers: Michaels among them. But Michaels can no longer do Max any harm. Max and his three companions present their revised map of Srinagar, and are praised. Then it is time to leave. Still Max has no answers. Dr. Chouteau has continued to elude him; Dima, fully recovered now, thanks him for all his help, gives him some warm socks, and wishes him well with his work.

Which work? Even to her he has not admitted what he is thinking about doing these next months. He holds her right hand in both of his and nods numbly when she says she will write him, often, and hopes that he'll write her. Hopes that they'll see each other again, when the surveying party returns to Srinagar.

More letters. Another person waiting for him. "Don't write," he says, aware the instant he does so of his cruelty. The look on her face—but she has had other lovers (how many lovers?) and she doesn't make a scene. Perhaps this is why he chose her. When they part, he knows he will become simply a story she tells to the next stranger she welcomes into her life.

And still he does not write Clara. Other letters from her have arrived, which he hasn't answered: six months, what is he thinking? Not about her, the life she is leading in his absence, the way her days unfold; not what she and their children are doing, their dreams and daily duties and aspirations and disappointments. Neither is he thinking about Dima; it is not as if his feelings for her have driven out those he has for Clara. He isn't thinking about either of them. This is his story, his life unfolding. The women will tell the tale of these months another way.

7

April 21, 1864

My dearest, my beloved Clara—

Forgive me for not writing in so long. I have been sick—nothing serious, nothing you need worry about, although it did linger. But I am fully recovered now, in time to join the rest of the party on our march back into the mountains. This season, I expect, will be much like the last. Different mountains, similar work; in October I will be done with the services I contracted for and the Survey will be completed. From my letters of last season you will have a good idea of what I'll be doing. But Clara . . .

Max pauses, then crosses out the last two words. What he should say is what he knows she wants to hear: that when October comes he'll be on his way back to her, as they agreed. But he doesn't want to lie to her. Not yet.

His party is camped by a frozen stream. The porters are butchering a goat. Michaels, in a nearby tent, has just explained to the men their assignments for the coming week; soon it will be time to eat; Max has half an hour to finish this letter and no way to say what he really means: that after the season is finished, he wants to stay on.

Everything has changed for me, he wants to say. *I am changed, I know now who I am and what I want and I can only hope you accept this, and continue to wait for me. I want to stay a year longer. When the Survey ends, in October, I want to wait out the winter in Srinagar, writing up all I have learned and seen so far; and then I want to spend next spring and summer traveling by myself. If I had this time to explore, to test myself, discover the secrets of these mountains—it would be enough, I could be happy with this, it would last me the rest of my life. When I come home, I mean to try to establish myself as a botanist. I have no hope of doing so without taking this time and working solely on my studies.*

But he can't write any of that. Behind him men are laughing, a fire is burning, he can smell the first fragrance of roasting meat. He is off again, to the cold bare brilliance of a place like the moon, and what he can't explain, yet, to Clara is that he needs other time, during the growing season, to study the plants in the space between the timberline and the line of permanent snow. How do the species that have arisen here differ from those in other places? How do they make a life for themselves, in such difficult circumstances?

Could Clara understand this? He will break it to her gently, he thinks. A hint, at first; a few more suggestions in letters over the coming months; in September he'll raise the subject. By then he'll have found some position that will pay his salary while leaving him sufficient time for his own work. Perhaps he'll have more encouragement from Dr. Hooker by then, which he can offer to Clara as evidence that his work is worthwhile. Perhaps he'll understand by then how he might justify his plans to her. For now—what else can he say in this letter? He has kept too much from her, these last months. If his letters were meant to be a map of his mind, a way for her to follow his trail, then he has failed her. Somehow, as summer comes to these peaks and he does his job for the last time, he must find a way to let her share in his journey. But for now all he can do is triangulate the first few points.

. . . I have so much to tell you, Clara. And no more time today; what will you think, after all these months, when you receive such a brief letter? Know that I am thinking of you and the girls, no matter what I do.

I promise we'll do whatever you want when I return: I know how much you miss your brother, perhaps we will join him in New York. I would like that, I think. I would like to start over, all of us, someplace new. Somewhere I can be my new self, live my new life, in your company.

Next to my heart, in an oilskin pouch, I keep the lock of Elizabeth's hair and your last unopened letter to me, with your solemn instruction on the envelope: To be Opened if You Know You Will Not Return to Me. *If the time comes, I will open it. But the time won't come; I will make it back, I will be with you again.*

This comes to you with all my love, from your dearest

Max

THE FOREST

L ATER THE SQUAT WHITE cylinders with their delicate indentations would be revealed as a species of lantern. But when Krzysztof Wojciechowicz first glimpsed them, dotted among the azaleas and rhododendrons and magnolias surrounding Constance Humboldt's kidney-shaped swimming pool, he saw them as dolls. The indentations cut the frosted tubes like waists, a third of the way down; the swellings above and below reminded him of bodices and rounded skirts. Perhaps he viewed the lanterns this way because the girls guiding him down the flagstone steps and across the patio were themselves so doll-like. Amazingly young, amazingly smooth-skinned. Sisters, they'd said. The tiny dark-haired one who'd appeared in the hotel lobby was Rose; the round-cheeked one driving the battered van, with her blond hair frizzing in all directions, was Bianca. Already he'd been clumsy with them.

"You are . . . are you Dr. Humboldt's daughters?" he'd asked. The sun was so bright, his eyes were so tired, the jumble of buildings and traffic so confusing. The step up to the van's back seat was too high for him, but neither girl noticed him struggling.

The small one, Rose, had laughed at his question. "We're not related to Constance," she'd said. "I'm a postdoctoral fellow at the institute." The blond one, who called to mind his own mother sixty years earlier, pulled out of the hotel driveway too fast and said nothing during the short drive to the Humboldts' house. He feared he'd hurt her feelings. For the last decade or so, he'd been subject to these embarrassing mis-identifications, taking young scientists for children or servants when he met them out of context. They all dressed so casually, especially in this country; their faces were so unmarked—how could anyone tell them from the young people who chauffeured him about or offered trays of canapes at parties? But these girls he should have known, he'd probably met them earlier. Now, as he stepped down into the enormous back garden and moved toward the long table spread with food and drink, the girl called after a flower veered toward a crowd gathered by the pool and left him with the girl he'd affronted.

"Dr. Wojciechowicz?" she said, mangling his name as she steered him closer to the table. "Would you like a drink or something?"

Reflexively he corrected her pronunciation; then he shook his head and said, "Please. Call me Krzysztof. And you are Bianca, yes?" He could not help noticing that she had lovely breasts.

"That's me," she agreed dryly. "Bianca the chauffeur, Rose's sister, *not* related to the famous Dr. Constance Humboldt. No one you need to pay attention to at all."

"It's not . . ." he said. Of course he had insulted her. "It's just that I'm so tired, and I'm still jet-lagged, and . . ."

Could he ask her where he was without sounding senile? Somewhere north of Philadelphia, he thought; but he knew this generally, not spe-cifically. When he'd arrived two days ago, his body still on London time, he had fallen asleep during the long, noisy drive from the airport. Since then he'd had no clear sense of his location. He woke in a room that looked like any other; each morning a different stranger appeared and drove him to the institute. Other strangers shuttled him from laboratory to laboratory, talking at length about their research projects and then moving him from laboratory to cafeteria to auditorium to laboratory, from lobby to restaurant and back to his hotel. The talk he'd given was the same talk he'd been giving for years; he had met perhaps thirty fellow scientists and could remember only a handful of their names. All of them seemed to be gathered here, baring too much skin to the early July sun. Saturday, he thought. Also some holiday seemed to be looming.

"Do forgive me," he said. "The foibles of the elderly."

"How old *are* you?"

Her smile was charming and he forgave her rude question. "I am seventy-nine years of age," he said. "Easy to remember—I was born in 1900, I am always as old as the century."

"Foibles forgiven." She—*Bianca,* he thought. *Bianca*—held out her hand in that strange boyish way of American women. Meanwhile she was looking over his shoulders, as if hoping to find someone to rescue her. "Bianca Marburg, not quite twenty-two but I'm very old for my age."

"You're in college?"

She tossed her hair impatiently. "Not *now.* My sister and I were dreadful little prodigies—in college at sixteen, out at nineteen, right into graduate school. Rose already has her Ph.D.—how else do you think she'd have a postdoc here?"

Would he never say the right thing to this bristly girl? "So then you . . . what is the project you are working on?" Americans, he'd been reminded these last two days, were always eager to talk about themselves.

"So then *I*—I should be in graduate school, and I was until two months ago but I dropped out, it was seeming stupid to me. Unlike my so-successful sister Rose, *I* am at loose ends."

She moved a bowl of salad closer to a platter of sliced bread draped with a cloth, then moved it back again. "Which is why I'm driving you

around. Why I'm here. I'm sort of between places, you know? I got a
temp job typing for an Iraqi biophysicist—see the short guy near the
volleyball net? He hired me because I can spell 'vacuum.' I'm staying
with my sister until I get enough money together to move. I might go
to Alaska."

"That's nice," Krzysztof said helplessly.

"Oh, please," she said. "You don't have to pretend to be interested.
Go talk to the other famous people. Constance collects them, they're
everywhere."

She huffed off—furious, he saw. At him? In the battered leather bag
that hung from his shoulder he felt the bottle he'd carried across the
ocean as a special gift for his hostess. But his hostess was nowhere to be
seen, and no one moved toward him from either the pool or the round
tables with their mushroomlike umbrellas. Already the top of his head
was burning; he was all alone and wished he had a hat. Was it possible
these people meant to stay in the sun all afternoon?

Bianca made a brisk circuit through the backyard, looking for someplace to settle down. There was Rose, leaning attentively toward Constance's camel-faced husband, Roger, and listening to him as if she were
interested. Entirely typical, Bianca thought; Rose submitted herself to
Roger's monologues as a way of pleasing Constance, who was her advisor.
Constance herself was holding court from an elegant lawn chair beneath
an umbrella, surrounded by graduate students and postdocs—but
Bianca couldn't bear the way Constance patronized her, and she steered
wide of this group. She considered joining the two students Constance
employed, who were trotting up and down the steps bearing pitchers of
iced tea and lemonade; at last week's reception, though, Constance had
rebuked her for distracting the help. The knot of protein chemists at the
volleyball net beckoned, Rick and Wen-li and Diego stripped of their
shirts and gleaming in the sun, but she'd slept with Diego after that
reception, and now they weren't speaking. Perhaps Vivek and Anisha,

easing themselves into the shallow end of the pool just as Jocelyn, already cannonball-shaped, curled her arms around her legs and launched herself into the deep end with a splash?

No, no, no. Vivek was charming but Jocelyn, impossible Jocelyn, was already whaling down on her young squire. Everywhere Bianca looked there was laughter, chatter, the display of flesh—much of it, Bianca thought, better left hidden—flirtation and bragging and boredom. A standard holiday-weekend party, except that all of these people were scientists, and many were famous, while she was neither. And had, as Rose reminded her constantly, no one to blame for this but herself.

Off by the fragrant mock orange tree, she spotted the institute's two resident Nobel laureates side by side, looming over the scene in dark pants and long-sleeved shirts. She drifted their way, curious to see if they were clashing yet. Arnold puffed and plucked at his waistband; Herb snorted and rolled his eyes: but they were smiling, these were still playful attacks. Last week, during Winifred's seminar on the isozymes of alpha-amylase, she'd watched the pair shred Winifred in their boastful crossfire. Arnold, sitting to her left, had favored her with a smile.

"Nice to see you gentlemen again," Bianca said.

The men stared at her blankly, Arnold's left foot tapping at the smooth green grass.

"Bianca Marburg," she reminded them.

"From Jocelyn's lab?" Arnold said now.

"Rose Marburg's sister," she said, grinning stupidly.

Herb frowned, still unable to place her. "Didn't I see you . . . were you *typing*? For Fu'ad?"

She held her hands up like claws and typed the air. "*C'est moi*," she said. What was she doing here?

"Ah," Arnold said. "You must be helping Constance out. It's a lovely party, isn't it? So well organized. Constance really amazes me, the way she can do this sort of thing and still keep that big lab working. . . ."

"But that last pair of papers," Herb said. "Really."

Bianca fled. From the corner of her eye she saw the man she'd driven here, that Polish émigré, physical-chemist turned theoretical structural-biologist, Cambridge-based multiply medaled old guy, standing all alone by the bamboo fountain, watching the water arc from the stem to the pool. Pleasing Constance inadvertently, she thought; Constance fancied her home as a place conducive to contemplation and great ideas. Krzysztof raised his right hand and held it over his head, either feeling for hair that was no longer present or attempting to shade his array of freckles and liver spots from the burning sun.

Quickly Bianca traversed the yard and the patio, slipped through the glass doors and across the kitchen, and ran upstairs to the third and smallest bathroom. The door closed behind her with expensive precision: a Mercedes door, a jewel-box door. On the vanity was a vase with a Zen-like twist of grapevine and a single yellow orchid. She opened the window and lit up a joint. Entirely typical, she thought, gazing down at Krzysztof's sweaty pate. That Constance and Arnold and Herb and the others should fly this man across the ocean to hear about his work, then get so caught up in institute politics that they'd forget to talk to him at their party. Had it not been for the lizardlike graze of his eyes across her chest, she might have felt sorry for him.

Krzysztof crouched down by the rock-rimmed basin and touched a blade of grass to the water, dimpling the surface and thinking about van der Waals forces even as Constance rushed to his side, burbling and babbling and asking if he was ill. When he assured her that he was fine, she asked about Cambridge, and then if he'd like a swim—but of course not, he should come sit here; he knew everyone, didn't he? She helped him into a long, low, elaborately curved chair, webbed with canvas that trapped him as securely as a fishnet. She couldn't have meant to let him languish there; that would have been rude, she was never rude. She must not have known that he couldn't rise from this snare unaided. Nor could she have known, as the faces bent toward him politely for a moment and then turned back to their animated conversations about meetings he hadn't attended, squabbles among colleagues he didn't know, that he'd forgotten almost all their names and was incapable of attaching those he did remember to the appropriate faces and research problems.

The sun had moved, was moving, so that first his knees, then his thighs and crotch were uncomfortably roasted. This was the throne room, he saw. This cluster of chairs, perched where an adrenal gland would be if the pool were really a kidney: himself and Constance, Arnold, Herb, Jocelyn, and Sundralingam. All the senior scientists. Directly across the pool the junior researchers stood in tight circles, occasionally glancing his way; the postdocs and students were gathered at the farthest end of the pool, where a group of bare-torsoed, highly muscled young men tended a grill that sent up disturbing smoky columns.

He made columns in his mind: faces, names, research projects. Then he tried and failed to match up the lists. The girl named Rose walked by and smiled at him. Although he smiled back eagerly she continued to walk, past him and between a pair of those low white cylinders standing among the glossy mounds of hosta like dolls in a dark wood. He knew he'd fallen asleep only when his own sudden, deep-throated snore woke him.

The sun had dropped and the sky had turned a remarkable violet-blue; perhaps it was seven o'clock. A few people still swam in the pool, but most were out, and mostly dressed, and the smell of roasting fowl filled the air. On the patio people milled around the grill and the table with paper plates in their hands. Bottles of wine, bottles of beer, dripping glasses, ice; he was, he realized, very thirsty. And past embarrassment, although the chairs near him were empty now, as if he'd driven everyone away. Somehow he was not surprised, when he rolled sideways in an unsuccessful attempt to pull himself from his lounge chair, to see Bianca, cross-legged on the grass, watching over him.

"Have a nice nap?" she asked.

"Lovely," he replied. She seemed happy now; what had he missed? "But you know I *cannot* get up from this thing."

The hand she held out was not enough. "If you would," he said, "just put your hands under my arms and lift . . ."

Effortlessly she hauled him to his feet. "You want to go over toward the tables?"

"Not just yet. I'll sit here for a minute." This time he chose a straight metal chair with a scallop-shell back. He sat gingerly, then more firmly. A fine chair, he'd be able to rise himself.

"I'll get you some food."

He sniffed the air, repelled by the odor of charred flesh. "Get something for yourself," he said. "Maybe I'll eat later. But I'm terribly thirsty—do you suppose you could bring me something cold? Some water?" He remembered, then, the bottle in his bag. "And if you could find two small empty glasses, as well," he said. "I have a treat to share with you."

When she returned he gulped gratefully at the cool water. "Do you like vodka?" he asked.

"Me? I'll drink anything."

He reached into his leather satchel and took out the bottle he'd meant to give Constance. In return, Bianca held out two paper cups, printed with blue and green daisies. "The best I could do."

"Good enough." He held up the heavy bottle, showing her the blade of grass floating blissfully inside. "*Zubrowka,*" he said. "Bison vodka, very special. It's flavored with the grass upon which the bison feed in the Bialowieza Forest, where my family is from. A friend brings it to me from Poland when he visits, and I brought it here from Cambridge."

"Cool," she said. "Should I get some ice?"

"Never," he said, shuddering. "We drink this neat, always." He poured two shots and handed her one. "Drink it all in one gulp—*do dna*. To the bottom."

"Bottoms up," Bianca said. Together they tossed the shots down. Almost immediately he felt better. Bianca choked and shook her head, her pale hair flying in all directions. He forbade himself to look at her smooth neck or the legs emerging, like horses from the gate, from her white shorts. He focused on her nose and reminded himself that women her age saw men like him as trolls. Even ten years ago, the occasional women with whom he'd forgotten himself had let him know this, and cruelly. How was it he still felt these impulses, then? That the picture of himself he carried inside had not caught up to his crumpled body?

"Take a sip of water," he said.

"It *burns*!"

"Of course. But isn't it delicious?" He refilled the ridiculous cups and they drank again. She had spirit, he thought. This time she hardly choked at all. He tried to imagine her as the granddaughter of one of his oldest friends, himself as an elderly uncle.

"Delicious," she agreed. "It's like drinking a meadow. Again?"

"Why not?"

Around the left lobe of the kidney came Rose, a platter of chicken in her hand. She seemed simultaneously to smile at him and glare at her sister, who was caught with the paper cup still at her lips. Was that a glare? He couldn't figure out what was going on between them.

"Welcome," he said. And then, reluctant to lose Bianca's undivided attention, "Will you join us?"

"I can't just now," Rose said. "But Constance wants to know if you'd like to come over to the patio and have something to eat." She thrust the platter toward his face. "The chicken's great."

"Maybe later."

"Bianca?"

"No," Bianca said firmly; she seemed to be rejecting more than just the food. The sisters glared at each other for a minute—*children*, Krzysztof thought; then remembered Bianca's earlier word. *No, prodigies.*

All grown up—before Rose made a clicking sound with her tongue and walked away.

Her mouth tasted of meadows and trees, Bianca thought. As if she'd been turned into a creature with hooves, suavely grazing in a dappled glade. The joint she'd smoked earlier was still with her but barely, palely; this warmth in her veins, this taste in her mouth, were from the splendid bison vodka. And this man, whom at first she'd felt saddled with and longed to escape, was some sort of magician. Now it seemed like good fortune that everyone else had abandoned him to her care. They rose from their chairs, on their way to join the crowd and examine the platters of food. But the voices on the patio seemed terribly loud and someone was shrieking with laughter, a sound like metal beating metal. Chased away, they drifted toward the Japanese fountain tucked in the shrubbery, where Krzysztof had earlier crouched until Constance captured him.

"Isn't this pretty?" he asked, and she agreed. Ferns surrounded one side of the fountain, lacy and strongly scented.

She peered down into the basin and said, "We could just sit here for a bit."

"We could," he agreed. His smile distracted her from the odd way his lower lids sagged, exposing their pale inner membranes. "If you wouldn't mind lowering me down on this rock."

This time she knew just how to fit her hands into his armpits. "So what is it you do, exactly?" she asked. When he hesitated, she said, "I did a couple of years of graduate work in biochemistry, you know. It's not like I can't understand."

"I know that," he said. "But I'm more or less retired now."

"What about before?"

His whole long life as a scientist stretched behind him, inexplicable to the young. He tried to skim over it quickly. "In Kraków," he said, "where I went to university, I was trained as a physical chemist specializing in polymers. I went to England, just before the Second World War"—he looked at her open, earnest face, and skipped over all that painful history, all those desperate choices—"and after I'd been there a little while I was recruited to work on a secret project to develop artificial rubber. Then I studied alpha helices and similar structures in polymers, and then did some fiber-diffraction work on proteins. Once I gave up running a lab I started doing more theoretical work. Thought experiments. Do you know much thermodynamics?"

"Enough to get by," she said. "But it's not my strong point."

"I like to think about the thermodynamics of surfaces, and the folding of globular proteins. The buried residues inside the assembly and all the rest. There are a set of equations—"

But Bianca shook her head. "Your bad luck," she said. "I'm probably the only person here who can't follow your math."

"I can show you something," he said. "Something that will make you understand at once."

"Yes?" she said. She was, she realized, wonderfully, happily drunk. Her companion reached into his magic bag once more.

"More vodka?" she said. "I could do another shot."

The paper cups were soft-edged and crumpled now, but he straightened them and filled them before delving again in his capacious bag. Sometimes, when he traveled to foreign countries, his audiences were so diverse that he had to bring the level of his standard lecture down a notch, use visual aids so the biologists could grasp what he was saying as well as the biochemists and biophysicists. Here at the institute, where the staff prided themselves on their mathematical sophistication, he hadn't had to use the toys he always carried. But now his hand found the coil of copper wire and the little plastic bottle.

"Perhaps," he said, "if there was a way we could get a bowl of water?"

Bianca pointed at the basin just below them. "Right here."

Had he not had so much *zubrowka* he might have considered more closely the relationship between the limpid water in the basin and the tiny stream trickling from the hollow bamboo. But he looked at the small pool and the eager, beautiful girl beside him, and without further thought he opened the bottle and poured some solution into the basin. From the wire he quickly fashioned several simple polygons. "Watch," he said.

The voices from the patio faded, the ferns waved gently, her vision narrowed until she saw only his hands, the basin, the rocks where they sat. He dipped a wire shape in the basin and blew a large bubble; then another, which he fastened to the first. More wire forms, more bubbles, more joinings—and before her, trembling gently in the air, rose a complicated structure supported by almost nothing.

"See where the faces join?" he said. "Those shapes the film makes as the faces join other faces?" He launched into an explanation of molecular interactions that seemed simplistic to him, incomprehensible to her. "You see," he said, "what a clear visual demonstration this is of the nature of surface tension. I stumbled on this some years ago, blowing soap bubbles for a friend's grandchildren."

"That was soap?" she said. "What you put in the water?"

"Not exactly—the film it makes isn't sturdy enough. There's glycerine in here, some other things. . . ." He added two more bubbles to his airy construction.

There was a theory behind all this, Bianca knew. An idea that this growing structure of soap film and wire exemplified; at this rarefied gathering, only she was incapable of grasping what he was trying to explain. Yet as she sat in the blue air, the bubble structure elongating while he expounded on his ideas, she felt almost purely happy. Soon she'd have to leave this place. Although she was closer to Rose than to anyone else in the world, so close they sometimes seemed to share a soul, they couldn't seem to get along now. At night, lying in Rose's tiny apartment, she could feel the fierceness of Rose's desire that she go back to school and continue the work they'd shared since their father gave them their first chemistry set. Or, if she refused to do that, that she leave Rose alone. Coming here had been a bad mistake.

Soon her whole life would change. But at that moment, sitting on the rocks with Krzysztof, she felt as if he'd led her to a castle from which she'd been barred, opened the front door with a flourish and then gaily flung open other doors one by one. The rooms were filled with sunlight and treasure. And although they were rooms she'd given up, rooms that from now on would belong to Rose and not her, this moment of remembering that they existed comforted her like balm.

She said, "I had a grandfather who did wonderful tricks. Maybe not as good as this but still, you would have liked him. He was from your part of the world, I think. I mean the part where you came from originally."

"He was Polish?" Krzysztof said eagerly. That she equated him with her grandfather was something he wouldn't think about now. "You have Polish blood?"

"Sort of," she said. "Not exactly. I'm not sure. Our grandfather's name was Leo Marburg, and the story in our family goes that he had a German name but was born and raised in Poland, near some big forest somewhere. Or maybe it was Lithuania. But somehow he ended up in the Ukraine, trying to establish vineyards there just before the revolution. And then—this is all confused, my mother told me these stories when I was little—he came to New York, and he worked as a janitor until he got sick and had to go live in the mountains. When he got better he found a job with one of the big wineries on the Finger Lakes."

"What are Finger Lakes?"

"Some long skinny lakes all next to each other, out in western New York, where I grew up. The glaciers made them. It's a good place to grow grapes. When he'd saved enough money he bought some land of his own, and established the winery that my father still runs. I know a lot about making wine. Grandpa Leo was still alive when Rose and I were tiny, and he used to bring us down into the corner of the cellar where he had his lab and show us all sorts of apparatus. The smells—it was like an alchemist's cave."

It was astounding, Krzysztof thought. What she left out, what she didn't seem to know. That Leo might have been hardly older than him, if he were still alive; what did it mean, that he'd made his way here, worked as a laborer but then reestablished himself and his real life?

"So was he German, really?" he asked. "Or Russian, or Polish . . . ?"

"I don't know," she admitted. "He died when I was five or so, before I could ask him anything. Most of what I know about him my mother told me, and she died when Rose and I were still girls. I don't know much history, I guess. My own or anyone else's."

How could she tell him about her mother, whom she still missed every day? And talked with, sometimes, although this was another point over which she and Rose quarreled bitterly. She felt a sudden sharp longing for her sister and craned her head toward the crowd behind her, but Rose, who was talking with Vivek, had her back to them. "It's because of Grandpa Leo," Bianca said, "that I studied biochemistry in the first place. Because of him and my father and the winery."

"But you stopped," Krzysztof said. "Why was that?"

She couldn't explain this to Rose, or even to herself: how could she explain it to him? The argument she and Rose had had, when they were working together on one of the papers that grew out of Rose's thesis—how bitter that had been. At its root was a small kinetics experiment that Rose interpreted one way, she herself another.

"It's so . . . *pushy,*" she said. The easy excuse, and at least partially true. "Science, I mean. At least at this level. When I started I thought it was something people did communally. Everyone digging their own small corner of the field, so that in the end the field would flower—I didn't know it got so vicious. So competitive. I hate all this hustling for money and priority and equipment. Actually," she said, "I hate these *people.* A lot of them. I really do."

"We're not very inspiring in groups," Krzysztof said. He pulled his hands apart and dropped the wire forms, disrupting the bubbles so that suddenly he held nothing, only air. Science was a business now, and sometimes he could hardly bear it himself. Yet he could remember the excitement of his youth, that sense of clarity and vision; it was this, in part, that had pulled him from Kraków to Cambridge. But not only this.

"Your grandfather," he said. "If what you remember about his youth was true, our families might have come from the same place. In northeastern Poland is this huge forest—the forest where the bison live, where this vodka comes from. That might have been the forest your mother meant in her stories."

"Do you think?"

"It's possible," he said, and he repeated the name he'd told her earlier: *Bialowieza.* Bianca tried to say it herself. "It's a beautiful place."

"And there are bison there? Now?"

"There are," he said. "It is partly because of my own mother that they still exist." The whole story swirled before him, beautiful and shapely and sad, but just as it came together in his mind Bianca leapt up from her seat and held out her hands.

"I could show you something," she said. "Something really beautiful, that you'll never see if we stay here. You probably think this country is ugly, all you ever see are airports and highways and scientists. Do you want to get out of here for a while? We'd only be gone an hour, and you could tell me about the bison on the way."

"I don't want to be rude."

"I promise you, no one will notice. I'll have you back so soon they'll never know you're gone."

No one had approached them this last half hour; the other guests had taken root, on the grass and the steps and the chairs, and were eating and drinking busily, arguing and laughing and thrusting their chins at each other. But a threat loomed, in the person of the woman—the wife of

Arnold?—standing closest to them. Although she was chattering with a postdoc she was sending glances Krzysztof's way, which made him shudder. He'd been stuck with her, at an earlier dinner, while she explained the chemistry of what made things sticky, but not too sticky: something to do with those small yellow paper squares that now littered all other sheets of paper, and on which his colleagues scribbled curt notes. She might sidle over if he and Bianca continued to sit by this fountain.

He held out his arms to Bianca. "If you would?" Just then all the cylinders in the shrubberies flared at once, casting a warm light on the paths and the pool and the patio—yes, of course they were lanterns, not dolls. Expensive, tasteful lanterns, meant to look faintly oriental.

"My pleasure," she said. She raised him and held her finger to her lips in a gesture of silence. Then, to his delight, she led him through the ferns and azaleas until they disappeared around the side of the house, unseen by anyone. Krzysztof was too pleased by their cunning escape to tell Bianca how badly he needed to urinate.

They drove toward the glorious red horizon, as if chasing the vanished sun. Although the road was narrow and twisted, almost like an English road, Bianca drove very fast. Krzysztof clutched the dash at first, but then relaxed; what was left of his hair rose in the wind, tugging at his scalp like a lover's hands and distracting him from the pressure in his bladder.

"Is there any of that vodka left?" Bianca asked.

He handed her the bottle and watched as she held it to her lips. "So," she said. "Tell me about those bison."

He stuck one hand through the open window, letting it cut into the rushing breeze; then tilted it slightly and let the air push his arm up. "I was born and raised in Kraków," he said. Had he told her that already? "But my mother grew up in the country, in this forest where perhaps your grandfather was from. It is so beautiful, you can't imagine—the last bit of primeval forest in Europe, the trees have never been cut. There are owls there, and roe deer and storks and bears. And it was the last place where the wild bison, the *zubre,* lived. When my mother was young the Russians controlled that part of Poland and the forest was the tsar's private hunting preserve."

"Your mother was Russian?"

"No—*Polish.* Defiantly, absolutely Polish." He almost stopped here, overwhelmed by the complexities of Polish history. But it wasn't important, he skipped it all; it was not Bianca's fault that she knew nothing and that, if he were to hand her a map, she couldn't place Poland more than vaguely. "After she married my father they moved to Kraków—he was an organic chemist, he taught at the university. During the First World War he was conscripted into the Austrian army and disappeared. We don't even know where he died. So it was just my mother and me after that. Later, when I started university myself, we heard stories about how the German armies trapped in the forest during the war's last winter ate the *zubre* after they'd finished off the lynx and wild boars and weasels. There were only a thousand or so of them left in the world. The forests had been cleared everywhere else in Europe and rich people had been hunting them for centuries. Then those German soldiers ate all the rest. What could they do? They were freezing and starving, and they butchered the *zubre* with their artillery. This made my mother bitter. Her father had been a forester, and she'd grown up watching the bison grazing on buttercups under the oaks."

Bianca interrupted him—he seemed old again, he was wandering. And crossing and uncrossing his legs like a little boy who had to pee. Was a bison the same as a buffalo?

"This is Meadowbrook," she said, gesturing at the gigantic houses and formal gardens tucked back from the road they whizzed along. "Isn't that a ridiculous name? Rose has a little apartment above the garage of one of these estates."

A tiny space, further cramped by mounds of books and papers and useless things—that was her sister, Bianca thought, trailing a whole life's garbage everywhere. From apartment to apartment Rose had toted relics of their mother: old clothes, mismatched earrings, broken dishes. A faded green book, which Suky had used to study mosses. A big wad of old letters and another, much older book, bound in flaking brown leather: antique geology, bent to prove God's role in the creation of the world. When Bianca, in a cleaning frenzy, had tried to throw it out, Rose had seized it and pointed to the handsome pictures. Engravings of fossils, stony fish and oysters and ferns—and wasn't the inscription inside the front cover marvelous? Unmoved, Bianca had examined the spidery handwriting:

I do this day, June 4, 1888, bequeath this most valuable book to my dear friend—to be by her kept all of her life—I also trust that she with her very brilliant mind may find great instruction therein, and that through her, the good contained herein may be spread far and wide.

> *Farewell—*
> *Yours devotedly—*
> *Susan A. Snead*

Who was Susan Snead? Who wrote that book, where had it come from? Suky's aunts might have known, but they were gone and had taken Suky's history with them. Now no one, not even their father, knew anything anymore—or so Rose had shouted at Bianca, wrapping the book in a sheet of paper and tucking it back in the corner. Someone has to save *something,* Rose had said.

The truth, Bianca thought, was that Rose kept the book simply because she'd found it in Suky's closet. That clinging to the past was the single most irritating thing about her. Why hang on to useless relics, when life was all about moving quickly, shedding the inessential?

"What did you say?" Krzysztof asked.

Had she spoken? "It used to be the gardener's quarters," Bianca said, gesturing vaguely in the direction of the apartment. "Over there, near that big stone house."

He ducked his head to see over her shoulder. Whatever house she'd pointed out had vanished. Suddenly she slowed and turned the van down a narrow lane between two stone pillars. "Almost here," she said.

He hurried on with his story, sensing that time was short. He skipped everything personal, all his struggles between the two great wars. He skipped the strange evolution of his mother's heart, the way she'd left him alone in Kraków and returned to the forest of her youth, yearning to rebuild what had been destroyed. The way she'd turned in disgust from his work, from every kind of science but forestry.

"The bison were gone by the end of the war," he said. "Almost extinct. But a Polish forester started trying to reestablish a breeding stock, and my mother moved back to the Bialowieza to help him. There were a few in a zoo in Stockholm, and some in zoos in Hamburg and Berlin. A few more had survived the war in the south of Poland. And my mother and this man, they brought some females from that little group to the forest, and borrowed bulls from the zoos, and they started a breeding program. From them come all the European bison left in the world. There are several thousand of them now—because of my mother, you see? My own mother."

They were in a forest of sorts right now—the lane grew narrower and turned into a dirt track, and trees brushed the side of the van. When they emerged into a small clearing, Bianca stopped the van without saying a word in response to his tale.

"I run here," she said. "Almost every night. It's a park, this place. But no one comes here, I never see any people. I like to run just before dark." For a second he pictured her pounding down the dirt paths. She came around to his side of the van and helped him down the awkward step.

"It's beautiful," he said. Why had he been telling her that story? The forest, his mother, the starving soldiers; the bison, so huge and wild, just barely rescued from oblivion. That part ended happily. The rest, which he would never tell Bianca, did not: the German army had overrun the forest in a matter of weeks. Then it had passed to the Russians, then back to the Germans; swastikas had flown from the roofs. The resident Jews had been slaughtered under those ancient oaks, and the farmers and foresters had been deported. His mother had disappeared. And all the while he'd been safe in England, unable to persuade her to join him. Unable to save her, or anyone. In test tubes he'd grown chains of molecules, searching for something that might be turned into tires for planes and jeeps.

"It's a park now, that forest," he said, unable to let the story go. Then the pressure in his bladder grew unbearable and he said, "Would you excuse me for a minute?" He stepped behind an oak and into a thorny tangle, disappearing in the brambles. Behind him, Bianca was puzzled and then amused as she heard the long splatter of liquid on leaves, a pause, more splatter, a sigh. The sigh was one of pleasure; even this simple act was no longer reliable, and Krzysztof felt such relief as his urine flowed over the greenery that he was hardly embarrassed when he emerged and Bianca gently pointed out the bit of shirttail emerging from his fly like a tongue.

After he tidied himself, Bianca led him across a muddy field and into the trees at the far edge of the clearing. The sky had turned a smoky violet gray, truly dusk, all traces of red disappeared, and with it the color of the leaves and Bianca's hair.

"No bison here," she said cheerfully. "But I think we made it just in time. This whole area—I hate this area, it's one giant suburb. This is the only bit of real woods left for miles. But something kept eating everything Rose planted in her garden, and when I started jogging here I found out what it was. Be quiet now."

He was. He was exhausted, remarkably drained, the vodka swirling through his veins. The marzipanlike taste of the bison grass; was it that flavor the secretive, lumbering creatures had craved as they grazed? The only time he'd visited his mother in the forest, just before he left for

England, she'd fed him a dish of wild mushrooms, wild garlic, and reindeer, washed down with this vodka. He'd tried to persuade her that war was inevitable. Her hair was gray by then, she no longer looked anything like Bianca. She lived in a low dark hut by herself and said she'd rather die than leave her home again.

A deer appeared in the clearing. He blinked his eyes; it hadn't been there, and then it was. Bianca inhaled sharply. "Oh," she whispered. "We made it just in time." He blinked again: four deer, then eleven, then seventeen. They came out of the trees and stood in the gathering darkness, looking calmly at each other and at the sky. How beautiful they were. He squeezed Bianca's hand, which was unaccountably folded within his own.

She stood very still. Night after night, during these unsettled weeks, she'd left Rose's apartment and their difficult quarrels, slipped on her running shoes, and sped down the long driveway, past the houses of the wealthy, across the busy suburban road, and into this park. Almost every night she was rewarded with this vision. She could hear her mother's voice then, as if the deer were transmitting it: *The good contained herein may spread far and wide.* The deer seemed unafraid of her and often stayed for half an hour. Tonight they were edgy, though. Their tails twitched and their ears rotated like tiny radar dishes; their heads came up suddenly and pointed toward the place where Bianca and Krzysztof were hidden. They were nothing like bison. They were dainty and delicate-footed, completely at home here and yet out of place beyond the confines of this small haven. Still she couldn't figure out either how or when they crossed the bustling road between the park and Rose's apartment, to browse on the lettuce and peas.

She didn't have to tell Krzysztof not to speak; he stood like a tree, wonderfully still and silent. But his face gleamed, she saw. As if he'd been sprayed with water; was he crying? Suddenly one doe leapt straight up, turned in the air, and then bounded away. The others quickly followed. Darkness had fallen, the show was over.

"You okay?" she whispered.

"Fine," he said. "That was *lovely*. Thank you."

"My pleasure. "

She slipped an arm beneath his elbow to guide him back through the muddy part of the field, but he shook her off. He was restored, he was himself. He strode firmly over the ruts. "It's hard to believe there's a place like this so close to the congestion," he said.

She was behind him, unable to make out his words. "What?" she said.

He turned his head over his shoulder to repeat his comment. As he did so his right foot plunged into a deep hole. For a moment he tottered between safety and harm, almost in balance, almost all right. Then he tipped and tilted and was down in the mud, looking up at the first stars.

In the emergency room, the nurses and residents were impatient. No one seemed able to sort out Krzysztof's health insurance situation: what were these British papers and cards, this little folder marked *Traveler's Insurance*? Then there was the vodka on his breath, and Bianca's storm of hysterical tears; for some minutes the possibility of calling the police was raised. X-rays, blood tests, embarrassing questions: "Are you his girlfriend?" one nurse said. From Bianca's shocked rebuttal, Krzysztof understood that, as he'd feared, she'd never seen him, not for one moment, as an actual man. Almost he was tempted to tell her how clearly, and in what detail, he'd imagined her naked. She sat in an orange plastic chair and sobbed while he was wheeled in and out of rooms, his veiny white legs exposed in the most humiliating fashion. And this exposure was what distressed him most, although several friends had met their deaths through just such casual falls. Somehow the possibility of actual bodily harm had not occurred to him as he lay calmly regarding the stars from the muddy field.

"The ankle's not broken," a young doctor finally said. "But it's badly sprained."

"So he's all right?" Bianca kept saying. "He's all *right*?" Unable to calm herself, she sat as if paralyzed while the doctors drew a curtain around Krzysztof and went to work.

Krzysztof emerged with his lower leg encased in two rigid plastic forms, each lined with a green plastic air-filled pod. Velcro straps clamped the shells around him, as if his ankle were an oyster. A boy young enough to be his grandson had given him two large pills in a white pleated cup, which resembled in miniature the nurse's cap worn by a woman he'd loved during the war; the woman's name had vanished, as had the pain, and his entire body felt blissful. Bianca carried the crutches, and a sheaf of instructions and bills. She opened the van's side door and tried to help as two men lifted Krzysztof from the wheelchair and draped him along the back seat.

All the way back to Constance's house Bianca drove slowly, avoiding potholes and sudden swerves. "Are you all right?" she asked every few minutes. "Is this hurting you?"

Drowsily he said, "I have not felt so good in years." Actually this long narrow seat was more comfortable than the vast bed in his hotel. The jacket Bianca had folded into a pillow beneath his head smelled of her; the whole van was scented with her presence. On the floor, just below his face, he saw nylon shoes with flared lumpy soles, socks and shirts and reeds and a bird's nest, a canvas sack and a withered orange. Behind his seat was a mat and a sleeping bag. "Do you sleep in here?" he asked.

"I have—but not these last weeks. I'm so sorry, I never meant—I can't *believe* this happened."

"My fault," he said. "Entirely. You mustn't blame yourself."

"Everyone else will," she said bitterly. "Everyone."

Should she bring him straight back to his hotel? But she had to stop at Constance's house, let Constance and the others decide what was best for him. Perhaps Constance would want to have him stay with her. It was past eleven, they'd been gone for hours; and although she'd had plenty of time to call from the hospital, the phone had seemed impossibly far away. Now the only honest thing to do was to show up, with her guilty burden, and admit to everyone what had happened. Behind her, Krzysztof was humming.

"Talk to me," he said. "It's lonely back here. All I can see is the back of your head."

"Those bison," she said. "Are they anything like our buffalo?"

"Similar," he said. "But bigger. Shaggy in the same way, though."

"I heard this thing once," she said. "From a friend of my mother's, who used to visit the winery when Rose and I were little girls. He was some kind of naturalist, I think he studied beetles. Once he said, I think he said, that the buffalo out West had almost gone extinct, but then some guy made a buffalo refuge in Montana and stocked it with animals from the Bronx Zoo. Like your mother did, you see?" For a minute her own mother's face hovered in the air.

The van slowed and made a broad gentle curve—Constance's circular driveway, Krzysztof guessed. "In Polish," he said dreamily, "the word for beetle is *chrzaszcz*."

Bianca tried to repeat the word, mashing together the string of consonants in a way he found very sweet. How pleasing that after all she'd paid attention to his stories. Their slow progress through the afternoon and evening had culminated properly among the deer, and all of it had been worthwhile.

"We're here," she said. "Boy, this is going to be *awful*—just wait for a minute, I'll tell everyone what's going on and we'll see what to do."

She turned and touched his head, preparing to face her sister.

"Don't worry," he said gently. "I'll tell everyone I asked you to take me for a drive. I had a lovely evening, you know. I'm very glad to have met you."

Neither of them knew that out back, beyond the rubble of the party, large sturdy bubbles had been forming for hours at the lip of the bamboo fountain, to the mystification of everyone. They did not see the bubbles, nor the inside of the house, because Rose and Constance came flying out the front door to greet the van. Terrified, Bianca saw. And then, as she prepared the first of many explanations, the first clumsy attempt at the story she'd tell for years, with increasing humor and a kind of self-deprecation actually meant to charm in the most shameful way, she saw their faces change: that was rage she saw, they were enraged.

In an instant she'd thrown the van into gear again and stomped on the gas. Krzysztof said, "Where . . . ?" and as they lurched back onto the road, leaving behind Constance and Rose and the fountain and the lanterns, the squabbling scientists, the whole world of science, she said, "Back to your hotel, you need to be in your own bed."

Back, Krzysztof thought. Back to the airport, back to England, back across the ocean and Europe toward home; back to the groves of Bialowieza, where his mother might once have crossed paths with Bianca's grandfather. Might have escaped, like him; might have survived and adopted another name and life during all the years when, in the absence of family or friends, her only son shuttled between his laboratory and his little flat and the rooms of the women who one by one had tried and failed to comfort him. Back and back and back and back. Where had his life gone?

He thought *back* but Bianca, her foot heavy on the accelerator, thought *away.* From Rose, their mother, their entire past, books and papers and stories and sorrows: let it sink into the ocean. She had her wallet and her sleeping bag and her running shoes and her van; and she drove as if this were the point from which the rest of her life might begin.

THEORIES OF RAIN

Kingsessing, on the Schuylkill
September 8th, 1810

HE RODE PAST EARLIER, that slip of a Sophie at his side:
James. If you knew what I feel when I see him . . . But why
shouldn't you know? If I can imagine you, not your face or
your gestures perhaps but your mind and your heart, why not imagine you capable of feeling all I feel? I picture us on the bank of the
river here, near the fieldstone bench, exchanging confidences. I think
how, when at last I find you, I will hand you these lines and you will
know me.

The aunts do not even look up as he passes. The hayfields surrounding
us, north and west, belong to James; the lush pastures to the south; the
oats and rye and cattle and sheep, the fine stand of timber between our
wedge of river-front land and the ramble of the Bartrams' botanic gardens—his, all his. He is nearing thirty, not yet married though rumored
to be looking for a wife. Wealthy, now that he's come into his grandfather's estate. And favored in all the other ways as well. About him there
is a kind of sheen, the golden skin of good fortune.

In the room below me the aunts ignore him as they work on their *Manual of Geography*: a book for school-girls, they have such high hopes. Lessons composed of questions and answers, which a classroom of girls with scraped-back hair may murmur in unison:

Q. What is the climate of the Torrid Zone?
A. *It is very hot.*

Q. What is the climate of the Frigid Zone?
A. *It is very cold.*

Q. What is the climate of the Temperate Zone?
A. *It is mild or moderate; the heat being not so great as in the Torrid Zone, nor the cold so severe as in the Frigid Zone.*

Aunt Daphne, Aunt Jane. If they knew what I think. If they were to step outside and hail James, and if he were ill-mannered enough (which he's never been, in his five years as our neighbor) to inquire about our unusual family, they would say they are cousins; they are not. That they are my aunts, which they are not. Not looking at his broad shoulders, the strength of his hand on his horse's reins; not looking at the planes of his jaw or the shape of his brow, because they care for the minds but not the bodies of men, they would point out the charms of our small stone house. Three women, and everything just so. They would not say that I was born on a farm near Chester, to a family with two parents, two sisters, three brothers all dead of the yellow fever when I was an infant; the surviving brother torn from my side while a few pigs and chickens wandered bewildered through the dirt. The aunts took me in, I belong to them. They think I will live here forever with them, sharing their studies, caring for them: I will not.

Their book is to have a section on meteorology. Why there is weather. What it is. From the papers and books their friends have loaned us, I am to collate the theories of rain. What will be left of all my work, after they simplify it? Something like this, which they wrote today:

Q. What surrounds the Earth?
A. *The Atmosphere; composed of air, vapor, and other gases.*

Q. What can you say of the Atmosphere?
A. *It is thinner or less dense the further it is from the Earth.*

Q. When water dries up where does it go?
A. *It rises into the air.*

Q. How can water rise into the air?
A. *It is turned to vapor, and then it is lighter than the air.*

THE EARTH.

Q. When vapors rise and become condensed, what are they called?
A. *Clouds.*

Anaximenes, I tell the aunts— offering this scrap much as our cat, Cassandra, brings moles to the kitchen door and lays them at my feet—Anaximenes thought air might condense first to cloud, then to water, then to earth, and finally to stone. Why not include, I asked Aunt Daphne, this:

Q: Why are raindrops round?
A: *One theory is this: Because the corners get rubbed off as they fall side by side. And because the round shape overcomes the resistance of the air;*

and because even the smallest parts of the world are obliged to represent and mirror the round image of the universe.

But the aunts are no more interested in these old theories than in the question of why Cassandra has extra toes on her paws. Aunt Daphne said, "Lavinia. When will you learn to keep in mind our audience?"

Yet why would the girls who will someday sit in a hot schoolroom, bored and weary with reciting these lessons, not feel the longings I feel? For the tantalizing theory, the mysterious fact—Descartes' assumption that water is composed of eel-shaped particles, easily separated. Urbano d'Aviso's proposition that vapor is bubbles of water filled with fire, ascending through the air so long as it is heavier than they are; stopping when they arrive at a place where the air is equally light. Why must all we write be *practical*?

September 13, 1810

He comes, he goes, he comes, he goes. The other one I would tell you about: Mr. Frank Wells. He is well enough favored, tall and slim, thinning brown hair, a nose as long and sensitive as a greyhound's. A bit older than James, with printer's hands. He has his own business and has built a house upriver from us, which I have never seen. Unlike James he likes the way I look. He comes, he goes, along with the others—botanists and geologists; a Frenchman named Rafinesque, fat about the waist, whose shirt escapes from his pantaloons and shows bare flesh as he lectures us; a shy and friendly entomologist named Thomas Say. They admire the aunts and their work and the way they have raised me. Our house of three virgins, so studious. So neat. Every hour occupied by something useful. We rise, cook, sweep, and wash, tend to the gardens and then study and study, always useful things. The aunts wear spectacles, their eyes are weary. At night they ask me to read to them. Their spirits are weary as well. Aunt Jane has spells.

"It is all too much for me," she says. April, often. Or September, like now. When everything around us is lush and damp and hot and fertile and florid. The box-hedges send out a powerful smell and the vines trying to strangle the trees send out another, even stronger; the mock-ingbirds sit on the roof and sing all night; a sound you would like, as I do. Aunt Jane takes to her bed, her skin muddy and cold and her limbs unmoving, with a cloth on her eyes and tufts of cotton blocking her ears from the bird-song. She gets sick for no reason, well for no reason. One day she rises, resumes her duties, declares that she is better. In a few months it will all be too much for her again. Her friends, those studious men, shake their heads in sympathy and whisper, *Melancholia.*

The aunts are Quakers, and have raised me the same. On our day of rest we go to Meeting, we sit in silence, we wait with the sun streaming through the windows for the spirit to enter and move us. In that calm still place I struggle not to leap from my bench and shout—but what is the use of talking about this, when you are not here to advise me? What is the use?

September 24, 1810

James again. He nods as he rides by, once more on his way to visit Sophie. The slip of a Sophie, in her house on the hill. Half my weight and half my brains and half my wit; and a hundred times my fortune and a father, who's a banker. Around her neck, a fine gold chain. Little rings on little fingers; little kid shoes on little feet. James could pick her up the way I might a spaniel, if we had a spaniel: the aunts do not like dogs. No doubt he has lifted her lightly into a carriage, or onto a saddle. I hear she plays the piano beautifully. In the garden I watch him passing by; I stand so he can see me and he nods. He rides on, lovely, taken.

If the aunts knew what I think. If the aunts knew what I dream. Aunt Daphne has her room and Aunt Jane hers but they bundle at night in the same bed—for comfort they say, for warmth—and they think I will settle for this.

September 8, September 13; October 1, 2, 3—what is the point of dating these words as I write them? They are for you, and when I find you, dates will mean nothing to us. You are in Ecuador, or in Cleveland; in England or Boston, the Rocky Mountains; or perhaps you are a few miles away, stripped as I was of our family name. Wouldn't I recognize you, though? No matter how you'd changed? If I saw you at the market, or passed you on the street. . . .

I have but the faintest memory of our last day. The aunts said the plague left only us alive: a little boy, barely five years old, and me, not yet turned two. Did you cry when the wagons came? When everything inside our home was burned, the bedding and furniture piled and torched but the things outside, uncontaminated, prudently saved and divided? The aunts took me, some hoes and hay-rakes, two pigs, a horse, a cart. Whoever took you, said the aunts—and how could they lose the name of that family who stopped on their journey to someplace else and, out of pity and charity, left with an extra, orphaned child?—whoever took you, also took the cow.

On September 13 I turned twenty: I am grown and what I write is mine; I may write whatever I want in any fashion. Wherever you are— perhaps you have headed out West?—you are now twenty-three. On an arid plain you may have picked up a glossopetra, shaped like the tongue of a man or a snake or a duck, and wondered if it rained from the sky on a moonless night. If you were here I would lift that triangular stone from your hand and say: *This has nothing to do with the rain; this is the tooth of a shark.*

A few times I have been alone with James. Once he arrived with a side of venison, a gift for the aunts, who were out. I was still a girl, perhaps sixteen; I was alone in the house. He arrived without servants and wouldn't let me touch the meat or help him convey it to the smoke-house. As if I were a young lady, as if I had never prepared a meal or handled a bloody bundle of ribs. Even then I felt something like lightning pass between us. It has nothing to do with who we are, who we think we are; he knows nothing of me and I know only what I can see of him, his actions and possessions: the mysterious current leaping between us comes from someplace deeper. Our bodies speaking. Or maybe our souls; it has nothing to do with our minds.

Once we met in the woods, his woods, he out marking trees for felling and I walking furiously away from the aunts, filling my lungs with air; around me the wild profusion of tulip trees and witch hazel and honeysuckle, the beeches and myrtle and sugar maples, magnolias and pitcher plants. He asked if I was enjoying myself and when I stopped to answer I blushed and broke into a sweat, the hollows of my armpits weeping: all this from the sight of him, standing like a tree himself in the cool dark shadows.

And once—it is this that wakes me at night—once we were together a little longer. The aunts keep bees, not just for the honey but for what they represent. Our visitors are trotted out to the hives, shown their neatness and order, subjected to Aunt Daphne's monologues about the virtues of bee-civilization. How the bees work as one, for a common goal; how they aid and nurture each other, raise their young, store up food for the winter; a community of females, the epitome of order. Into this model of virtue come the king-birds, who love above all else to eat bees. Once, last August, the aunts appealed to James for help and he came with a shotgun and slaughtered twenty birds. The aunts fled from the carnage, but I stayed. One bird, James said, was leading all the others; he pointed out a beautiful creature who snapped with great determination at a line of bees returning from the clover. This bird he brought down with a single shot, then retrieved it and laid it at my feet.

"May I show you something?" he said. "You're not frightened of blood?"

"I am not," I said.

He knelt with a penknife and slit the bird from throat to vent, plunging his hand in the craw. On a bit of smooth grass he laid handfuls of bees, shaking his head at their number. The sun was blazing bright, the air heavy with the scents of grass and clover; in that syrupy atmosphere the blanket of bees began to stir. To my astonishment half of them rose like Jonah from the whale, licked clean their rumpled golden down, and flew back to their hives apparently undamaged.

"All those," he said with satisfaction. "In that single bird."

I couldn't say a word. I think he knew what I felt. A cloud passed over the sun as the bees vanished into their hive; the sky darkened and mosquitoes rose from the pond and arrowed toward us. I was looking at James, watching hypnotized as he lifted his arm and reached in my direction. Gently, firmly, he pressed his palm against my forearm, flattening the creature who had already penetrated my skin. When he lifted his hand we both stared at the streak of blood, so red against my whiteness. He was the one who blushed that time; he picked up his gun and bowed. "I am glad I could be of use to your aunts," he said; and then he left. I wanted to lick the blood from my arm, I wanted to lick his arm. Oh, what use is this?

Mr. Wells again today.

He sat with us, we all drank tea; the aunts showed him part of the *Manual.* "And Lavinia?" he inquired. His hands on the papers were long and intelligent.

"She helps with every step," said Aunt Jane.

"But also," I said, "also I am working on something of my own."

Aunt Daphne sniffed; Cassandra entered, bearing a grasshopper, and busied herself in tearing it apart.

"What is it that interests you?" Mr. Wells said. Which no one ever asks me.

"What you would expect," I replied, and told him what I would tell you, if you were here. "How a cloud floats, when water is much heavier than air. How cloud particles form from vapor; and how raindrops grow from those particles. Whether the winds drive the particles together, coalescing them."

He looked puzzled yet also, I thought, interested. "There are rains of manna and quails in the Bible," he said. "And in Pliny the Elder, rains of milk and blood and birds and wool."

What I wanted to say was this: *It was raining the day they took us from each other.*

Q. What kind of rain?
A. *A light rain, a drizzling rain.*

Q. You remember that?
A. *It is almost all I remember. On the muddy ground our household burns without flame, the smoke rising up through the fine rain falling down. You have no face. Your figure, clad in damp homespun, disappears into a cloud.*

What I said was, "Rains of fish." The aunts, who don't remember the rain, have no idea what asking me to collate these theories has meant. "And of frogs and hay and grain and bricks," I continued. "But almost everyone agrees that those result from whirlwinds."

Mr. Wells bent down to Cassandra, meaning I think to rescue the grasshopper; too late, she had left nothing but the wings. He straightened with these in his right hand. "Rains of stone," he said, augmenting our list. "Do you know the theory of the lapidifying juice?" Aunt Daphne struggled to maintain the expression of deferential interest she feels is proper with such men.

"Through the earth's crust moves a fluid body, or juice, that can turn various substances into stone," said Mr. Wells, nodding in the aunts' direction but addressing me. Really his face is very kind, almost handsome in its own way. His linen is clean, his hands as well; but on the middle finger of his right hand is a callus always stained with ink. "It is also found in the sea, and in the atmosphere, in a gaseous form: moving through these layers as blood moves through the body. In the air this lapidifying juice makes pebbles, which fall to earth."

"I have never heard of this," I said.

"A sixteenth-century theory," he said, setting down the broken wings. "An attempt to account for the generation of stones, and a distinct advance on the theory of the petrific seed."

Another phrase I had never heard. The aunts turned the conversation toward their textbook before Mr. Wells could finish his thought, but later I was able to thank him for teaching me something new.

"It's nothing," he said. "Do you investigate the theories of snow and hail and dew, as well as rain?"

When I told him I was interested in all the hydrometeors, he made me spell and define the word. "It's just as you would expect," I said. "If 'meteor' is any atmospheric phenomenon—think of *meteorology*—so we speak of the aerial meteors, or the winds; the luminous meteors, such as rainbows and halos; the igneous or fiery meteors, such as lightning and shooting stars. Among the watery or hydrometeors are all those things you mentioned."

"Now we have made a fair trade," he said. "You have taught *me* something new."

He is kind enough, smart enough. If you were here, would you tell me what to do?

Q. What is it I feel for James?

Q. What is it James feels for me?

Q. What theory accounts for these feelings, which can come to nothing?

Q. What?

In the garden Mr. Wells held out a sheaf of papers. "From my Charleston cousin, William Wells," he said. "He practices medicine in London now, and in his spare time studies nature. He is writing an essay on the dew."

Perhaps you are in London as well, perhaps you are leading the life I long for, rich in friends and good conversation, the universe unfolding before you. I smoothed my skirts against the bench, aware that Mr. Wells was watching me as he talked about dew as rain that falls very slowly, particles of water moving toward the objects that attract them. He stuttered and looked down at his lap, at the papers in his lap.

"Does dew come from the earth, or from the air?" he read from his cousin's notes. "Does it rise or fall? What is the source of the cold that condenses the vapor? At first I thought that the deposition of the dew might cause the cold we observe on those objects. But I have come to realize that the cold *precedes* the dew."

He turned to another page. "My cousin did an experiment," he said. "Which we might try to repeat."

We gathered uncarded wool from the aunts' stores, and on the balance they use to weigh mordants and pigments for dyeing, we weighed out two equal amounts. One sample we spread in a loose circle on the grass. Inside a long, thick-walled piece of clay drainage pipe, set on end so that it was open to the darkening sky, we spread the other sample in a circle the same size. The aunts watched, unimpressed but polite. They have borrowed many books from Mr. Wells.

"I'll return in the morning," he said. "Quite early, if you don't mind."

When the aunts didn't offer him a bed, he rode off to his own home. The legs of his horse disappeared in the mist, then the horse's head, and then his own, leaving only the silver rays of the moon and the clear, cold air. Aunt Daphne made me come inside but then she and Aunt Jane kept me awake, arguing in the fierce, airy whispers they think I can't hear through the wall between our rooms. Their words were lost but not their tone and I knew they had settled into their favorite topic:

Q. What shall we do with Lavinia?
A. *Is there an answer to this?*

I slept, and dreamed of you. In the morning Mr. Wells arrived and we gathered and re-weighed the samples. Just as his cousin had found, the sample out on the grass had collected more dew.

"Which it would not," I said, "if dew fell from the sky like rain; an equal amount should have fallen within the cylinder as without."

"My cousin's point exactly," said Mr. Wells. "He contends that the cooling of the earth's surface causes water vapor to condense from the air. What matters is how much heat is radiated into the atmosphere. What matters is the exposure of the objects on the surface to the air. The sheltering walls of the drainage pipe lessened the radiation to the sky; it was colder outside the pipe than within, hence there was more dew outside."

My skirt was wet, our hands and arms were drenched, there was damp wool everywhere and the smell of sheep. "I'll borrow some thermometers from my friends," he said. "We'll set them around and see if the dew is heaviest where they read lowest."

As I spread my arms, pointing out a sheltered hollow and a promising rise, I caught him looking at me. I forget sometimes how long my limbs are, how fleshy I am in the shoulders and bust. You are built the same, I expect, tall and strong and capable, like James. Mr. Wells looked me over shyly and said, "Forgive me, I don't mean to stare. But you have such *amplitude.* You are very different from your aunts in this way."

They are not my aunts, I wanted to say. Instead I reached over to brush off the bits of wool on his coat, which caused him to color up to the roots of his soft brown hair.

A rain that moves in swirls and gusts, pushing the leaves against the limbs, pushing my hair away from my face; then a rain hardly more than a mist, seeming simply to condense on my skin: it is raining today. And although you disappeared in the rain, perhaps because I last saw you in it, I love the rain. In it I am sleek and slender and smooth, attractive as Sophie is attractive, a woman someone might love. The wide span of my hips reduced, the thick mat between my legs tamed and trimmed and my monthly bleeding dried to a few dainty drops—oh, forgive me for these thoughts. You will know what I mean by them.

Out of the rain stepped James. Behind him his wagon, and on it two boxes: two solid, well-made wooden hives. Gifts for the aunts. But once more they were absent. "I thought they might like to enlarge their apiary," James said.

When I told him they had gone to consult with a printer about their book, he murmured something about their industriousness. "A pleasure," he said. He smelled of wood and wool and leather harness, of honey, and himself. "To have such neighbors."

"I'm sure they'll be grateful," I replied.

He nodded and stood at the door for a moment, before hoisting the first of the boxes and hauling it past the barn and the sheds, to join the others among the apple trees. A second trip and he was done, back before me, sweat slipping down beneath his heavy hair. He did not refuse the glass of water I offered. He drank slowly, steadily, the muscles moving in waves beneath the smooth skin of his throat. After he passed me the empty glass, he stepped back. "Why are you looking at me like that?" he asked.

"There is something," I said faintly. "A little spot of something, on your cheekbone."

The gesture with which he raised his hand—index and little fingers spread, ring and middle fingers together, the whole strong shapely hand displayed—was that of a beautiful woman. Two fingertips brushed his cheekbone, where I would place my tongue. He knew that, knew there was nothing to brush away but a few drops of sweat. That was pity passing over his face, and fear at the hunger in my gaze, and pleasure, just a little, at being so sharply admired. He started to say something, stopped, shook his head, and left.

I cannot have James. This is perfectly clear. In my mind I know he belongs to Sophie and I accept this, I understand it. In my mind. Still my heart lags behind. Though even if my heart wants to be broken, if part of me wants to be brought to my knees, it is not to be my choice. For James I will never be more than one of the three virgins he passes daily.

The aunts have no idea of this, but it is from the likes of James that they have wished to preserve me. From that giving in, that going under, they would preserve me as they've preserved themselves. Not the children born every year, half or more of them to die; not the daily bowing down, the loss of my own thoughts and my independence; not the loss of my mind nor (the thing the aunts can't envision) the loss of that clear separate place in me where I dream of you, and long for you. Through that channel of longing, the world enters me.

Yesterday Mr. Wells took me to visit our elderly neighbor, William Bartram who has grown so reclusive. We've met before; when I was a girl, still in short skirts with my hair in a braid, the aunts occasionally trotted me over to him. *Great man,* they said, introducing him to me. Then me to him: *Our niece, whom we are raising. She is very studious.* A few questions they would put to me, so Mr. Bartram might see how well I answered. After those I was expected to be silent.

Mr. Wells brought me there as someone like an equal. On a seat in the garden, near the giant cypress Mr. Bartram's father brought back from Georgia, with Mr. Bartram's menagerie disporting about us, snakes and frogs and salamanders, two dogs, a possum, a crow named Virgil—there, Mr. Wells had me describe our experiment with the dew.

Mr. Bartram listened attentively, Virgil perched on his shoulder and pecking at his spectacles. "This is most interesting," he said. Then he rose and beckoned us to follow him down the gentle slope from the house to the river, touring us through the persimmons and walnuts, the odd vines tangled high in the chestnuts, the cider press perched above the water, and the pond he'd deepened and banked with stone.

As we walked around the pond something went plop and plop and plop: "My little green frogs," Mr. Bartram said fondly. "At night their croaking keeps us awake." When he waved his arms about, fending off the clouds of mosquitoes and gnats, the strands of white hair left on his head rose and danced in the sun. He walked quickly for such an old man but I kept up with him, delighted with the black calf boots Mr. Wells had given me as a belated birthday gift. At the peach grove Virgil leapt down from Mr. Bartram's shoulder and pecked inquisitively at my boot buttons. "Was he hard to train?" I asked.

"Not at all," Mr. Bartram said. "His wit is prodigious. The first time he saw me pulling weeds from the vegetable garden he watched for a while and then hopped over and began plucking blades of grass from the ground with his beak. When I am writing, and he would rather I came outside, he pulls the pen from my hands. You might train a crow yourself, if you desired a companion."

"My aunts," I said. "I think they would not . . ."

Mr. Bartram nodded. "Worthy women," he said. "But very . . . tidy." He gestured toward his specimens, which live in a tangle that might seem chaotic had he not explained it. For each plant he'd made a place imitating its natural home: a split rock if he'd found it in a mountain cranny, a moist spot under briars if it lived under briars in the woods.

"When those ladies used to visit," he said, "they always suggested I might want to *neaten* things a bit. I'm glad they haven't wholly neatened you." His gaze on me was clear and straight; I think that, like our other older neighbors, he has always known that the aunts are not my aunts. If he knows too that they're not kin to each other he hasn't betrayed this to me; though who knows what he'll say to Mr. Wells. Perhaps, when they next meet, they'll speculate over a glass of whiskey. What do men think, when they see women living together? Do they imagine the aunts sleeping side by side, wrapped in flannel, untouched?

Back in the garden, cool glasses of cider before us, Mr. Wells complimented Mr. Bartram. "The riches you and your father have gathered—

such a marvelous array of species," he said. "No visitor can fail to be impressed."

"I've had good company," Mr. Bartram said. "Men from Russia and France and England and Germany have all honored me with their visits, even Peter Kalm from Sweden; this has been a great pleasure."

Virgil flew past us, carrying something bright, and landed beneath the cypress. With his beak he tossed scraps of bark over his toy, until it was hidden.

"What Kalm wrote about Niagara Falls," Mr. Wells said. "Such a powerful description—the blinding fog and the cascading water, the birds losing their way in the cloud of vapor rising from the rocks. Ducks and geese and swans, their wings weighed down by the mist until they drop from the air and tip over the cataract. . . ."

"Feathers," Mr. Bartram said dreamily.

They can't imagine the aunts: or not the aunts young and caught together in a current. Instead they think about the sliding layers forming the current itself, conversing as if jointly creating the falling birds and the rising water. Where is the theory, I wanted to ask, that might make sense of this?

"When Kalm visited," Mr. Bartram continued, "he said he found below the Falls each morning enough feathers to stuff many beds. And fish, all broken and writhing, and sometimes deer, once a bear."

They weren't ignoring me; they were talking to each other but also to me, perhaps in part *for* me; they were so happy that I felt happy too. From the table I slipped a little knife, which Mr. Bartram had used to sever the stems of the grapes. Virgil, who'd been creeping closer while the men spoke, was staring beseechingly at my boots; from the left one I cut the topmost button, which I never use, and held it out to him. He bent his head, his beak grazed my hand; the button disappeared. At the base of the cypress he tossed it up in the air and down again, up and down until he tired and buried it near his other treasures.

When we rose to go, Mr. Bartram asked us to wait and went into the house for a minute. He returned with a book, his own famous *Travels*. Mr. Wells rested his hand on my arm and looked at Mr. Bartram; I saw Mr. Bartram nod. "A small gift," he said. "In return for the pleasure of your company, and for what you gave Virgil."

I had thought myself unobserved. Inside the front cover Mr. Bartram had written: *For my new friend, who can listen to the birds.*

Another of Aunt Jane's spells. She took to her bed, pale and damp; when I brought a tray with her supper she turned her face and said she couldn't eat. "I have no appetite," she sighed. "Not for food, not for work. Not for anything." I looked at her and wondered what I am *except* appetite.

"Shall I read to you?" I asked. What I should have done was smooth her hair and say I loved her. Say I would live my life like hers, that I am grateful for all she has taught me and do not judge her.

"Read," she said. "Please."

And softly, so she could hardly hear me, I read about the wonders of the planetary system, the perfections of the Deity, and the plurality of worlds. I read about igneous meteors. "'Another species of phenomena, on which a great mystery still hangs,'" I read, "'is the singular but not well-attested fact of large masses of solid matter falling from the higher regions of the atmosphere, or what are termed meteoric stones. Few things have puzzled philosophers more than to account for the large fragments of compact rocks proceeding from regions beyond the clouds, and falling to the earth with great velocity.'"

"Oh," Aunt Jane moaned. "What has this to do with anything?"

Beneath the counterpane her body made barely a ridge. I wondered what she was like at my age, what she longed for and couldn't have.

"Listen," I said.

I read about luminous meteors over Benares, a large ball of fire followed by falling stones; it was you I was reading to. About a huge stone that fell in Yorkshire, burying itself deep in the ground; about an extraordinary shower of stones that happened in Normandy. "'In the whole district,'" I read, "'there was heard a hissing noise like that of a stone discharged from a sling, and a great many mineral masses, exactly similar to those distinguished by the name of meteor stones, were seen to fall.'"

Outside her window the frogs were singing. "'The stones,'" I read— but I had done something good after all, she had closed her eyes and entered the dead sleep from which she'd emerge, twelve hours later, washed clean and a little stupid. "'These stones,'" I read, "'have a peculiar and striking analogy with each other. They have been found at places very remote from each other, and at very distant periods. They appear to have fallen from various points of the heavens, at all periods, in all seasons of the year, at all hours both of day and night, in all countries of the world, on mountains and on plains, and in places remote from any volcano. The luminous meteor which generally precedes their fall is carried along in no fixed or invariable direction; and as their descent usually takes place in a calm and serene sky, and frequently in cloudless weather, their origin cannot be traced to the causes which operate in the production of rain.'"

Here I paused and closed the book. Into the still night air I said:

Q. But what are the causes which operate in the production of rain?
A. *We do not understand even those; how should we understand a rain of stones?*

I was talking to you, I was asking you. Lapidifying juice, petrific seed, volcanic spume, the tears of the moon—somewhere, wherever you are, do you too look at the world and ask question after question?

You have no face, but sometimes I can hear you. Not as a human voice but as a pulsing hum, lower in pitch than the tree frogs' note, higher than the cicadas; pure intonation, no information. When I think about Mr. Wells I hear the hum deepen, as if with pleasure, while I imagine a life. Sons and daughters and a large airy house, a garden soft with ferns and herbs and a long drive bordered by peonies. His work—he works hard, he will not be home much—and mine. Much of mine the education of children; but *my* children, not the children of strangers. At night a hand on my breasts, a thigh between mine; and if that body doesn't belong to James, if it is not James who bends to me, if it is not James . . .

While Aunt Jane slept I leaned out the window, looking up at the cloudless sky and the ring around the moon. All that is there, all that hangs suspended in air, suspended above the air: rain and hail and fire and stone, the mind of God, if there is a God; the stars and planets and comets and our fates. Sleep well, my dear. Wherever you are.

"What makes you happy?" Mr. Wells asked. We were out in the garden again. This is a question no one has ever asked me. The question you might have asked, might someday still ask.

"To be out here at night," I told him. "On a clear cold night when the dew is heavy, to walk on the grass between the marigolds and the Brussels sprouts and feel my skirts grow heavy with the moisture. Or to go further, into the hayfield, where the mist hangs above the ground, rising nearly to my waist. . . ."

I should not have said that, he looked startled. But although it was burning hot and the sun was shining I could feel myself in that field, timothy and clover and young wild grasses knee high and soaking wet, my wet skirts clinging to my legs and before me the low cloud spreading and spreading, white in the light of the moon and the stars above. On a ridge in the distance a white house is shining; this is the house where James lives. At night, long after the aunts are asleep, I have stood in the field, sopping wet, gazing across the sea of mist to a porch set with tall columns. Behind the columns are rows of windows, two of them softly lit; and in the golden slots a chair is outlined, a rocking chair with a wooden back and a woven rush seat. Sometimes the chair is empty. Sometimes the chair holds James. I stand in the cloud, invisible to him, moving through the damp green growth like a deer, my height and heaviness cut in half, suspended above the suspended water. As the mist rises to my waist, my shoulders, my head I am standing in a kind of rain: and in that rain I am beautiful, at least to one man. Above me a meteor cuts the air and hot stones shower down. In that light, across the field, is all I will never have. Next to me is all I will.

"Will you marry me?" Mr. Wells asked.

I placed my hand in his and thought how I would say to you, how I would say . . . Oh, my brother, where are you? In the hum that is you, or my longing for you, I heard an answer.

"I would be honored," I said.

TWO RIVERS

The Ruins

A S A YOUNG WOMAN, she had written letters only infrequently. But now, in aid of her sister's work, Miriam found herself writing letters almost every day. To the geologists, soldiers, government officials, and river traders on whom she and Grace depended, she wrote requesting cargo space for their crates, or reporting progress on their project, or itemizing their expenses: *freight on 1422 lbs @ 6 cents/lb: $85.32.* She wrote to her son, in whose hands she'd left the Academy months ago, and to her daughters, who taught there. She wrote to bank officials, freight agents, book dealers, and, late in the afternoon of one bright, clear day, to her dead husband Caleb's dearest friend:

June 29, 1853
Mauvaises Terres of the Dacota Country

Dear Stuart—

Forgive me for taking so long to answer your last. I do mean to answer promptly, I know you like to follow our progress. I can only plead the constant press of work. You would understand if you could see this place; the season for collecting is short, and we are busy every minute. Do you remember what Caleb used to say about the ruins of an older world being visible all around us? He might have had this strange ugly landscape in mind, so jumbled and jagged. Box canyons, big cliffs, a river bed that looks as though God hacked through the plain with a giant axe.

Grace, who loves all of this, maps the sites where we dig and correlates the strata to similar formations elsewhere. In the cliff walls, she reports, the relics are arranged by age, youngest at the top and oldest at the bottom, neat as a filing cabinet: the clearest possible demonstration of the ideas you and Caleb shared. The fossil skulls and shinbones we stumble across on the basin floors are more difficult to place, and we have to guess at how they were arranged above.

My work is the usual: interpreting for her as necessary, otherwise helping as I can. Everything she chips out with her chisels and hooks I pack and ship to Dr. Leidy, the vertebrate paleontologist in Philadelphia. He tells us who the bones once belonged to—a gigantic quadruped with three pairs of horns, an antique camel, miniature horses, saber-toothed felines, a ruminating hog. He is writing a book ("Of course," I can hear Caleb saying wryly. "Of course he is writing a book.") A complete account of the extinct local creatures, classified and given Latin names. He promises acknowledgment in a footnote: "Thanks to Miss Grace Dietrich, who gathered these specimens."

She doesn't complain, so neither will I. The lithographs of her finds are beautiful, and we both understand, every day, how lucky we are to be able to do this. . . .

Here Miriam stops, not sure what else she wants to say. She and Stuart are separated now by more than geography; the letters they've exchanged since her departure from Pittsburgh are friendly but also constrained. She takes pains to present Grace's accomplishments in the most positive light, as if to justify their absence. In turn, Stuart amplifies every sign of progress at the Academy. She suspects he is at his desk even now, a pile of student papers before him and a glass of lemonade nearby. Still he teaches part of each day, although it tires him. And still, after all the years they worked together, her feelings about him are complicated. He is her oldest and in some ways her closest friend, now that Caleb is gone. Yet they have often quarreled and hidden things from each other.

Are there not always conflicts, though? The best friend and the second wife of such a well-known man; they were bound to disagree. After Caleb's death, Miriam had felt burdened by Stuart's pleas that she continue to share the responsibilities of the Academy with him. In turn, Stuart had been hurt by the speed with which she and Grace detached themselves from their duties, proposed their project to several eminent geologists, and found a place at the unofficial edge of this surveying expedition in the Bad Lands.

"I wish you wouldn't," Stuart had told her. "All Caleb's hard work, the work we have *all* put in—we have twenty-three pupils, what about them?"

"They'll be fine," Miriam had replied. "William is anxious to take on a larger role, and you know what a good teacher he is. Both his sisters are coming along nicely. And you've been Caleb's essential lieutenant. . . ." She'd tried not to flinch at the expression on Stuart's face.

Why has he always been surprised by her? The day they met, when he first saw her and Grace conversing, he had stared as if they'd fallen from the moon. She can't imagine what he thought when Caleb explained the idea behind his plans—that the deaf might have a particular *affinity* for the study of plant and animal shapes—or when, after Grace's friends arrived, the angry parents took their hearing children away.

Whatever Stuart felt during that tumultuous time he confided to Caleb, not her. From the moment their first new pupil walked through the door, his hands signing a greeting while his anxious eyes said, *What if no one understands me?,* she had known that they were doing the right thing. She couldn't worry about Stuart's feelings, or wonder what it cost him to set aside his own plans and throw himself into Caleb's grand project.

Miriam rises, sets aside the board on which she's been writing, and considers the jagged landscape surrounding her tent. One formation, not far away, looks like a giant molar waiting to be pulled and would, she thinks, delight Caleb nearly as much as would her and Grace's presence here. Ignore the gossip, he would tell her. Concentrate on your work. But it isn't always easy being the widow of such a man; everyone has opinions about his life as well as hers. In the schools that their former pupils have founded, portraits of Caleb hang in the halls, along with miniature biographies that might refer to someone else's life.

No one knew him, Miriam thinks. Not as she and Stuart did— and no matter how the two of them disagree, this crucial bond remains. She picks up her pen again.

You should see Grace's face and hands: very brown, dotted with freckles. Against these her hair, powdered with rock dust, is so white that strangers sometimes take us for twins. They ask what we are doing, where we have come from. Sometimes, when they persist, I pretend I'm as deaf as Grace.

As I write, she's at the base of a ravine. Big birds whirl around above her; I should go call her, dusk comes suddenly here. I miss my dear children, I miss the Academy, I miss all of you. I know my life doesn't make sense to you. It makes sense to me and to Grace; it would have made sense to Caleb. Please ask my William to write and tell us how things are with him and his sisters, also how many new students he has enrolled for the autumn classes. I think of you often, always fondly.

—Miriam

The Origins of the World

In Pittsburgh, as Miriam knew, people continued to talk about Caleb after he was dead. They spoke of the great swerve he'd made in midlife and the dedication his family showed to his cause; of the visitor from Hartford he corralled into training them all and the pupils who became such a credit to him. But no one spoke of the years that laid the course for those events. The obituaries made no mention of Caleb's original family in Philadelphia, nor of his adoption by the Bernhards. Samuel Bernhard appeared only as the Academy's founder and Caleb's father, never in the context of his other work. And Caleb's best friend, Stuart, who might have corrected certain mistakes and omissions, kept his secrets.

Before Miriam set off for the West, she too had refrained from adding to the accounts of Caleb's life. A few private moments she hoarded for herself. Other things she was not equipped to speak about. Caleb was fifteen years her senior, a young man before she was born. And for all they shared in their years together, he never told her much about his first home, or about the endless nights, after he moved, when he stayed up with his new father.

He was in a house in Pittsburgh during those nights, his feet cold and his eyelids drooping while the river at the end of the block murmured, *Ohio, Ohio.* Everyone else was asleep. Rosina, his new sister, was too young to be up so late; Mrs. Bernhard, his new mother, went to bed early, still mourning the children who, if they hadn't died as infants, would have been the rest of his new family. Behind the house was Bernhard's Academy for Boys, which Samuel Bernhard ran with a single assistant—but there were neither dormitories nor boarders then; those pupils went home at the end of the day. As Caleb turned eight, then eleven, then twelve—1800, a fresh new world—he bore the brunt of Samuel's enthusiasms alone.

Listen, Samuel said to him. *Listen to this.*

What Caleb heard was new and often enchanting, despite his exhaustion; it helped distract him from all he'd lost. Unlike his first parents, who had been farmers, Samuel talked about geology, theology, the origins of the world and all its creatures. About fossils, which some people called figured stones. In the old days, Samuel claimed, when he was a boy in Germany, rocks formed like animals or plants had been grouped with those shaped like axes or pots or hats.

With the rest of the household fast asleep, in a room cold except for a space near the stove, Samuel would hand over gray slabs that dusted Caleb's fingers. "That shape like a fern," he said, "is a miracle of nature."

"Where did it come from?" Caleb asked. In his old life, people had talked about the weather. "How did it get here?"

"There is only one true and simple explanation," Samuel said gravely. "But despite this men have had many notions. I keep track of them in these pages."

As Caleb admired the basswood box containing the papers, Samuel eased forward a single sheet. "Here is one idea," he continued. "Perhaps the figured stones are sports or jokes, which a capricious God developed in the rocks."

Perhaps, Caleb heard, *perhaps, perhaps.* Swooning with lack of sleep, still he struggled each night to be a worthy confidant. There were vapors, he heard, which might have risen from the sea, bearing the spawn of organic life and then condensing into rain. Or God might have endowed the earth itself with some extraordinary plastic virtue, capable of imitating existing forms. Some men, Samuel said, believed that in the secret, hidden parts of the earth, fossils might have been created as ornaments, just as tulips and roses, also useless, had been created as ornaments for the surface.

"Suppose they grew," Samuel said, smiling as if the idea had a savor on his tongue, "and reproduced accordingly—as plums beget plums, so might a stone bearing a snail-like figure beget a second snail."

All those stories, all those words, swirling around in Caleb's mind. When he admitted his confusion, Samuel said, "You must learn not just to listen, but to think for yourself."

Am I to listen? Caleb thought then. *Or am I not?* On another night, after carefully considering more of Samuel's stories, he asked, "But what is the *truth?*"

"The truth," Samuel said quietly—it was very late, and dark red halos shimmered around the coals— "is that fossils are relics of the Flood, the petrified remains of creatures drowned in the Deluge. When God punished the sinners and the waters rose, the earth's surface was converted into a fluid jelly. Think of the jelly around the pickled pigs' feet your mother makes."

"I like that," Caleb said, although he still had trouble thinking of Mrs. Bernhard as his mother.

"While the jelly is warm and still liquid, she can stir in bits of meat. But once the jelly cools, everything is set in place. Exactly so," he continued, while Caleb's stomach rumbled, "was everything living frozen into the rocks when the Flood receded. The just along with the unjust; plants and fishes and snails, who after all had committed no sins, petrified equally with the humans who offended God."

"But that's not fair," Caleb said indignantly. "Why should the innocent be punished?"

Instead of answering, Samuel led Caleb to a long, heavy arch of gray rock resting on the windowsill. "From an elephant, who did no harm," he said. "This is part of a rib. A man I know found it at a salt lick in Kentucky." As Caleb held his candle closer to the petrified bone, Samuel raised his hand and cupped Caleb's chin. Since Rosina's birth they seldom touched; Caleb leaned into the unfamiliar warmth.

"We cannot know what God sees," Samuel said. "Nor how He judges. We can only accept that all He does is both just and merciful."

Sometimes, in the following months and years, Samuel read to Caleb from the Bible. Sometimes he read from his growing pile of pages, in which—the better to set off his true knowledge—he detailed the erroneous theories of the past. And sometimes he read from the papers of other men who studied the secrets buried in the ground. Although no one had ever seen the giant creature called Megalonyx, it was not extinct, simply undiscovered. "For if one link in nature's chain might be lost," Samuel read, "another and another might be lost, till this whole system of things should vanish by piecemeal."

Caleb wondered if he might not vanish himself, his former ways and habits buried beneath the flow of Samuel's ideas. He felt most in danger of disappearing, but also most intrigued, on the nights when Samuel put down his papers and stared into the fire, describing his own vision of the Deluge.

When the rain ended, Samuel said, when the great masses of cloud finally parted, how astonished Noah and his family must have been! The water shimmering under the first pale sun, the clouds first black then gray and then finally white in an open and radiant sky. Under the water, Samuel said dreamily, lay lost cities, drowned mountains, entire forests uprooted from their tenuous hold on land to float horizontally.

The Flood sounded lovely then; Caleb listened raptly. Only during the day, when he paused to consider the stories he'd heard in the dark, did he think of what Samuel hadn't mentioned: the lost people also floating through that calm liquid, tangled with lizards and birds among the branches.

One of Samuel's gifts was his power to conjure such vivid pictures in Caleb's mind. But Caleb had a gift as well, which he discovered during those years: he could pick out secret shapes where others distinguished nothing. Where had this come from? Not from Samuel, whose eyesight was very poor. Perhaps his first parents had shared a similar sharpness of vision. Outside, along the cliffs and streambeds, Caleb was drawn to the hidden fossils as if they were iron and he a magnet. When he found a new specimen, his joy made up for his gritty eyes and the way his classmates mocked him for his old-fashioned speech and his love of rocks.

Bernhard's heartburn, some of them sang. *Headmaster's bonehead son.*

He shrugged them off, they were ignorant. For friends, until he met Stuart Mason, he had his much younger sister, Rosina, and a bent-tailed yellow dog.

On a rainy spring afternoon in 1810, when Caleb was twenty-three, he visited Dr. Mason's office on behalf of his mother and left with a prescription for a tonic.

"See my nephew," Dr. Mason said. "Next door. He'll make this up."

In the space between the two low buildings Caleb, already wet, was so thoroughly drenched that even the roots of his hair felt refreshed. Behind him, as he ducked through the door, the rain fell and fell for the third day in a row. The streets were streams, the empty lots were ponds, the river was pushy and loud. The yellow dog was dead by then; Rosina, who'd turned from an eager, long-legged girl who liked to run through the woods into a miniature copy of her mother, hated to get muddy now and would never go out on a day like this.

Caleb, who liked the rain, shook himself off. Inside the cool dark room, perched on a stool before bottles of rhubarb bitters and witch hazel, hanging dried herbs and mysterious twigs, was a compact, sweet-faced young man he'd met briefly several times but not yet gotten to know. After they reintroduced themselves, Stuart inspected the note and said, "For your mother?"

How clear and frank his eyes were. "The rain makes her melancholy," Caleb replied, stifling an impulse to add that she wasn't actually his mother. Recently he'd been startled by how little he resembled his adopted family, and how sharply his long, wiry limbs and his consuming curiosity set him apart.

He looked down at the newspaper lying open on the counter, leaning closer when Stuart pointed out an article and asked, "Did you see that?"

The Rappites, Caleb read—hardworking religious ascetics, calmly awaiting the end of the world—had built a new woolen mill. What could it be like, Caleb wondered aloud, to work a loom in the expectation of being lifted bodily, any minute, into heaven?

"Unnerving, I imagine," Stuart said. "Every time you heard a strange sound you'd be thinking, *This is it.*"

When Caleb laughed, Stuart offered a tale about a man named Symmes who claimed that the earth was hollow and filled with nested concentric spheres, each one habitable and awaiting settlement. In Russia one might find mammoths in the frozen river deltas. In Egypt there were mummies underground, in Oregon relics of ancient tribes—and so who could say for sure what else might not be hiding inside the earth?

"You'd like to travel?" Caleb asked. "So would I."

The lines of a possible life fanned out—two companions exploring here, adventuring there—and just as quickly reeled themselves in: Stuart was already married, Caleb learned. Already tied to the infant fussing in a basket at his feet.

"Talk is my form of travel," Stuart said wryly. "At least for now. That and reading whatever I can." As Caleb pondered the contrast in their situations, Stuart bent over the basket and then deposited the squalling bundle in Caleb's arms.

"Elias," he said, as Caleb inspected the infant's charming ears. "He's teething. He wants to be held, and I need both hands to work."

While Stuart ground and stirred, he said he'd meant to be a doctor but now made a living compounding potions for his uncle and experimenting with leaves and roots. A sharp smell rose from some herb he crushed. "My father's legacy to me," he said, wincing. "An oversensitive nose." What would it be like, Caleb wondered, to *know* who had given him certain traits—his sharp eyes, his cowlick, his sense of not quite fitting in anywhere? The smell of living blood, Stuart said ruefully, was what had turned him away from medicine.

Caleb jiggled Elias gently and eyed a huge tooth lying behind the bundles of willow twigs. "Mastodon?" he asked, prodding the conical cusps with his foot. "My father has part of a rib, from a place down the river."

"The salt lick in Kentucky?"

Caleb nodded. "His speculations about the Elephant of the Ohio are almost the first things I remember."

A lie, already; no way to make a friend. He crouched, balancing Elias, and touched the tooth's curved roots. What he first remembered, hazily, was an entirely different life. If his true parents had not died of the yellow fever when he was a child, he thought. If the Bernhards, making their way from New Jersey to Pittsburgh, had not stopped near the smoking heap that until that morning had been his home; if their eldest son had not died a few weeks earlier and if he himself had not been pulling against the hand of the doctor, shrieking as his first sister, Lavinia, was placed in a wagon with two women. . . . *Grateful*, the doctor had said. *Always, to this family willing to take you.* He'd been five when he was chosen. He had never seen Lavinia again.

"My father told me the ground near the salt spring is filled with giant bones, all mixed together," he said. At least that part was true. "Some from creatures that no one has ever seen."

Stuart looked up and nodded. "The great American incognitum, now extinct."

"Or simply, as my father believes"—Caleb had his own doubts about this—"a living nondescript we haven't seen *yet*."

Stuart raised his eyebrows, which Caleb found both reassuring and alarming. "So where are these behemoths now?"

"Out West," Caleb said cautiously. He returned Elias, who had fallen asleep, to the woven basket. "Or at the tip of South America, or hiding in the arctic. Somewhere, my father contends, mastodons are still roaring."

"That's one possibility," Stuart said. "Myself, I think they are long extinct—and I don't mean by the agency of any biblical event." Through a rolled cone of paper he poured a stream of ground bark. "I heard from my uncle that your father is writing a tract about fossils."

"He is," Caleb admitted. "An historical overview of all the old theories, followed by his own account." Was this a betrayal?

"I'm interested in the relationship of fossils to geology," Stuart said. "My uncle lets me borrow from his library. I'd be glad to share some books with you, if you're interested."

They talked for another hour, a rush of ideas that left Caleb both grateful for all he'd learned from Samuel and, as he wandered outside through the last feeble rain, afraid of his new friend's opinion of Samuel's work.

In Stuart's company, among the delectable rows of Dr. Mason's excellent library, Caleb developed his own ideas about the earth's beginnings. Stuart passed books, stuffed with scribbled notes, to Caleb; in turn, Caleb passed the least objectionable of these on to Samuel. After all, Caleb told his father, the earth's crust did not so much resemble a fluid pudding in which raisins were randomly mixed. Rather it resembled a squashed and tilted book, each page bearing a different form of writing. And this sequence of strata might *mean* something; the neatly stacked layers, all bearing their characteristic fossils, a signal that different kinds of life had over time appeared and then disappeared. Not one Deluge, Caleb suggested. But a long series of inundations.

Although Samuel dismissed that idea with a laugh, their arguments, which often included Stuart, in general seemed to please him. "I have always kept up with the times," he said proudly. "I have always been open-minded. Reconcile your theories with the truth of Scripture and you will have my full attention."

It was enough, Caleb thought, to see Samuel caught up again in the pursuit that had once been his greatest pleasure. In recent years he'd grown sluggish, seldom going on the collecting trips that had punctuated Caleb's childhood. Work on his book had slowed as well; he was growing old, and sufficiently vague that his assistant master, exasperated, had recently resigned. Caleb, with little warning, now found himself teaching half the classes.

What a relief, in light of this, to see some of Samuel's old energy and enthusiasm return. Once again he was scouring the local cliffs and creekbeds, and if at first he returned with the same familiar fossils, still his ardor was touching. A small, solitary figure climbing clumsily up a rock face, scarf flapping over his shoulder as his bruised hands fumbled for treasures: how could this pleasing sight lead to so much pain?

During the weeks when Samuel found the first of the peculiar stones, Caleb, who was swamped with teaching duties, knew only that his father vanished at awkward times and seemed gleefully secretive. He would have been horrified to see Samuel on that cliff, charting the positions of his finds before removing and squirreling them away. Had Caleb known what was going on, he would have asked the questions that became obvious later: Why did Samuel find only counterparts—the impressions, the prints—and no corresponding parts? Why were all the impressions intact, and all of the same depth? But Samuel saw, instead of these problems, a grand solution.

His stones, which depicted bees caught in the act of sipping nectar, birds frozen in midflight, a spider consuming a fly, were not mingled together but layered, birds above bees above the spider until, near the top of the cliff, the sequence was crowned by pictures of the sun and broken shapes that resembled letters. Relics of men, Samuel decided. A civilization drowned in the Flood. Without telling Caleb anything, without showing the stones to a soul, Samuel commissioned an artist to draw illustrations of all he'd found. Only then did he confide in Caleb.

What was it like, that first sight of the stones? Like a blow to the head, like the onset of a fever. Caleb knew, he knew right away; Stuart agreed with him instantly. The stones are fake, Caleb told his father. Can't you see?

But Samuel locked himself in his study, emerging with fresh chapters for his book. These discoveries, he claimed, proved that fossils were arrayed in layers not because they'd been laid down over time during successive inundations, but as a result of their differing degrees of intelligence and closeness to God. Little creeping things had drowned in the first days of the only Flood, while the more intelligent, flying or fleeing uphill, had been caught by the water later. Of course human beings had drowned last. By this arrangement, God demonstrated order even in the midst of chaos.

By then Samuel wasn't speaking at night, pacing before the fire; by then he was preaching to his family or bursting into Caleb's classroom. Nothing has altered since the Deluge, he claimed, nor will it ever, as God's first plan was perfect. Consider the sturgeon, that very odd fish. "From the Monongahela," he told Caleb's history class, "I once pulled a specimen five feet long, with a mouth like a hose." Who could have expected God to fashion such an improbable creature?

All this, and more, he wrote down. Soon his book assumed its final shape and a title that, repeated on brown calf covers, would haunt Caleb for years:

God's Hand Apparent
in the Figured Stones
of the Allegheny and Monongahela Valley Region;
Illustrated with Folio Plates of these Marvelous Creations

Eighteen months after finding the first stone, three months after he'd sent copies of his book to all the best scientific societies and journals, Samuel found, in a crevice at the top of the cliff, a flat slab inscribed with his name.

In the schoolyard, among the whispering boys, were a few who betrayed the culprits: three recent graduates who, before leaving the Academy, had carved the impressions into bits of soft shale. Caleb tracked them down and made them apologize to Samuel. They'd never meant, they said, for Mr. Bernhard to take those stones seriously. They had thought he'd see their joke at a glance. Their bland blank faces and callused hands, their fumbling explanations: Caleb had wanted to strike them.

Samuel stopped teaching, he stopped going out, soon he stopped leaving his bed. He spent all he'd saved, and more he borrowed, buying back copies of his book. During the days Caleb, now running the Academy by himself, could not be with him. But at night he sat by Samuel's bed, the two of them once more awake together while the rest of the household slept. This time it was Caleb who read: at first out loud, when Samuel could still listen. Later, near the end, he read to himself.

The Academy of Sorrow

A herd of schoolboys dropping books, reciting their lessons, bungling grammar and simple sums while exuding a smell—not unpleasant, completely definitive—that hadn't changed since he was a boy himself: for a decade, except for a brief, glowing year, this became the shape of Caleb's life. He worked to restore the Academy's reputation and to repay the debts which, along with a tower of brown books and a clear sense of his father's errors, he'd inherited. To the curriculum, which he'd also inherited, he slowly added algebra, astronomy, a smattering of geology. Still he wasn't teaching what he wanted, but each small change was a revolution to the parents he courted and couldn't afford to offend.

Young Harry Spires, who joined the Academy as assistant master seven years after Samuel's death, was all for tossing Livy and Horace aside completely and adding botany, chemistry, French, and German. Patience, Caleb counseled. We must move cautiously. He didn't say what he sometimes thought: that he'd inherited a kind of factory, stamping out adequately learned, sufficiently tractable young men. Men like him. He'd loved teaching, when he was younger and had first started helping his father. Now he sometimes dozed in class, waking to find suggestive drawings on the slates and the boys smirking as if he'd turned into their last, collar-frayed visions of Samuel. *A widower*, parents whispered, excusing his lapses.

Briefly, through his courtship of Margaret Harper and their simple wedding, through the lush days of August and the months when Margaret was carrying their child, he'd felt as clear and radiant as a glass bowl lit by a beeswax candle. Then something snapped or fell or cracked, a wind blew, a storm raged—who ordered this?—and he was sitting in the kitchen, staring at Stuart while his son struggled and failed to be born and left Margaret burning with fever. He roasted straws in the stove and removed them, burning holes with the fiery tips in a sheet of paper. From the pattern of charred holes, letters emerged: *The Academy of Sorrow.* Stuart seized the paper; Caleb singed spots on the back of his hand. Stuart seized his hands. During the rest of that terrible week, Stuart left his own work to help Harry with the classes, while Rosina managed the house so that Mrs. Bernhard could tend to her daughter-in-law. Caleb prayed, everyone prayed; and still, Margaret followed her son four days later.

After that Caleb turned away from whoever tried to help him. His pupils' well-meaning mothers—the widows especially—sometimes asked why he didn't remarry; it wasn't right for a man to be alone. He might have replied that the Academy, and his remaining family, required his full attention. Or he might have told the widows the truth: that once, not long after he and Margaret were married, he'd complimented her on a pot of yellow blossoms near the front door. She'd laughed, and blushed, and then confessed that weeks earlier, watching him walk around the vegetable garden, she'd slipped out, dug up a brick-sized clump of earth which held the clear impression of his right foot, and tucked it into a flower pot. In that earth she'd planted a chrysanthemum, hoping that as it bloomed year after year so would his love for her. How should he marry again, after that?

He told the widows nothing. In the constant absence of Margaret he worked, and looked after his mother and Rosina, and missed his old lively friendship with Stuart; Stuart had two more children now and when they met they spoke wryly of the tasks—the endless, tedious tasks—that kept them, almost all the time, apart.

The spring of 1825, they agreed, was more than usually harassing. Stuart's daughters both had the measles; two of Caleb's pupils were caught stealing and had to be expelled. Rosina, who for years had managed the Academy's accounts and helped her mother with the housekeeping, was suddenly useless. She and Harry, surprising everyone, had decided to marry; she was so happy she wandered around in a daze. While she stood in the hall outside Caleb's classroom, smiling down at the bust of Homer beneath her unmoving feather duster, he led his youngest pupils in a geography lesson and imagined giving her away. Rosina's hand relinquishing his arm for Harry's, Harry moving into the house with them, sharing the family duties so that his own burdens finally lightened—why, then, did he feel so unsettled?

To the boys in his classroom, he read, "For what is Asia remarkable?" The boys said:

It is the division of the Earth that was first inhabited.

Who were the first persons on Earth?
Adam and Eve, who were placed in the Garden of Eden.

At what time was the Deluge?
Nearly seventeen centuries after the creation of man.

What then became of all living beings?
All living creatures died, except those that went with Noah into the Ark.

A sharp tight pain, which resembled a cramp, seized the base of his lungs just then. He dropped his eyes to the textbook, which he'd used for more years than he cared to remember. In the back of the room, Ian Berger pushed his lank brown hair aside, revealing freckles that merged into coin-sized splotches over his nose and left cheek.

"Question," Ian said, as someone did each term. "Where did the water go *after*?"

Caleb had no answer. Wasn't this endless repetition, wrestling each day with the same tasks, same words, same weak and squalid self, enough to make anyone yearn for change? After the boys had gone home, he made his way to Stuart's house. There he found his friend in equally bad spirits, sitting on the brick stoop and prying loose scraps of mortar.

"Tired?" Caleb asked.

"Of every single thing," his friend replied. He flicked a scrap disdainfully into the air. "I'll be thirty-eight next week—my father was dead by then. Yours has been gone for a decade. And here we're still stuck in the same place, doing the same things, never seeing anything more than this tiny corner of the world—look at this stoop, it's falling apart."

"Something could change," Caleb said. "*We* could change."

"Our natures don't change," Stuart snapped. "If you had children of your own, you'd understand." As Caleb flinched, Stuart reached for his hand. "Forgive me," he said. "I wasn't thinking."

He went into the house and returned with a bottle of rum, which a grateful patient had given him, and a single glass, which, like their discontent, they shared.

Classes ended at the Academy and the boys disappeared; Mrs. Bernhard and Rosina, absorbed by the wedding plans, failed to notice the anniversary of Margaret's death. As the trees leafed out and the dense heavy heat descended, Caleb spent hours down at the wharves, fascinated by the jumble of boats and barges. He saw Frenchmen, and Indians, and a group of emigrants heading west—where was everyone going?

The movement and bustle cheered him briefly, as did Rosina and Harry's wedding, but afterward, watching the new couple settle contentedly into their household routines, he couldn't help thinking of the life that he and Margaret had lost. All summer he dreamed of Margaret; often he saw her holding his sister Lavinia in her arms. Lavinia's face, which had dimmed in his memory as he'd grown up, had mysteriously regained its color and definition after Margaret's death. Now he saw both of them clearly, the tiny scar on his first sister's chin as vivid as the dark speck Margaret bore on the rim of one hazel iris.

Those dreams brought a cloud of melancholy that even the start of the new term couldn't dispel. Stuart was downright gloomy; in November, when Caleb brought him a book they'd both coveted and couldn't afford—Rembrandt Peale's *Historical Disquisition on the Mammoth*—Stuart only shrugged. The long, intense conversations of their youth, their arguments over philosophy, history, the nature of science: how these had shrunk, Caleb thought. Shriveled to almost nothing. He set the precious volume on the table.

"What we need," he said, "is a trip."

"I can't go anywhere," Stuart said flatly. "How could I? Barbara, the children, my uncle, my mother: everyone needs me."

The crumpled skin around his eyes, the softness below his jaw—how old they'd gotten, Caleb thought. "A few weeks?" he asked.

He tried to convey to his friend the ferment he'd detected in the air. At the wharves he'd glimpsed an enormous keelboat, still under construction, that belonged to a group of naturalists and teachers headed for Robert Owen's utopian community on the Wabash River. Other boats were crowded with emigrants headed for Illinois, merchants loading and unloading goods; everyone had a plan. The papers were thick with appeals—for a Fourierist phalanx, a haven for freed slaves, a rational utopia; for asylums to benefit the deaf, the blind, the insane. Even the Rappites, less than twenty miles away, had established a new community called Economy. Couldn't the two of them step back from the history of their own lives and embrace the larger history of the earth?

"I had a thought," Caleb said. "We could go to Kentucky together and visit the Big Bone Lick. I'd love to gather some fossils for the classroom, I think I'd have better luck teaching the boys if they could actually *feel* one of those giant tusks. And I'm curious to see for myself how the fossils lie where they haven't been disturbed."

Stuart reached for the book on the table but offered no comment. And why should he? Caleb thought. Even to his own ears, the excuse for the trip sounded feeble. Something else was pressing at him: a sense, which he couldn't articulate, that in rummaging through that bone-filled pit he might finally make sense of his history with Samuel. More forcefully, he continued, "At the right site, we might be able to demonstrate a clear column of succession."

But still Stuart looked at him wearily. *Our natures don't change,* he'd said: but he hadn't meant that, he wasn't himself. Not so many years ago, they'd argued happily about the possibilities of a world still developing, still in progress. But if the world was fixed as God first created it, forever immutable; if nothing ever changed or became extinct but persisted and persisted—

"I know it's winter," Caleb said. Was that what Stuart was worried about? "But the lick is south of here, and the ground is saturated with salt. If it's frozen at all, it will only be on the surface. And no one else will be there—a great advantage."

"I really can't travel now," Stuart said. "I just can't. But why don't *you* go?"

Traveling alone seemed unappealing, but if he could bring back something that would cheer his friend . . . Caleb jumped when Stuart smacked both palms against the table.

"Go *somewhere,*" Stuart said. "Harry can take care of the Academy for a few weeks. Learn what you can and come back and tell me everything. I'm so tired of being stuck here—bring me something *new.*"

———

Everything happened quickly after that. A pupil's father, a commission merchant, owned a flatboat being loaded with linen and ginseng and nails, which was leaving for New Orleans; Caleb was welcome, the merchant said, to passage as far as he desired. A three-week break was scheduled for the end of term, and although Caleb expected to be gone at least six weeks, Harry said he could manage with a temporary replacement. Surely that small inconvenience was nothing in light of the useful and instructive fossils Caleb might bring back. "If you happened to find any plant fossils as well, that would be excellent," Harry said enthusiastically. "And when you return, maybe we could order a new globe, and some botany manuals."

Rosina, leaning up against Harry, said to Caleb, "But don't be gone *too* long, will you? There's so much to do here."

While Caleb packed shirts and socks and waterproof boots, a gun and a measuring stick and two shovels, he considered, and then set aside, the fact that Samuel's bitter last months had also begun with a fossil-gathering trip. Yet at the wharf a few days later, shivering in the cold wind and regarding the roughly built boat heaped with kegs and tarpulin-covered mounds, he felt an instant's panic.

Why was he leaving? A smell he couldn't name rose from the river, and in the confusion of saying his farewells he dropped a trowel into the water and then failed to thank Stuart for the book pressed firmly into his hands. Sally, Stuart's youngest, had brought a gift as well: three sprigs of holly tied with a white bow. With the crisp green leaves in his buttonhole, Caleb stepped onto the boat. Once not he but Samuel had said, teaching the boys some local geography, *If we could fly, we would see from the clouds the clear waters of the Allegheny flowing down from the north, the muddy waters of the Monongahela flowing up from the south, two rivers merging into the Ohio at our home and forming a great Y. By that enormous letter we are meant to understand . . .*

He'd forgotten the rest, the most important part; always he remembered the wrong things. At the railing he watched a band of black water expand between him and the shore. In some language, an Indian language, Ohio meant "beautiful river." From the sky something cold, part rain and part sleet, began to fall.

Beautiful River

A few miles past the Rappite settlement of Economy, a farmstead set back from the river housed an informal school quite different from the Academy. On this December afternoon all the pupils—Grace Dietrich, her two older brothers, and four little girls from the neighboring houses—were walking toward the water, intent on their weekly nature lesson. Forget the snow, forget the cold. Or so said Miriam, who was their teacher. If the animals pranced about in it, why shouldn't they? Every week they made this journey, in every kind of weather. On this day they romped in the woods for an hour before they emerged at the river's edge and saw a boat being pushed toward the shore by rafts of ice. Men were shouting and long oars were flailing while the bow ground against tree roots already tangled in ice. The other pupils exclaimed at the noise and confusion, but Grace heard nothing.

Had the boat not appeared, Miriam would have pointed out deer scat, or a woodcock's feather, or a fallen cardinal bright against the snow. Instead, as a man jumped from the boat to the ice to the ground, a rope in his hand, a hat on his head, Miriam directed Grace's gaze to the scene unfolding before them. Twice the man passed the rope around a tree, tying a complicated knot before he opened his mouth and spiraled a finger through the air. Another man lowered a plank from the deck to the shore. On the deckhouse roof a third man, tall and thin, stood amid the bristling oars and looked curiously down at the scene.

Grace held her arms straight out, in imitation of the oars, and then pulled them in and asked her sister a question. Miriam said, "Travelers," at the same time shaping a gesture with her hands.

"Going where?" asked three of her pupils at once.

Miriam called a question to the man who'd secured the boat.

"St. Louis, then New Orleans," he called. Once more Miriam turned to Grace and gestured.

"Where's the nearest village?" asked the man who'd lowered the plank. Carefully he made his way across the gap between the boat and the riverbank.

Miriam stepped toward him, drew a map in the snow—the river here, a farmhouse there, a stand of willows, the sandbar—and told him where he might buy flour and cheese. The sun was setting, the children were cold. Grace, who was watching her actions intently, was shivering.

"We won't be here long," the boatman said cheerfully. "I'm sure the ice will break up soon."

"I wish you good luck," Miriam said. Everyone was busy with something, she saw, except that odd figure still peering down from the roof. Uneasy beneath his inquiring gaze, she herded her students together and began the long walk home.

Caleb had been tagged as an oddity even before his boat was forced ashore; not in the old, familiar way, but in an unexpected way. Only those with a purpose, he'd learned—traders transporting cargo, families looking to settle new land—traveled at this time of year. What, the boatmen asked him, was he thinking? They were unimpressed by his account of the fossil graveyard awaiting him downriver.

"You want to dig in this weather?" one asked. "For petrified bones? Good luck."

Caleb slept alone in the first and smallest of the cabins, while the boatmen, crowded into the other cabin aft of the big space heaped with cargo, laughed and talked and smoked their pipes, never inviting him to join them. On their fourth day out, when ice forced the boat to halt, they pushed him aside and moved through their tasks in an easy synchrony.

Unable to find a single useful thing to do, Caleb had watched the children racing like rabbits across a small clearing, the slender woman who spoke to the boatmen, and the little girl whose hands moved rapidly in the air. The woman's hair was almost white; the girl's hair was equally pale; they looked, not like the sister with whom he'd grown up, but like his real, lost sister. He'd raised a hand partway, a hesitant greeting, but they didn't respond and a minute later they vanished.

Later that afternoon, while the crew settled into a routine of chopping wood and playing cards, Caleb fiddled with his equipment and worried about the weather, so much colder than he'd expected. The river seldom locked up like this, one boatman said. But they'd probably be freed in a day or two. After dinner Caleb wrote a letter to Stuart describing his predicament: which included the fact that the mail wouldn't move until the river had thawed. *I could walk home in two days,* he wrote. *But it's too soon to give up.* Then he stuffed the letter in his satchel, wrapped himself in his blankets, and went to sleep.

When he woke the boat was still frozen in, and the boatmen were still playing cards. Determined to be useful, Caleb left very early with his gun. The birds and bushes and trees near the boat were the same, he saw, as those he'd left less than twenty miles behind him. Also the same were the rocks poking up through the snow and the hawks spiraling through the sky. Farther away from the river's edge, where the snow was deeper, he found the tracks of deer and possums and pheasants. Enormous trees, black and bare, and the sun so low in the sky; he walked for miles, beguiled by the light and shooting at nothing. Only when he crossed his own tracks did he realize he'd traced a great circle.

Off he went again, on a line diagonal to his first route. Near noon he came upon a modest house, where he thought to beg a few minutes by the fire. The young woman he'd seen near the river a day earlier opened the door.

"Oh!" she said. "You—was that you on the roof of the boat?"

"I waved," he said. "You didn't see me."

Her face colored slightly. "I was talking to my sister. I didn't have a free hand."

He took off his hat and introduced himself, both confused and touched by her embarrassment.

"Will you come in?"

Behind her was the girl he'd glimpsed, along with six other children. Twining among them were a black cat, a tortoiseshell cat, and a large splotched dog. From the kitchen an older woman, Mrs. Dietrich, came forward to greet him. Miriam took his coat and gun and settled him by the fire.

"Grace is deaf," she murmured as her mother withdrew. Then she continued with the introductions, Grace's hands following her words. For her older brother, who had large ears, Grace pinched her right earlobe gently and tugged it. For her younger brother she stroked her eyebrows: his were dark and full, the most striking thing about him. She had similarly eloquent gestures for the girls Miriam introduced as their neighbors and her pupils. As she shaped them Grace studied the stranger who'd finally arrived.

Not a stranger, exactly: she'd seen his awkward gestures on the boat. Along with the fresh smell of snow and the deeper notes of his wet boots and woolen clothes, he carried an odor of sadness. As he stretched his boots toward the fire, Miriam pointed at him and raised her eyebrows in a question. Grace put her hand to her forehead, palm out with two fingers raised and curled forward, imitating his tuft of springy hair.

"What does she mean?" Caleb asked.

Miriam laughed and repeated the gesture. "She told you her names for everyone here; then she gave you a name-sign as well."

Clumsily he tried to imitate her movement. "This?"

"Turn your wrist," said Miriam. "That."

"How do I make her name?"

Miriam passed her left hand, palm in, over her left ear and then her mouth, as if with that gesture she sealed them both shut. Caleb shaped the sign for himself, correctly this time; then pointed to Grace and smiled and shaped the sign for her. Mrs. Dietrich appeared with a tray.

"Your daughter has a whole language of signs?" Caleb asked. Mrs. Dietrich nodded.

"*We* do," Miriam replied, helping her mother pass around cornbread and coffee and peach preserves. The children stared at him and the splotched dog licked his hand. "Our whole family."

She did most of the talking; Mrs. Dietrich was quiet and the gestures she used to converse with Grace were cramped and halting. Soon she excused herself and returned to the pies she was making.

"Grace lost her hearing when she was two," Miriam offered. "Most of our signs she invented, though we also use some she's picked up from her friends." She passed Caleb the last fragments of the cornbread. "But tell me about your journey," she said. "Where you're headed."

Even as he tried to describe his plans—the salt lick in Kentucky he hoped to visit, with its famous graveyard of ancient bones; his hope of digging out some of these relics—part of his attention was also with the children, who'd returned to their lessons. A schoolmaster's trick, pounded deep within. As he spoke he eyed the few worn books they shared and the open picture-primer, its oversized words paired with drawings: HAT, RAT, POT, CAT, HEN, TOP, BOY. At the moment Grace was drawing a map of Pennsylvania while the others shared the history text. With a gentle word, Miriam quelled the fit of giggling that swept through the room when the big-eared boy dropped the book on the floor.

"Forgive them," she said. Her attention too was split, Caleb sensed. As it should be. "We're taking three days off from our lessons for Christmas, and they're so excited they can't concentrate."

"You do very well with them," Caleb said. He looked down at his wet boots, imagining himself back at the Academy a few weeks from now, pushing the younger boys through their readers and ignoring their yawns. "I'm a schoolmaster myself."

"You enjoy the work?"

He nodded and then, encouraged, described the Academy. He barely mentioned Samuel and at first, flattered by her attention, didn't notice how little she offered about herself. Nothing about how Grace had lost her hearing, nor how she'd started this school. As he spoke, Grace continued drawing her map.

With her beloved colored pencils she made a blue river, brown mountains, patches of green forest. This river, her river, without the ice but with Caleb's boat. The cat walked to the window, placed her front paws on the glass, and stood staring sway-bellied out at the snow until, without transition, she was perched on the sill and the dog was walking back and forth below her, considering all that the cat might be seeing. The dog moved toward the door and waited for one of the boys to release her. Their visitor, whose crest resembled that of a female cardinal, crossed and uncrossed his legs. What would her father make of him? Over her map she unconsciously shaped her father's name-sign, one hand holding and guiding an invisible chisel while the heel of the other pushed. He'd gone to a neighbor's to build them a table but would soon return. When the cat pressed a paw to the window, trying to touch a passing crow, Grace pinched the air near her upper lip with two fingers, drawing them in an eloquent movement through the place where her whiskers would be, if she were a cat.

Caleb, who'd been watching her, laughed and said, "Even I can understand that." The children, or the fire, or the fragrant woodsmoke, Miriam's easy conversation or Mrs. Dietrich's restful silence, the sight of Grace—perhaps especially Grace—had cheered him. Only now did he realize how off balance he'd felt since leaving home. Through the window he saw the dog leap up in a startling curve, snapping at something beyond the frame. A beautiful day, one of those days for which the world had been created. He had almost missed it entirely.

He rose, flexing his toes in his nearly dry boots. "I should head back," he said reluctantly. "Thank you for making me so welcome."

"We're glad for the company," Miriam said. "The bad weather's cut us off from everyone." The children waved and the cats serpentined around his legs. Mrs. Dietrich, who hadn't spoken directly to him since they finished their meal, came forward, smiling, to offer a pair of mince pies.

He shared these with the boatmen on Christmas Day, when they asked him to join their quiet celebration. The captain led the men in some hymns; Caleb read from the Bible when asked; rain fell, harder and harder, melting the snow until it seemed that they must soon be freed. But after their dinner of pheasant and biscuits and pie, the rain stopped, the sky cleared, and a cold wind swept down the river, freezing everything again. Caleb excused himself from the boatmen's cabin and retreated to the pleasures of Stuart's farewell gift: John Filson's essay on the natural history of Kentucky. A book older than he was, but still very useful—and how like Stuart, he thought fondly, to give him not the most up-to-date scientific volume but this early description of the area. Stuart had marked one page with a piece of paper; the passage described the salt lick—still so far downriver that Caleb could hardly imagine it—and the finds of astonishing bones.

The celebrated Dr. Hunter, Caleb read, had observed from the form of the giant teeth found there,

> that they must have belonged to a carnivorous animal. . . . These bones belonged to a quadruped now unknown, and whose race is probably extinct, unless it may be found in the extensive continent of New Holland, whose recesses have not yet been pervaded by the curiosity or avidity of civilized man. Can then so great a link have perished from the chain of nature?

Where had Stuart found this book? And when—and why hadn't they read it together? Perhaps they had: there'd been long stretches, during Samuel's last months, when Caleb had sat by his father's bed with the books Stuart loaned to him, passing the words before his eyes but registering nothing.

Every morning, Caleb thought, Samuel had eaten the same kind of porridge at the same time, from the same bowl; then washed his hands and said a prayer and entered the same classroom full of boys essentially if not actually the same. After teaching the same Scripture lessons he dissected the same passages from Horace and Virgil and ate the same midday bread and cheese, eagerly awaiting the late-night hours when, surrounded by his trays of fossils, he might seek an answer to the riddle of Creation. What kind of a life was that? The same kind, Caleb feared—he was back in his bunk, unable to sleep—that he'd been leading himself.

Yet look what happened when he tried to broaden his horizons. In Pittsburgh, a few months earlier, he'd gone by himself to a party. The room had been filled with strangers, most from the same group of teachers and naturalists whose keelboat Caleb had seen being built at the wharves. They were headed for New Harmony, someone said; they meant to change the world. Intrigued—where did they find the nerve?—but also hugely skeptical, Caleb had eavesdropped on several conversations. A Frenchman attached to the group, a naturalist named Charles Lesueur, spoke eloquently about his earlier travels. The astonishing falls at the Niagara River, new species of sturgeon and pike; proudly he displayed his sketchbook to Mr. Wright, their host.

Caleb, edging up to the circle of listeners, admired the beautiful drawings until Mr. Wright, to his embarrassment, pulled him inside the circle and presented him to Lesueur. After repeating Caleb's name, Mr. Wright added, "Caleb is the son of Mr. Samuel Bernhard, who some years ago published a remarkable book about the nature of fossils and their role in God's creation."

This again, Caleb had thought. Always this. What did Mr. Wright have against him? Lesueur pouted his lips and blew, a small explosive puff that Caleb would forever after think of as definitively French. "That book," he said. "I have seen that book. Your father . . ."

Caleb flushed and looked at his shoes. The moment would pass, he thought, if he said nothing. He had lived through similar moments before. "My father is dead," he said.

"I don't mean to insult him," Lesueur continued. "Or this backward country. Merely to suggest that we consolidate the truth in opposition to a knowledge of the false—and so your father after all had a role to play. Cuvier proved last year that Scheuchzer's famous fossil skeleton, the one he called *Homo diluvii,* was the front part of a giant salamander. Your father probably believed it was a man who drowned in the Flood."

Caleb had made some clumsy excuse and fled; but the damage was done. It had taken Stuart days to calm him.

Still thinking about that party, and of the Frenchman who'd insulted him, he slept fitfully and woke with an aching head. After breakfast he went walking again, this time making a beeline for the pleasant house in the woods. Once more, Miriam opened the door. Both would remember this, later: her surprise, which deepened so quickly to pleasure. Gratefully he settled down again beside the fire.

"My parents are out," she said. "It is just us. But we're glad to see you."

Grace sat on the floor, busy with her colored pencils; after Miriam signed to her that she and Caleb were going to talk privately, her hands were still while they chatted. The weather, the moving ice; her mother's pies, which had been delicious, and her father's work, which was all around them: table, clothespress, walnut chest of drawers. The house itself. Grace and her brothers had been born here but Miriam was old enough to remember the journey from northern New York and the isolation of their early days, before they'd had neighbors. Her parents had taught her to read and write and, later, when she'd proved to have a particular gift for teaching, had encouraged her to take in pupils.

Although Miriam's words flowed in a straight line, still Caleb thought they skirted something essential. About to ask a question, he subsided as she explained that the key to Grace's education was the language of gestures, which, mysteriously, she'd been able to grasp more easily than had her parents. Through it Grace had already learned so much.

"She's beginning to read," Miriam said. "It's a second language for her, written English—I explain it by way of signs, and by drawings. Her written vocabulary isn't very large but she learns new words every day."

"Astonishing," Caleb said.

"Is it? Some days it simply seems like what we make together. What *is*. Since she first lost her hearing I've been able to understand her gestures almost instinctively, even though my mother stumbles and my father can't express himself that way at all. I'm not good at remembering ideas from books, but I remember shapes. It was her own idea to learn her letters. One morning she carried a book to me, pointing at the lines, then herself, then the lines. She was holding it upside down."

The warm glow that lit her features made him think of Margaret. "She makes signs in her sleep," Miriam said. "I think she must dream in gestures. And when she's reading she sometimes shapes the corresponding gestures with her hands, as you or I might have moved our lips when we were first learning."

He repeated a story he'd heard over Christmas dinner, about a young man, born deaf, whose father had been a boatman here on the Ohio. "When the boatman drowned," he said, "a deaf beggar took the child to Philadelphia and used him to help solicit alms. There's a school for the deaf there—"

"I know of it," Miriam interrupted eagerly. "There's one in Hartford as well, we use their signed alphabet."

"—and someone from that institution saw the boy on the streets and took him in, where he learned to draw wonderfully. Later he was apprenticed to an artist and learned lithography. Now he makes his living doing that and is much admired, especially for his skillful renderings of fish."

"I have to tell Grace this part," Miriam said.

Caleb couldn't see, in her liquid movements, where one word ended and another began: how did one learn this? He and Lavinia had been separated before she learned to speak, when she was about the age at which Grace had lost her hearing. But he had always known what she was thinking.

When Miriam's hands returned to her lap Grace began to draw a school of fishes: red and green and blue and brown, with huge fins and beautiful golden eyes. "She's fond of fish," Miriam said. "She likes to wade in the river."

"My father was enchanted by fish," Caleb replied. In this warm safe house, it seemed possible to mention Samuel without betraying him. "Not only live ones, but the images of dead ones in the rocks. There was a book he loved, when he was old—I've forgotten the Latin title, but in English it was something like *Complaints and Justifications of the Fishes*. A Swiss naturalist named Scheuchzer wrote it."

How peculiar to say that name out loud, after all these years. After hearing it roll, so unexpectedly, from the mouth of the Frenchman at the party. When he was young he'd sometimes wondered if anyone but he and Samuel knew the contents of Samuel's old books.

Miriam was looking at him expectantly, and he continued. "The hero is an enormous fish who swims close to shore and addresses the humans. In excellent Latin, no less."

He paused while Miriam conveyed this to Grace. With a pencil Grace sketched a giant fish pushing his head above the water, openmouthed and wearing a look of utmost concentration.

"Perfect." He smiled at Grace. "The fish complained that his ancestors had suffered the effects of the Deluge, although they were innocent themselves. That the tribe of fishes had paid for human sins, some being left to perish on dry land when the waters subsided. And that it was wrong for people, uncovering the impressions of their bodies in the rocks, to deny that those were the remains of actual creatures."

"Did people deny that?" Miriam asked.

"Some did," Caleb said. "My father used to study the different explanations men have come up with over the centuries. He was always convinced, himself, that the remains were relics of the Flood."

"And you? The bones you hope to find in Kentucky—how do you think they got there?"

Instead of answering Miriam's question, he looked down at Grace's drawing. She'd done something to the front fins, drawn lines suggestive of their movement—the fish was gesturing with his fins? The fish was signing?

Beneath it, in blue pencil, Grace wrote F I S T.

Miriam leaned over, changing T to H. Grace scribbled again: FISH.

"How well you draw," said Caleb.

Miriam translated Grace's swift reply. "She says she likes you, very much. And your story about the fish." She pointed at Caleb and made five slow, separate shapes with her right hand. Above the drawing of the fish, Grace proudly printed CALEB.

He tapped his chest and then formed the name-sign she'd given him at their first meeting. "Have you thought about one of the deaf-and-dumb schools for her?"

"My parents and I have talked about it. But she wouldn't want to be away from me, nor I from her. I try to teach her here the best I can, I have books and pamphlets from some of those schools but I know it's not enough." Her face clouded over. "I wish you could see how she is with other deaf children. The Rappites are taking care of a few, who've become Grace's friends. On Sunday we're going to Economy, where they live. Would you like to come?"

"I hope I'll be gone by then," Caleb said. Although he felt strangely at peace in this house, still he hated to see the point of his journey slipping away. With each passing day his goals were further deflected by the wretched weather, his own poor planning, his need to return to his duties by a certain date. How had he thought this could work?

"But if we're still stuck," he added, remembering the thickness of the ice and the morning's bitter cold, "I'd be delighted to join you."

Lightning

A ridge, a path, some black-barked trees. All of this was pleasing to Caleb, and helped make up for the fact that Kentucky lay hundreds of miles away, down a stalwartly frozen river. Mr. Dietrich, taciturn but kind, had saddled his own bay gelding for Caleb and then settled his daughters, Grace clinging to Miriam's waist, onto a sweet-tempered dappled mare. More trees, an open field. They neared a cemetery almost buried in snow. The horses walked side by side as Miriam tried to explain what she thought Grace had thought before she could understand prayers. How she'd conceived of death as coming from the moon, which until their dog had sickened and died she'd believed had watched over their family. Then she'd stood beneath the trees, a tiny, furious figure throwing rocks at the sky. Not until later, when they shared a language, had Miriam understood that gesture.

Grace rode with her cheek pressed against her sister's back, Caleb saw. With her head turned toward him. "How do you teach an idea like death?" he asked.

"By example," Miriam said patiently, as if speaking to one of her pupils. "By generalizing from the specific." Grace caught his eyes with her own, the green-gray irises uncannily flecked with gold.

As their horses stepped between rows of small stone tablets topped with sleeping sheep, Miriam talked and Caleb listened without listening. Under similar miniature stones, he thought, lay his stillborn son and the four children his second mother had seen born dead or watched die within days. Under larger stones lay Margaret and Samuel and his first parents, perhaps his sister—where was his sister? Samuel had prized a shard of English limestone, made entirely of fossil ammonites. Each the shape of a coiled snake but no bigger than a human eye, all of them pressed together without a scrap of plain stone showing—the fossils *were* the stone, the stone a mass of petrified shells. How could someone think that they weren't shells? Or that human nature might be ductile, when each season laid down another layer of stony compacted coils?

"You were right," Samuel had whispered on his last day. The figured stones on the cliff were fake and he should have seen it; he should never have accused Caleb of being an unsympathetic son. But still there *was* a message in the stones: the forms inscribed by the boys had been wonderful in themselves, representative of the effects of the Deluge. In them his pupils had incarnated exactly the knowledge he'd tried to transmit—and wasn't that, in itself, astonishing? A sign from God?

The reverse, Caleb had wanted to say. They were simply doing what they'd been trained to do. Brothers, the sons of an Aberdeen stone carver, they worked hard in the family shop and were often late for their lessons. For them, already skilled at chiseling names and pairs of dates, scratching the outlines of spiders and bees into crumbling mudstone had been a simple exercise. In a few weeks they'd made the counterfeits, in a day salted the cliff with their work. Then hid their amusement as Samuel uncovered them.

"I failed you," Samuel had whispered. "I have failed everyone. My inability to reconcile the truths of Scripture with those of geology was God's punishment for my sins. I have gone over and over these in my mind, trying to understand the huge offense that merited such punishment. So many sins. My worst wrong was to you."

"You rescued me," Caleb remembered protesting. "You took me into your home and brought me up as your son."

"I *acted* toward you as toward a son," Samuel said. "But when I took you from the wreck of your parents' house and remade you in my own image, I acted out of pride. And in my heart—once Rosina was born and I had a living child of my own I could not conceal from God that I loved her more."

The feeling that passed over Caleb then, that feeling—he had known that Samuel spoke the truth, confirming something he'd always sensed. Rosina shared with her father few habits of heart and mind; a fossil for her was a dusty rock. She shared his blood.

Beneath him the gelding walked easily, keeping pace with the mare. The wind blew, the sun glanced off the snow, and he chatted quietly with Miriam, the smallest part of his mind engaged and the rest lost in the past. Economy, when they finally reached it, stretched along the river like a picture of a village. So clean, so neat; empty of people at first. "They're in church," Miriam said. "They'll be finished any minute." And suddenly there were people everywhere, pouring from a door and moving purposefully in their neat plain clothes. Despite the cold, Miriam moved not toward but farther away from the central buildings and the crowds.

A few people nodded politely; no one approached them. Long ago, on a day when four of Caleb's classmates had pummeled him, Samuel had wiped blood from his nose and told him about the Rappites, who strove to live in harmony with one another. Equal in their stations, possessing their property in common; their hard work in this world meant to prepare them for an easy transition to the kingdom of heaven. You might try to live a bit more harmoniously yourself, Samuel had said. The boys, Caleb might have replied, were mocking *you*. Years later, Stuart's jest about the Rappites had made Caleb want to befriend him. It was a consolation to see this place at last.

Without warning, Grace flew to the three children playing along the river's edge. Immediately their mittens were cast aside; their hands darted and leapt in the air, arms whirling, eyebrows moving, mouths open, laughing, frowning, set in every sort of grimace.

"The tall boy," Miriam said, "with the shock of black hair—that's Joseph, the one who's taught us so much. When he was small, his father gave him into the care of some charlatan preacher who claimed he could teach him to talk. Joseph ran away and was found by one of Mr. Rapp's flock in the woods; they took him in, and brought him here when they moved. At first he bit whoever touched him."

She waved at Joseph and returned his elaborate bow. "I've been able to act as an interpreter for him," she continued. "The things he's told me— people have such remarkable ideas about the deaf. His preacher believed that since the deaf are without a voice, which is the breath of God, they must also be without souls. That their language of signs is no language at all, but the mimicry of trained animals. He tormented Joseph, trying to get him to speak. Tubes in his ears, hot stones in his mouth, a long probe and hot water down his nose . . ."

"Terrible," Caleb said.

"It was a great thing for Joseph when this community took him in. Although they couldn't understand him at first, they believed that his language of signs was itself a divine gift, permitting entry into his soul of the word of God."

Listen, Caleb imagined the Rappites saying. *To this.*

Still the children were conversing intently. "I don't know where Conrad and Duncan came from," Miriam said. "They're both so secretive. But I know Joseph taught them too. As he's taught us."

"You've been lucky," Caleb said.

"Lucky we live on this river," she said. "If nothing else. It gives me a chance. Boats stop here at Economy, and sometimes at the clearing where you're tied up. A few of the boatmen take an interest in the children. They bring them presents, and gestures they've seen other deaf people make."

Three crows soared up the river and settled into a bare box elder. Without any warning Miriam added, "Shall I tell you how Grace lost her hearing?"

Caleb, startled, turned his gaze from the crows to her flushed cheeks. "If you want."

Moving her hands, she said, "We were at a neighbor's wedding. Me, my parents, my brothers, and Grace. She was two and a half, and I was fifteen."

As Miriam spoke, Grace ignored her gestures. This was a story she already knew—but here were Joseph and Conrad and Duncan, the four of them free, with so much to say. What had happened to each of them that day, that week, that hour. What they could remember of the time before they found each other; the ways the world appeared to them, then and now. I have learned to bake bread, I have read a book. On Wednesday I rode by the river and saw a snake. Rain falls down through holes in the sky, said Duncan; from clouds, Joseph said. From clouds. Then Duncan again, who had never heard: At night, when I could understand nothing, I learned that others saw in the darkness with their ears.

With her eyes cast down, and her voice so low that Caleb could hardly hear her, Miriam spoke of a hot August day, a heavy meal, pitchers of strong cider from which they all drank thirstily. Dancing, different games, her parents laughing with friends they seldom saw and Grace sitting in Miriam's lap and then toddling next to her when she rose and, with a friend named Harriet, followed an older boy into a broad meadow. An enormous hickory stood all alone in the center of the grass. So safe, so sheltering. They ran for it when the thunderstorm flashed; the leaves kept them almost dry. Miriam held Grace in her arms and turned her head from Harriet and the boy, who were embracing.

Her hands, apparently without her knowledge, had continued to move as she spoke. Now she looked down at them and paused. Joseph, who'd been watching her, asked Grace a question.

I remember sounds, Grace told him. Then I fell in a big white light and when I woke someone carried me. At home there were people but I couldn't hear them. The cat sat on my chest and miaowed but I heard nothing, the dog barked and I couldn't hear her, a crow flew down beside my window and I saw her beak open and open again but everything was silent and has been since then and I didn't know what that meant.

She dropped her hands to her sides as Joseph nodded. Once he'd told her about the shining instruments of pain. So little time they had to catch up with each other—what was life and what was death and who was God and who were they; when the wind blew, what did that mean? Why did the mare have spots, or the pike such teeth? Somewhere, far away, were there others like them? All these thoughts passed through her hands and face and it was blissful, pure bliss to know herself understood and to feel, pouring back into her, other stories in such swift and shapely forms. Miriam was her sister, her life; but she signed slowly. The man who'd come to them couldn't sign yet at all. She flashed his name-sign at Joseph and explained that her family had taken him in, as they might a lost dog. Joseph laughed and beckoned toward the river.

"And then what happened?" Caleb said.

"And then a big bolt of lightning hit the tree." Miriam grasped her right hand in her left and held it still. "Harriet and the boy she was kissing were killed, although I didn't know that until later. I felt the lightning come up my legs, I felt it flow down my arm like fire, and I tried to drop Grace before it reached her but my hands wouldn't work. When I woke there were people all around us. Harriet and her beau were gone, someone had covered their bodies with a blanket. I was unharmed except for one long burn." She rolled back her sleeve and exposed to the cold air a forked scar branded between elbow and wrist. "Grace had a bruise on her cheek where she'd fallen, but she seemed fine. Then after a while we knew she wasn't."

Always, he thought, the blow was felt after a while. After Samuel's death he'd continued to see the guilty boys in town—almost grown, then truly grown, then with children of their own. While the oldest one had trebled the family business, replacing his father's flat chiseled slabs with three-dimensional angels and willows carved in high relief, he himself had lost Margaret and their son.

"It should have been me who was punished," Miriam said. "Not her."

Before Caleb could object to this, a man appeared beside them, gliding up so silently that his greeting made Miriam jump. Gray-haired, rosy-skinned, too gaunt. Miriam introduced him as Brother Eusebius. "The schoolmaster here," she said. For a few minutes they talked politely, catching up on the past two weeks.

"And how are our wonderful children today?" Eusebius asked.

"As you see," Miriam said, gesturing toward the animated group streaming away from them.

To Caleb, still pondering the vision of Miriam electrified, the sky's fire pouring through her arms and into Grace's ears, Eusebius said, "You're enjoying your visit?"

"Very much."

"Any friend of Miriam's is welcome here."

While Miriam excused herself and followed the children, now running along the river and poking at the heaps of ice, Eusebius began to talk about the advantages of this settlement. Silkworms, merino sheep, the cider press and the wine cellar; he spoke too fast, his eyes were too bright. Caleb barely listened to him. The look on Miriam's face when she mentioned that boy she'd followed, when she spoke of him and her friend embracing—perhaps she'd wished herself in her friend's place. When Eusebius paused, Caleb asked how Joseph and his two friends had come to join the community.

"It is our tradition," Eusebius said obliquely, "to welcome all who arrive here destitute and ask for help."

"Everyone?" Caleb asked. "Even tramps?"

Eusebius frowned. "We prefer to call them pilgrims," he said. "Or unfortunates. But yes—we house and feed whoever arrives, no matter what their state, and even though some people think we're foolish and call this place 'Tramp's Paradise.' But better to take in a hundred unworthy than to turn away the one who is worthy. Some—like Joseph—have clearly been sent to us by God. When they ask for work, we give them work. If they ask to join us, we welcome them."

He peered more closely at Caleb. "You, for instance," he said. "You have not said why you arrive here on a Sunday, unattached to family and friends, accompanying our beloved Miriam and Grace—perhaps you are without a home?"

"I *have* a home," Caleb said, startled.

"Yet you aren't there," Eusebius said. He tucked his hands inside his sleeves, seeming at the same moment to tuck his lips inside his mouth. "You are not there, tending after your own, nor are you in church. I pray for your soul."

Who made you? Samuel had asked at prayers each night. *In whose care is your soul?*

"My soul is in the hands of my Maker," Caleb said.

"You could lose it this day," Eusebius replied. "This very hour. We expect the Second Coming at any moment, certainly during Mr. Rapp's lifetime. Then a general harmony will rule, as it did before disorder entered the world."

Caleb felt his face contort, the muscles twitching without his permission.

"You think we are fools to await the millennium here," Eusebius said angrily. He barely acknowledged Miriam, who had just returned to them. "But I tell you this: we are not so foolish as you who believe that the world is fixed as you see it." He stalked away.

"You upset him," Miriam said quietly. "I think he has hopes of me and Grace joining their group."

"Would you really think of joining them?"

"Would you?"

For a moment they gazed at each other curiously, and then she smiled. "I'm grateful for the interest they've taken in Grace. But to live here . . . I want a family of my own. And I don't share their beliefs."

She beckoned to Grace, who waved but stayed with her friends. Inside me, she was explaining to Joseph, is a little person, the size of a thumb, who looks exactly like me. You have one too, yours looks like you. When we sleep they fly out of our chests and go here and there, then come back. When we die, they leave for good. These are our souls.

"I want *more* for her," Miriam continued. "More than I can give her—look how her face lights up around her friends. Look how their hands fly. I want to start a school for the deaf near our home, I want someone to come here and train me and a few other people, so we can teach all the children we can gather."

She turned toward a stand of willows, denying Caleb any hints he might have gleaned from her expression. Did he know then? Perhaps he knew. Beyond the willows a scraping, repetitive noise, which he'd heard faintly for some time, grew louder. He followed Miriam through the screen of hanging branches toward a frozen creek framed by steep low banks. A solitary man was skating there. An enormous wild bird. No, a man. Moving forward at great speed and then, after a smooth pirouette, backward just as quickly, his hands clasped behind his waist and his head thrown back with pleasure. Just when Caleb was about to call out a warning—a hole in the ice, where rapids bubbled—the man spun again, took a few strong strokes, and leapt over the darkness. Landing, he reversed once more, slipping over the plain.

As Caleb moved forward, his arm was tugged backward: Grace, pulling his sleeve and gesturing at the skater's intricate patterns. She clasped her hands behind her back and leaned forward: *Teach me, teach me.* The skater slid backward, disappearing, as Samuel had disappeared, behind a bend. Caleb could not remember, anymore, the real details of their fiercest arguments, the language of his accusations, the precise texture and smell of the sheets beneath Samuel's wasting body. He could not remember all the pages he'd turned to distract himself, nor all Stuart had done to comfort him. *The Earth,* Samuel had once read to him, *was more fruitful before the Deluge. The temperature of the air was more equable, without burning summers or piercing winters; the air was more pure, and subtle, and homogeneous, and had no violent winds or agitations. The Antediluvians ate only vegetables; their lives were more equal, and vastly longer, than ours.*

From the creekbank, which Caleb found he was kicking with his right foot, a spray of smooth, reddish brown stones tumbled down. Click, clack, clonking against each other and the ice. When one split, he knew what he'd find. The stone had cleaved neatly, revealing the impression of a palmate leaf. Beautiful, if not a surprise. He held the halves out to Grace, part and counterpart, and said to Miriam, "Would you help me explain it to her?"

She bent over her sister's hand. "What is it?"

"A fossil," he said, waiting while she finger-spelled the word. Joseph was watching her hands as well, although Conrad and Duncan had been diverted by a goose. "The word refers generally to anything dug out of the earth, and more specifically to the petrified remains of something once living, like this. Some are species that no longer exist."

He relied on her to translate accurately. "They're quite common," he said. "Not just the remains of plants, but shells and sea creatures and larger animals too, some of them enormous—at the place I'm headed to, people have found the fossil remains of a giant creature with the tusks of an elephant and the teeth of a hippopotamus. We call that creature *Mastodon* now—"

Miriam halted him with a raised hand. "And where," she said, "should I find a name-sign for *that*?"

What a complicated smile she had! And still he kept talking, unable to stop himself. It was like being in the classroom of his dreams, saying exactly what he meant in the light of someone's full attention. He must have known then. As he spoke, Miriam's hands moved swiftly. Grace's eyes never strayed from her sister's gestures.

Beneath her feet, beneath the river, Grace thought, the world was as densely layered as a leek. Was that what Caleb meant? Her geography book had said nothing of this, that beneath the superficial film of dirt and vegetation were layers of fish and serpents and bugs and plants, frozen lives, life she hadn't known was alive—anything might exist in the rocks and that she hadn't seen it before was only because she hadn't thought to look. She bent down, searching through the rusty pebbles fanned across the ice and then cracking a smooth oval the size of her palm against a large rock. Shocked and disappointed, she held the pieces out to Caleb.

"They're not *that* common," he said gently, speaking to Miriam but looking at Grace. "Tell her they're only in special stones."

Joseph was staring at him, he saw. As intently as Samuel's pupils had once stared—what had those boys with their figured stones meant to say? He watched Grace crouch on the shore, inspecting the bank behind her. The boys might have forged the stones, he thought, as much for *him* as for Samuel.

For years he'd listened without complaint as Samuel described, first to him, then to them, the earth's unchanging perfection. Some of the boys, clean and well dressed, had listened attentively. But the shabby ones, those with dusty hands and shadowed eyes, missing parents, irregular households: what had they known of such order? Perhaps, Caleb thought, like him they'd seen evidence of a Maker whose attention wandered. One day, after taking over the afternoon class, he'd offered them an alternate view of the earth's history.

Not just *his* view, he said, regarding the boys' dropped eyelids and sullen mouths. The modern view, the *real* view. He'd presented to them what he'd just tried to share, in a simplified version, with Grace: a vision of an earth immensely old and subject to natural processes, the sea floor heaved up into mountains, the mountains ground down by rivers and glaciers, evidence of change and movement visible everywhere in the strata. In the newest layers of the earth, he told them, barely below the ground on which they walked, might be found the bodies of mammoths and the bones of mastodons. Below those were other fossils, and still other fossils, each layer more ancient than the last. He drew on the stories Stuart had told him; the books they'd read together. The fossils that Samuel had shown the boys were, Caleb claimed, the remains of plants and animals which lived no more.

"From the Flood?" asked a boy to his left. And from the back bench,

in a tone that might have been disrespectful, or merely tired, a voice
Caleb had never pinned to its owner whispered:

At what time was the Deluge?
Nearly seventeen centuries after the creation of man.

What became of all living beings?
All living creatures died, except those that went with Noah into the Ark.

"There are different theories regarding the origin of fossils," Caleb
said, trying to locate the voice. "Many of these my father has explained
to you. He believes what you just suggested: that they're relics of creatures destroyed in the Flood. For myself, I think they are evidence of the
earth's antiquity, and of the antiquity of life."

The boys whispered in twos and threes, one coming forward to ask
what he was supposed to think when his teachers contradicted each
other.

"Think for yourself," Caleb calmly suggested.

And a few months later there was Samuel, coat flapping in the wind,
hair flapping over his eyes, happily grasping counterfeit stones which
he wrapped in paper and hid from his son. After his death, when Caleb
finally told Stuart about his impulsive lecture, and about the disturbing
timing of the stones' appearance, Stuart had groaned and said, "Couldn't
it have been coincidence?"

Miriam touched his arm. "What are you thinking about?"

He pointed to Grace, who was still rummaging through the stones.
"Her."

He had not been honest with Stuart either, when they first met. Why
did he start this way?

When they left, the horses once more stepped quietly along the river.
The trees were quiet. The birds were quiet. The sun had dropped, the

sky was gray, and it was, suddenly, very cold. On the horses the riders were silent. Grace was clutching both Miriam and the handkerchief knotted around her cache of rocks. Miriam held the reins in one hand, with the other trying to imitate a new sign she'd seen Duncan make. Caleb, behind them both, stared down at his own hands as if they might suddenly begin to speak, revealing what he was meant to do with his life. So he'd once stared, when he was a boy, at a beautiful stone Samuel gave him, which was marked with coin-sized reticulated disks.

One minute these were decorations, elegant and mysterious. The next—the sun was glaring through the window, the cicadas were shrieking their hot-weather song; it was three days before his thirteenth birthday and his pants were itching the tops of his thighs—the disks were the stems of plants, seen in cross-section. What had happened to his eyes? The familiar turned strange and the strange familiar: Margaret's face would later turn overnight from an appealing arrangement of features into the countenance of the woman he loved, her skin enclosing blood and bone and a light he couldn't name, which had seemed like life itself. Lavinia, who'd been folded into a stranger's arms when he last saw her, her small self pressed against the woman's cloak, had twisted her head as the wagon began to roll and gazed directly at him.

He looked up from his hands, at the horse ahead, at Miriam's straight, slim back and her pale hair. At Grace, who had turned around and was looking back at him.

Fire

Out here, surrounded by the evidence of vanished rivers, Miriam thinks of that evening riding home along the frozen Ohio. At what moment had the stream of Caleb's life bent and merged with hers? The people she's left behind in Pittsburgh know nothing of this; nor does Stuart. When she finds herself signing, almost unconsciously—*Was it what you wanted, was she like a daughter, was she more to you than your own daughters?*—she is more reassured than surprised.

She and Caleb were married for twenty-five years, and although it is Stuart to whom she's been writing, she can't help but reach at the same time toward the companion of her heart. Caleb was proud, she knows, that he made the Academy for the Deaf into a place known throughout the country. Five of their first students have themselves become teachers of the deaf, one opening a school in Kentucky and another in Missouri. A long way from the early days of the children teaching her and Caleb and Stuart their home-signs while they taught back everything else they knew, history and geography and botany, the way to roast a joint or dress a loom. How bold they'd been, and what unexpected gifts Caleb had turned out to have!

In her opinion they were lucky despite meeting so late in his life: their school's success, and their three healthy children, more than many get. Was that enough? It was never like him to complain. She always knew that his fascination for Grace was part of his bond to her. As he always knew what she most wanted. And if he didn't feel for her exactly what he felt for Margaret, if his mind wasn't braided as closely with hers as it was with Stuart's—what did that matter? They worked together, they made a life. In the dormitory they built for the boarders, they sometimes found the children, late at night, huddled around an illegal candle with their hands flying urgently. Despite the risk of fire, Caleb could never bear to snuff the flame.

She walks to the edge of the bluff, lifts her skirt calf-high, and sits with her feet dangling into the cool, sweet air. It is almost dark, and although Grace has a lantern with her and always works until the last minute, Miriam likes to watch over her sister's final ascent. She waves her arm, signaling across the ravine to where she can see one shoulder, one lifted arm, a fraction of Grace's gleaming head moving up the narrow trail. When Grace signals back, Miriam rises, shakes the dust from her skirt, and prepares to start a fire.

The people around them, concealed by the twisting bluffs and canyons but near enough as the crow flies, will read in the column of smoke, she knows, the news that they're still here. Soldiers uneasily surveying the Bad Lands under the eyes of the Lakota; the acquisitive geologist, meant to keep an eye on her and Grace, whom the Lakota call *picks-up-stones-running*; the Lakota themselves, with whom she and Grace converse in an Indian sign language somewhat similar to their own—all of them, Miriam thinks, wishing the inconvenient women would leave. Or perhaps they wish something else entirely, their true desires as hidden as the paths by which she and Caleb reached the decisions that shaped their lives.

Were you happy? she signs to Caleb. Under this vast and steely sky the world seems ancient, and very large. She feeds more grass to the little flame and adds this: *I was.*

THE MYSTERIES OF UBIQUITIN

WHEN THEY MET, ROSE was standing in the cool, airy kitchen of the house on Keuka Lake, peering with fierce concentration into a yellow pottery bowl. Her mother's fingers were wrapped around hers. "This is folding," Suky said, and together they guided a rubber spatula through the egg whites and into the batter, turning two phases into one. Beside them Rose's sister, Bianca, licked the chocolate pot and said, "*I* want a turn." Then there was a gentle knock at the screen door, and when Rose looked up from her task she saw, against a background of hollyhocks and hills, a tall man letting himself into their house as if he belonged there. Her mother sprang into this stranger's arms, leaving Rose openmouthed.

"You're here!" Suky said. "And just in time. Girls, you remember Peter Kotov?"

But they did not remember him at all. Rose was eight and a half that summer, Bianca seven; and even when Suky reminded them that they had glimpsed Peter a few years earlier at their grandfather Leo's funeral, they could not recall him, they had been babies then. This was the afternoon that Rose, forever afterward, would count as their first meeting. She would remember the way Suky fit so easily in Peter's embrace and how, after the cake was cooled and frosted, her father, Theo, tromped in sunburnt and smiling and shouted with glee at the sight of his friend.

Dinner that night was late and joyful; they ate on the porch, overlooking the vineyards and the hanging mist above the lake. Red wine from their own grapes shimmered in plump glasses, next to trout that Theo had grilled and a salad of soft early lettuce. Suky's hair shone and the men's teeth gleamed. The men resembled each other, Rose saw. Although their features were different they were similar in their coloring and carriage, and in their easy vigor. She saw that Theo was a little older than Suky and Peter, somehow in charge; that Suky and Peter directed their comments to him and were bound by a shared desire for his attention. All this Rose registered from where she sat with Bianca in the shadows, long past their bedtime. Bianca had fallen asleep in her chair, plump with the cake that still clung to her lips, but Rose stayed awake.

Was it that night, the first night, when she grasped how long her parents had known Peter? So much talk, so many stories. Perhaps the fragments of their history fell together during the two weeks he stayed with them. But certainly before she went to bed that night Rose understood that Peter and Theo had met when they were no older than she and her sister. More peculiar was the revelation that Peter's parents had known her own Grandpa Leo and were somehow responsible for helping him establish the winery. And thus, in some way, responsible for the fact that she lived here, in this house she had always known? Each time Rose considered this, her mind spun and stopped. It was through Peter that she first understood that the world existed before her, without her. For a few days she could not forgive him for this.

But who could resist him? He came out of the bathroom wearing only his pants, with a towel draped around his neck and tufts of shaving cream beneath his ears; he picked Rose up by one wrist and one ankle and whirled her around like an airplane. He played records and taught Bianca to dance while Rose resisted in an agony of self-consciousness. Around him Suky and Theo were radiant, cheerful, sweeping the girls up for sudden kisses and twining their arms around each other's waists. The bustle of early summer work in the vineyard seemed fun in his presence, and when Suky and Theo were occupied Peter entertained the girls.

He was an entomologist, he told them gravely. His specialty was beetles and he meant to collect some here. He had spent the last few years collecting in Costa Rica, which was why they hadn't seen him in so long. From a trunk he pulled vials and killing jars and nets and forceps, hinged wooden boxes and packets of slim black pins.

"We could help you," Bianca offered. Rose blushed and pinched her sister under the table. She was already in love with Peter, although she wouldn't be able to name this feeling for a decade. It was infuriating to have Bianca ask so easily for what she herself most wanted.

"You could," Peter agreed. "I am in dire need of assistants." Black hair sprouted through the open collar of his shirt in the most intriguing way.

He tacked a sheet inside an old black umbrella so that, as Rose held it under the shrubs and he beat the branches, the falling beetles might show up clearly against the white scalloped bowl. But Bianca, to Rose's secret delight, was not enchanted by this. Nor was Bianca impressed when Peter entrusted them with knives and small hatchets and showed them how to whack bark from fallen logs, revealing the beetles bustling just below.

"Are they *all* black?" Bianca said. "Like those?"

Already she was as tall as Rose, although she was a year and a half younger; and Rose, so small and dark and full of dismay at Bianca's blond charm, shrank inside herself. But for once she didn't have to compete with Bianca. Bianca declined to come on further expeditions, and Rose had Peter to herself.

After dinner one night, she and Peter set off with portable lights.

Her parents smiled and yawned, drowsy with food and wine; Bianca lay on the couch with a book. Peter carried the black light, the fluorescent tubes, the battery, and the killing jars. Rose carried the white sheets and the notebooks and the clothesline.

"Some species are attracted to ultraviolet light, and others to white light," Peter explained, while he suspended the sheet between two limbs of the basswood near the edge of their backyard. He hung the black light a few feet in front of the sheet, the fluorescent tube beside it. "Can you spread that other sheet here on the ground, so it forms a right angle?"

Rose smoothed the sheet over the grass. Peter connected the lights to the battery, switched them on, and guided Rose outside the circle of mingled light. When he plopped on the grass he pulled Rose down beside him, and for the next few minutes she sat without moving, her left leg only an inch from his right thigh. The beetles arrived quickly, whirring out of the darkness and striking the hanging sheet with a sound like hail.

"Can you write yet?" Peter asked. "Are you old enough to write?"

"I am almost *nine*," Rose said indignantly. "And I already skipped a grade in school. Of course I can write, I don't even have to print anymore. I can do cursive."

"Well," Peter said, laughing. "*Cursive.* But maybe just for tonight you could return to printing. If I gave you my notebook and spelled what I wanted, could you print it out clearly for me?"

"You don't have to spell," she said. "I am a very good speller."

But after all she needed his help when he began crawling around the hems of the sheet, turning over beetles and flicking specimens into the killing jar. The black light made his teeth and his collar glow and Rose sealed her lips, afraid she too would look like a jack-o'-lantern. The names he called out were long and complex: Latin names, he said. *Macrodactylus subspinosus, Phyllophaga rugosa.* She'd heard her mother mouth other, similarly complicated names for the mosses she collected. Humbled, Rose concentrated on printing clearly what Peter spelled.

"Ha!" he said, pouncing on a body clinging to the sheet. "The elusive *Nicrophorus*—see what good luck you bring me, Rose?" He held out a large beetle, black with beautiful red bands on its wing covers. Those covers, Peter said, were called elytra.

All the following day Rose sat next to Peter at the impromptu laboratory table he set up outside. There was little she could do to help; she could not persuade her hands to do the fine work of inserting the delicate pins through the beetles, and her attempts at transcribing the names onto small paper labels failed as well. She concentrated on keeping Peter's glass of iced tea filled, and on handing him paper points and glue as he called for them. When he pinned the *Nicrophorus* he said, "I didn't expect to find this here. If we set a carrion trap we might get more—would you like to help me with that?"

For him she would have cast herself adrift all night in a leaky boat. "Yes," she said.

"What we need," he continued, "is something small and dead—a mouse, a mole, something like that."

Here was her chance to be a hero; she excused herself and ran off as fast as she could. The cellars of the winery buildings were meticulously clean, full of shining tanks and tidy racks, casks and bottles and corks. But the white house was half a century older than any of the outbuildings, and although the upper floors gleamed with polish and care, the basement, which she and Bianca usually avoided, was stone-walled, dirt-floored, low-ceilinged, dark. Rose gathered the broom and the dustpan and descended the stairs. How terrible it smelled down here! She breathed shallowly and watched her feet, praying she wouldn't step in something horrid. Past the great brick pile supporting the chimney, past the furnace with its octopus arms; there was a corner under the soapstone sink where she had not been able to avoid seeing both small corpses and busy cats. She bent down and peered into that secret space—and yes, there was something there. She reached with the broom and flicked the body into the dustpan, then sprinted across the floor and up the stairs.

In the kitchen she forced herself to look and found that her prize was a little gray mouse, not long dead.

"Perfect!" Peter said when she returned to him.

That afternoon they set the trap: the mouse, trussed with a bit of fishing line, laid carefully in the thin grass of a shady bit of ground below the vineyard. On the limb of a shrub overhanging the site Peter tied a red cloth. "So we can find the place later," he said. Then he stretched the fishing line from the mouse's hind legs along the grass.

Trudging back up the hill to the house, Rose believed she might become an entomologist herself. Her mother dabbled at botany, specializing in the mosses; Grandpa Leo and her father were both chemists of a sort. The grandmother she'd never known—Eudora, Grandpa Leo's wife, who'd died before Rose could meet her—had left behind a cache of letters from her own grandfather, a surveyor who'd studied plants from giant mountains on the other side of the world. Rose had seen how Suky cherished those, savoring their connection to her own work and sometimes speaking wistfully of her desire to travel. Holding those letters in her hand, sniffing the yellowing, earth-smelling pages and trying to imagine that ancient figure, Rose had sworn she'd never vegetate in one place as her mother had.

Dear Sir, her great-great-grandfather had written to some famous British botanist. *Your examination of the Tibetan lichens is of great interest to me. I enclose some notes on the Kashmir irises.* That could be Peter, Rose thought now. Or herself. Through Peter's eyes, she saw that her family was packed with scientists. The next time they were together, she asked, "How did you start doing this?"

"Ever since I was tiny I was interested in all the animals around me, particularly the insects," he said. "It's hard to explain, it seems like I've loved them since I was a baby."

"Me too," Rose said. "That's what *I'm* like." Although until that moment, this hadn't been true. Already she was vain about her intelligence, about reading better than her classmates and skipping second grade entirely because her teachers didn't know what else to do with her. But until recently, although she'd been drawn to her father's small laboratory, where the tests on the wine were carried out and where her Grandpa Leo had entertained them with chemistry demonstrations, she'd found nature boring.

"Are you?" Peter said. "No surprise, I guess; you're Leo's granddaughter. I owe him a lot." He bent to examine a stream of ants filing across their path. "When I was growing up we lived in Ovid, not far from here, around the other side of Seneca Lake."

"I've been there," Rose said. "Near the park."

Peter nodded. "My parents were apple farmers, and friends with your grandparents. They thought my interest in insects was silly. But your father and I used to play together, and Leo always paid attention to us. He must have noticed me lugging around the bottles and matchboxes I stuffed with bugs. The Christmas I was ten, he gave me some books by a wonderful French naturalist named Jean-Henri Fabre, and those were what turned me into a entomologist. I could dig them up, if you're interested. You seem to really like this stuff."

"Oh, I do," Rose said fervently. "I do."

Two days later they returned to the site. The ground was blank beneath the red flag, but Peter brushed aside some litter to show Rose the bit of fishing line protruding from the ground. Carefully they scooped away the loose dirt to uncover the mouse, already hairless and mummified, and below it the gleaming pair of burying beetles who had so assiduously dug the grave.

"Fabre called the species of *Nicrophorus* native to France 'transcendent alchemists,'" Peter said. "For the way they convert death into life." He let Rose hold the beetles briefly before he placed them in his vial. "You always find them in couples—a male and a female, digging together to provide the family larder. They push away the dirt below their quarry until the corpse buries itself. And all the time they do that they secrete chemicals that preserve the body and keep other insects from eating it. Then they copulate—can I say that word in front of you?—and the female lays her eggs nearby. When the larvae hatch they have all the food they need. Aren't they pretty?"

At the library, a few days after Peter departed and her heart broke for the first time, Rose looked up "transcendent" and "alchemy," ransacked the card catalog for books on entomology, and stole outright the one volume of Fabre's she could find. Against her stomach, held by the waistband of her shorts, the warm book pressed on her like a hand.

It was just as well she stole that book, because Peter never sent the books he'd promised. And why should he? Why should he remember her, small and slight and short-haired and breastless? She was almost nine, and then really nine—but Peter was nearly thirty, as old as her mother: a grown man with a complicated life. And girlfriends, as she was forced in the following years to understand.

When he left Hammondsport after that first visit in 1964, Rose pined for weeks: so obviously, so melodramatically, that her great-aunt Agnes shook her head at the sight of Rose pushing peas around her plate. "Puppy love," Agnes said, which caused Bianca to snort into her milk and Rose to resent both of them. That night Suky sat on the edge of Rose's bed and said, "You're very fond of our friend Peter, aren't you?"

Rose writhed and buried her head in her pillow.

"I'm fond of Peter too," Suky said. "He's an old friend; he was at our wedding. When I first started seeing your father, we did things with Peter all the time; and he was part of how your father and I fell in love with each other. He has this way of making everything and everyone around him seem more interesting."

She stroked what she could reach of Rose's hair.

"It's the *beetles* I'm interested in," Rose snapped. "The *beetles*."

Suky bought her some schmitt boxes and a lovely hand lens, and said nothing more about Peter. Rose pored over her stolen book and made her own first collection of beetles, a clumsy imitation of her mother's neat array of dried mosses. Suky's praise she found condescending; she couldn't identify most of her specimens beyond the family level, and she waited impatiently all through the fall and winter for Peter to reappear. He'd taken a teaching job in North Carolina, she learned from her parents. And would visit again when the school year was done. She was crushed when Peter arrived that May with a young woman, and disgusted by the sleeping arrangements.

"I could stay in the living room," Rose offered. "She could have my room."

Suky said, "That's sweet of you, but it isn't necessary," and put the couple together in the guest room. Two rooms down the hall from them, Rose lay rigid and sleepless, too young to know what she was listening for but sure that she must listen.

Rose forgot that young woman's name, as she did the name of the one who showed up with Peter the following summer. During both visits she alternated between sulking alone in the vineyard and making furious efforts to pry Peter away from these usurpers. She spread her beetles out alluringly, piled heaps of books next to her forceps and vials, and bent to her work in a way that could not, she thought, fail to bring Peter to her side. When she succeeded and he drew a chair next to her, casually naming the beetles she had tried and failed to classify, her heart beat so violently that she plucked her shirt away from her chest lest the pounding show. But when he turned from her, when those women, identical in their despicable ripeness, walked by so casually and drew Peter away by raising their arms in their sleeveless shirts, revealing bristly shadows beneath their armpits, and bra straps, and the curves of their breasts: then Rose flew into furies that puzzled everyone except, perhaps, her mother.

Suky found her one afternoon, after Peter's third visit, pulling beetles from her boxes and savagely stripping them and their labels from the pins. Rose was almost eleven then, and almost had breasts of her own. On the floor near her feet was a disheartening cone of dried bodies and small paper points. She had jabbed herself several times and her fingers were bleeding.

"Oh, *Rose*," Suky said. She tried to pull Rose's head to her shoulder but Rose would not be comforted. And by the following summer, there was no comfort anywhere.

A hundred times, a thousand times, Rose would try in the following years to reconstruct her mother's life and mind, her mother's death. What was science for, if not for this? In her mother's closet she turned the same things over and over again. An old brown book, falling apart, filled with interesting drawings of fossils but stubbornly silent regarding the nature of its path to Suky. A slightly less decrepit green book, *Mosses with a Hand-Lens,* which Suky had consulted almost daily. The letters, those crumbling letters, among which a few leaves and lichens had been pressed. And, incongruous among all that paper, one ancient, tiny lady's boot, black and moldy, balanced on a ledge as if the woman whose foot it had once sheltered had scaled the side of the closet, passed through the ceiling, and simply disappeared.

There was no understanding, Rose thought, why her mother had saved the odd things she'd saved. No knowing what had really happened on Suky's last day.

On that day, Rose would think, her mother had been walking along the lakeshore road near Hammondsport. Happy, or not; thinking of her daughters, or not. Cars were speeding along the road, tourists, some of them driving too fast; Suky, wearing a red shirt, held something green in her hand. On the lake the sailboats sailed. On the hill a dog with a brindle coat was barking at Rose and Bianca, who were holding their arms above their heads, lengths of thread stretching tautly from their hands and sweeping out the shapes of invisible cones. The threads were tied to Japanese beetles, who in straining to escape only orbited the pair of girls; who were shrieking with happiness. Could Suky hear them?

She could, Rose would decide each time. She could hear her daughters and, listening to them, hardly noticed the cars moving too fast along the road. She was watching the starlings swoop over the telephone lines, the swallows flicking over the lake, the light on the trees, the light on her shoes, the light.

On the lake the sailboats were heading for shore; the wind had picked up and the sky had darkened; a few drops of rain were falling. In the vineyard gleaming above her the tractor was running again and the brindled dog still barked. Near him Theo worked happily, holding Suky in his mind; he was thinking they ought to buy shoes for the girls, he was thinking about the rain. As he turned he saw the dust spout up, greeting the drops splashing down. On the lake Suky saw a shining patch, the shape of a door, smooth on the rippling surface.

It was as if a door were floating there, opening into the depths below. The door between this world and the next, the door to the rest of her life. Years later, as Rose looks up from her microscope, she'll see something like that door and will hear the sentence, always the same, which confines her mother's death: *Walking along a lakeshore road, she was struck by a speeding tourist and killed instantly.*

Those are the words, always those words. Behind them lie all she's forgotten. A noise Rose didn't hear and then a moment she couldn't name: the moment when Suky disappeared. Theo, stuck in his well of grief, was no help afterward, and although Peter showed up briefly, and alone, for Suky's funeral, Rose was blind to him and clung to Bianca. Their differences mattered less then than their shared loss, and they drew together and closed out everyone else.

Into a trunk—a smaller version of Suky's closet; even Rose could see that she closed the lid exactly as she'd sealed that door—went the hand lens, the stolen library book, and the mysterious stew of feelings she'd once had for her parents' cherished friend.

When Rose and Peter met again, Rose was draped over a pair of chairs in the Detroit airport, looking over some notes for a talk and drinking coffee from a cardboard cup. She was waiting for her friend Signe to arrive from Oslo, so that they could share a rental car. This was a kindness on her part; they were both headed for the same enzymology meeting, and she knew Signe would be too exhausted to drive. Rose was in one of her airport trances. Her home near Boston left behind, the meeting and the prize she was to receive for her research still in the future; the air stale, the day still young, her thirty-first birthday a week away. Legs looped over the arms of one chair, feet braced against another, she was wondering if she'd reached the age when she could no longer sit like this, like a teenager, in public places. Then a hand touched her shoulder. She looked up and there was Peter Kotov.

"Rose?" he said. The tone in his voice was pure wonder; they hadn't seen each other in almost twenty years. He was much changed, and yet still himself: the mustache grizzled, the black hair half gray; thicker at the waist and shoulders yet still with the same eyes. She'd changed more, she knew; she'd been a weedy girl when they last met and was amazed that he recognized her.

"How did you know it was me?" she asked.

"Your mother used to sit just like that—remember? With her legs draped over the arm of the couch? And the way you push back your hair with your left hand is so like her. . . ."

The oddest feeling passed over her, as if Suky had breathed in her ear. When she gazed into a mirror she saw only broken shadows of her mother, and it hadn't occurred to her before that habits of body and gesture might link them, visible only in motion, and only to others.

In the hour they had before Signe arrived and Peter had to catch his flight to Arizona, she was further amazed to learn that they'd been nearly neighbors for the last six years. All the time she'd been at the Institute, he'd been at the Museum of Comparative Zoology in Cambridge; he lived in Watertown, not far from her apartment in Waltham.

He was on his way to a huge entomology meeting in Tempe, he said;

and she, in turn, revealed that she was headed for a gathering so small and prestigious that he raised both eyebrows when she named it. Briefly, she told him about her research, which didn't seem to surprise him. Although he hadn't been in touch with Theo in years, he'd heard that she'd gone to graduate school in biochemistry, done a stunning thesis, and set off for a postdoctoral fellowship in Philadelphia when she was still very young.

"But I didn't know where you went after that," he said. "I had no idea you'd ended up around Boston."

She didn't tell him about the prize she was about to get, nor her grants and her embarrassingly large research budget, nor the fact that she was the youngest Senior Fellow at the Institute. "Is it still beetles with you?" she asked.

"Still. Unfashionable beetles." They talked briefly about his trials; how the money for whole-animal biology had dried up, and how the molecular biologists who'd taken over at Harvard and elsewhere scorned his kind of science now.

"For a while I thought maybe I'd recruited you into the fold," he said wryly. "Do you remember how much you liked my beetles?"

She stared, amazed at how little he'd understood of her violent feelings. "Somehow I drifted away from that."

"It's a shame," he said. "You had a real flair for taxonomy. But it's just as well, I guess—here you've ended up working in a hot field, and I've been relegated to the sidelines. I didn't even have enough money this year to fly a graduate student to the meeting with me."

Rose changed the subject before the difference in their professional lives became more embarrassing. "Are you married?" she said. "Family?"

Peter looked down at his legs and plucked at invisible lint. "I *was* married," he said. "You must have known—I got married the year your mother died."

How could she have forgotten that? "I'm sorry," she said. "I can't remember much from those years."

"Lauren," he said. "You met her, I brought her to the house. We split four years ago, in '82. Lauren wanted children, but we were never able to have any." He looked up here, he looked right into Rose's eyes. "She lives in Missoula now."

His hands were still plucking at the cloth on his legs, tenting then releasing the material, and Rose reached over and covered his fingers with hers.

"I am fifty-one years old," Peter said flatly. "And all alone. How about you?"

"The same," Rose said. Although this was something she never thought about, which she normally forbade herself to think about. Her life was interesting, and very busy.

"But," Peter said. "You know. . . ."

And then Signe appeared in the distance, bowed beneath her backpack and struggling with a suitcase; and it was time for Peter's flight to Tempe. A flurry of introductions and almost simultaneous farewells, an awkward hug, everything left hanging and Peter suddenly distant, clearly embarrassed by what he'd revealed. He rushed away, his stride still that of a young man, bouncy in running shoes.

He called her, though. Two weeks later, after they'd both returned from their meetings, he called her at work and asked her to meet him for dinner. She was on her way to Italy and had to put him off. When she returned he was in Costa Rica with a group of students, gone for the rest of the semester. But finally they were both in town at the same time, and they did get together. He visited the Institute and she toured the Museum; he cooked a mushroom risotto for her and she made a complicated dish with eggplants and pine nuts and goat cheese for him. The first time they went to bed together was in her cluttered apartment, and it was not a bed they shared but a futon. Peter knocked over the lamp. Later he showed her the oval, slanted holes in the slab of tree trunk she used as a coffee table. "Longhorn-beetle larvae," he said. From the floor the underside of the table was easy to see.

By a stroke of coincidence Rose preferred to ignore, their love affair began in May, just when Peter had always visited her family in Hammondsport and at the height of beetle season. Deadlines for grants and papers loomed, talks for meetings later that summer had to be prepared, her students all had examinations, and in the lab, where she'd always worked far into the night, her research took a surprising turn that ought to have captivated her entirely. Yet still she made time for Peter. Whole Sundays she spent with him, driving into the forests of western Massachusetts in search of specimens. And evenings too, as the days lengthened. The names of the beetles returned to her, and she found pleasure in this—although for some years now she had, like every molecular biologist her age, spoken scornfully of descriptive biology and taxonomy. Peter, she came to understand, was one of the two or three people in the world most expert in the Silphidae; and within that family he knew more than anyone else about the burying-beetles.

That expertise, she thought—it might not be science, but it was something. She couldn't hold it against him that he didn't understand her own work: who did, beyond a handful of people in her field? In June she looked up at a dinner party—his friends, not hers; all a generation older and so cultured she felt barbarous—and caught him listening as she tried to explain her research to an elderly cellist.

"I look at a protein called ubiquitin," she said. A college girl in a crisp white shirt cleared the arugula salad and laid clean plates, making Rose uncomfortable; who was she to be waited on? There were flowers embroidered on the linen napkins, and cushions on the chairs. "It has that name because it's so abundant, and found in all kinds of cells—in people, beetles, yeasts, everything. And it's almost identical in every species."

The cellist cocked his head attentively and touched his salmon with a silver fork. Rose wasn't sure he even knew what a protein was. "What it does," she said, "—in your cells, in any cell, proteins are continuously synthesized and then degraded back into their component amino acids. The degradation is just as important as the synthesis in regulating cellular metabolism. Ubiquitin molecules bind to other proteins and mark them for degradation. Without that marking and breaking down, nothing in the cell can work. I try to sort out the details of the protein-degradation process."

She'd left out everything important but still the cellist looked mystified. She was about to change the subject when she saw Peter eavesdropping across the table. To Rose and the cellist, to the table at large, Peter said, "You see, our research isn't so different after all. My beetles and Rose's molecule both break large dead things into smaller bits, so new things can be made."

The link he'd made between their research problems made her hands itch; surely he wasn't implying that she'd chosen her work because of him and his beetles? But he did grasp her work after all, Rose thought. Or at least its point. Although later, when she tried yet again to explain the enzymatic pathway devoted to the covalent conjugation of ubiquitin to cellular proteins, he smiled and held out his hands palm up, in a gesture of incomprehension. "Different generation," he said. "And a whole different field." But if the fractionating columns and chromatography setups littering her benches were alien to him, what he missed were only the details. He knew a part of her as closed off to the rest of the world as the cupboard where she hid her mother's relics.

They made love in a dark museum attic, accompanied by the faint ticking of deathwatch beetles calling their mates through the old oak beams. They made love in dusky groves and on hot river rocks, in Rose's lab and on her kitchen table, in Peter's office surrounded by dead bugs. All of this—the conjunction of pins and papers and Latin names with flesh and hands and tongues, the mingling of past and present—was thrilling to Rose. Peter pointed to the hard, shell-like front wings of some dermestids scurrying around their colony and said, "Do you remember the name for these?"

She said, "Elytra?" and felt her knees grow weak. When he kissed her neck and buried his fingers in her and said, "Rose, Rose, Rose, *Rose,*" she closed her eyes and she was a girl again, he a young man again, and she came with startling violence. Closing her mouth around his cock, which was curved and smooth but sometimes reluctant, she did not see his paunch but rather the tight muscles vanishing into the pants in which he'd emerged from her parents' guest room.

How confusing all this was! One night, after too many margaritas, he licked the palm of her hand and said, "When I close my eyes and listen to your voice, it's as if I'm back in Hammondsport, listening to your mother."

And she, made careless by the liquor, said, "Were you in love with her?"

"We were never lovers," Peter said, moving his hand slowly over her breast. "If that's what you mean."

It wasn't; she had never considered this. Only now did that disturbing image pass behind her eyes and then disappear.

"Your parents were happy together," he went on. He touched the mole in her armpit. "I would never have interfered. But it's true I loved them, both of them. And if it hadn't been for my friendship with Theo—I adored your mother, I did. When the three of us were together your father thrived on the charge between Suky and me. It made him feel even luckier to know that he was the one she'd chosen."

But that wasn't right, Rose thought with surprise. Or not wholly right; there had never been a real contest. On the night she'd first seen Peter, Theo had clearly been the sun in which Suky and Peter both basked. Nothing Suky had ever said or done had suggested anything different to Rose. Whatever Peter's feelings for Suky had been, Suky's bond with Theo had been unambiguous. Was it possible that Peter, after all this time, still read that wrong?

She sat up and folded her arms around her knees. "What happened between you and my father?" Until now she'd assumed that her mother's death had separated the men. Some sadness that could not be bridged.

"After I married Lauren, he didn't seem to want me around anymore," Peter said, rising reluctantly. "Or not me and Lauren as a couple, anyway. You know how bitter he was, he couldn't stand to see someone else happy—and we *were* happy those first years. The last time I saw him, he accused me of marrying Lauren just to comfort myself for the loss of Suky, and we had a fight. Then when he got married again I was in Costa Rica and couldn't go to the wedding, and I guess he thought I was still angry with him."

Who had taken comfort from whom? Rose wondered. Was it wrong? "I was in love with you then," she said. "Did you know?"

Peter bent and kissed her leg.

They were apart that summer more than they would have liked. Rose had meetings in Atlanta and Montreal and Spain; Peter lost the last bit of funding for his lab and was forced to begin a humiliating campaign to pry money from the Museum. Each day seemed to increase the disparity in their professional situations, and neither could help knowing that Rose's star was rising fast while Peter was struggling just to stay in place. When Rose traveled she thought of Peter constantly, but not Peter as he was; away from him, she constructed a being half the Peter she'd known as a girl and half the Peter she knew now. Returning, seeing him move toward her down one of the long corridors at Logan Airport, she was surprised each time to see how old he was. On these occasions, before his arms wound around her and she sank back into her enchanted state, she felt briefly that there was something shameful in their coupling.

She admitted this to no one; she avoided the issue entirely by avoiding anyone who'd known her as a girl and might have remembered her family's connection with Peter. She called Theo dutifully once a month, as she had for some years, but said little about her personal life. As she had not for some years. There was nothing so straightforward as a quarrel between them: only a long separation, and Theo's continued depression, and Rose's sense, since his remarriage, of no longer mattering to him. That she had not attended his wedding, and that she had not forgiven him for selling the winery; that he had spoken to her sharply when she objected to the sale—well, perhaps it was a quarrel after all, but she couldn't bear to describe the distance between them this way. When she called she spoke coolly about her work and never mentioned Peter. She took it for granted that Peter, after all these years, wouldn't reopen his friendship with her father now. To friends she presented her relationship with Peter as one of responsible adults. Bianca aided her inadvertently here; she'd returned to Alaska and was working that summer as a fire-jumper. She could not be reached, and so Rose could not be blamed for keeping her secret.

That it was a secret she finally understood in August, when Peter, pounding basil in olive oil as she cooked linguine, looked up and said, "Do you ever think about marriage? About having kids?"

"*No*," she said. Although of course she did, or had now and then; but not with him, never with him. What was this dreadful feeling in her chest? The heat, the humidity, overwork. For weeks the city had been sunk in a heat wave, and her apartment was airless and sticky. She tried not to mind when Peter flung his sweaty clothes over the chairs, left bristles and shaving cream in the sink, tossed an arm across her chest in his sleep and then left it there hot and moist. But she did mind, she minded fiercely. As she was beginning to mind the disruption to her work, his bad digestion, her sense that, however patiently he waited up for her at night, he was *waiting*. And then there was the way he expected her to remember everything he'd taught her as a girl: as if her own work might not have driven out some of his. While she was down at the pond with him, helping him capture some *Necrodes*, he stopped her hand just as she was about to drop a specimen into the killing jar.

"That one just molted," he said. "It's still teneral—see how pale it is, and how soft? If you kill it now, it'll shrivel as it dries."

"How would I know that?"

"I *showed* you, years ago. . . ."

It was true, she realized. They'd had this conversation two decades earlier, down near Keuka Lake. One of his girlfriends—Lauren?—was with them, lying languid on a rock, and Rose wasn't paying attention to Peter's instructions. "I was nine," she said irritably. "Maybe ten."

"But mature for your age." He kissed her shoulder and she twitched away. "Let it harden before you kill it."

She held the beetle as it darkened and aged before her eyes. Egg, grub, pupa, adult, egg. Holometabolous development, the most advanced form of insect metamorphosis. When Peter wasn't looking, she tossed her specimen into a shrub. That night, or perhaps the next day, he said, "It was Lauren, you know. I mean the reason we couldn't have children of our own—it was never me."

"I'm sorry," she said. "That it didn't work out, that everything happened the way it did."

A few weeks later she went to a meeting in Maine and slept with a graduate student from a San Diego lab, who rode a mountain bike and wore his hair in a ponytail. When she returned to Boston Peter had bronchitis and emerged from her shower hacking and steaming, each cough making the loose flesh around his nipples shimmy. Something must have shown on her face, because Peter raised his head from a wad of tissue and said, "What? *What?*"

"Nothing." But she continued to stare. It was not so much that he looked like her father as that he was so obviously of her father's generation.

"It's no big deal," he said, coughing again. "I know you hate it when I'm sick, but it's not a sign, or a symbol, or a warning. It's bronchitis. Anyone can get it."

"I know," she said. The biking biochemist had meant nothing to her, but she found herself thinking of his smooth legs.

She turned and went to her desk, where a huge stack of paper awaited her; she'd been asked to write a chapter for a book devoted solely to the mysteries of ubiquitin. It was absorbing, and very complicated. Nothing Peter could understand. *Can you write? Are you old enough to write?* In the other room, Peter settled onto the futon with a groan.

When they parted, after a quarrel she manufactured, it was like losing her childhood all over again. It was not his fault, exactly, that he'd altered her last vivid memories of her mother, nor was he to blame for the secret she'd kept from Bianca, which increased the distance between them. She had chosen all this, she had chosen him. But years later, when she went to visit her dying father, she found her old trunk in the storeroom. Long ago she'd ransacked her mother's closet, hauling the contents around with her even during the years when she'd owned almost nothing else. But the trunk she'd left behind, the trunk she left with Theo. Inside it she found the hand lens Suky had given her after Peter's first visit, the stolen library book, some beetle pictures Bianca had crayoned—when was that?—and a postcard (she had forgotten this too) which Peter had sent on her eleventh birthday.

Hugs and kisses to my favorite beetle-girl, he'd written. *Love, Peter.* She mentioned none of this to Theo. But when she sat by his bed and stared at his creased tired hands, it was their shared past she mourned for as much as him.

THE CURE

E VERYTHING, THINKS ELIZABETH, is in order.

Everything is as it should be, exactly as she would wish it: nine o'clock, on this December day in 1905, and already breakfast has been cooked and served and cleared, Livvie and Rosellen are at the dishes, and all nine of her boarders are resting, wrapped in blankets and robes, on the lower veranda or the private porches of the upstairs rooms. In the light, airy dining room, the new napkins look well in their rings and the cloth is crisp on the table. In the kitchen—the girls look up as she walks by, smiling without interrupting the dance of dishes passing from basin to basin and hand to hand—and also in the mudroom, the woodshed, the smaller shed where the laundry is stored in enormous lidded crates until the boilers are fired up twice each week, everything is as it should be for this hour and minute of the day.

Everything, Elizabeth thinks, except that she hasn't found a nurse to replace Mrs. Temple, who left three days ago. And that Martin Sawyer is dying; and that Andrew refuses to believe this.

Outside Andrew is burning trash in a big metal bin; the essential task he does each day after breakfast. Through the frosted window in the laundry shed she can see, after rubbing the glass with her apron, her husband poke the vents, shake the grate, and then toss in the contents of two more covered tins. One scrap of paper catches fire midair, but Andrew—no gloves, she notes with a rueful smile, no hat no scarf no coat no socks, ankles bare above his low boots and thick white curls flopping dangerously—bats it down before it flies away. A few weeks from now, she knows, he and his oldest friends will strip naked for their annual New Year's celebration, smashing through the ice on the lake to leap, shouting and pounding their chests, into the frigid water. Along with the rest of the crowd, she'll applaud the grizzled, wrinkling, suntanned heroes.

For now she goes back through the walkway, back through the kitchen (Rosellen and Livvie are almost done; she reminds them the woodwork needs washing down), and into the empty nurse's room, where she tilts her head and listens thoughtfully to the ceiling. Both this and the room next door, which she and Andrew have always shared, are crowned with porches, two among those she added to the second-floor guest rooms. Everyone wants to sleep outside now; no one will rent a room without a cure porch. Sometimes she hears footsteps crossing the ceiling above her head. Today, she hears nothing.

She waits; still nothing. Not a glass clinking down on a coaster, not the sounds of a body shifting in bed. Martin, so lively when he first arrived, these days hardly moves. He's gone back to sleep, she thinks. Otherwise she'd hear him coughing. She decides to bring up his midmorning tray herself, before she visits her friends. Dorrie and Emeline, who also run private homes for health-seekers, grew up helping their mothers and aunts; they know everything that goes on in the village. One of them may know of a plausible candidate for Mrs. Temple's vacant place. Or they might, on this particular day, mention Nora, from whom all three of them learned their trade.

Dorrie's mother, Bessie Brennan, was the first to rent a room to a sick stranger. During the summer of 1875, a slender Baltimore banker named Mr. Woodruff spent six weeks at a sportsmen's hotel here in the northern Adirondacks. His cough improved, his fever decreased; he felt better than he had in months. At the end of the season he decided to stay on, only then learning that all the hunting and fishing lodges closed down for the winter. He asked advice from Bessie's son, the guide who'd rowed him through the lakes, built his lean-to, and cleaned and cooked his fish.

Once Bessie agreed to let the room behind her kitchen, she made Mr. Woodruff's meals and did his laundry, mended his woolen coat and provided a chair and horse blankets for the days when, despite the frigid weather, he sat outside for hours on the porch. He gained ten pounds and lost his cough entirely. The following September, Bessie took in a Boston professor who'd summered at the Northview Inn and had the same idea as Mr. Woodruff. Her cousin Olive, eager for the extra income, then rented a spare bedroom to a young man training to be a lawyer. Other neighbors joined Bessie and Olive and soon there were eight women housing invalids through the winter.

Sturdy and competent, the daughters and mothers and wives of guides, they were perfectly comfortable tending to a finicky eater, a late sleeper, one who shivered and needed an extra log on the fire. If a boarder's cough worsened, if his fever rose or he spat blood, then the women sent to the Northview Inn for Nora, the only one among them to have experience as a nurse. There wasn't a doctor, then, within sixty miles.

Nora, like the men who first wintered there, was a stranger to the village. During the long hours of their exile in the freezing air, the strangers talked. Nora learned how the men had discovered they were consumptive, who they'd left behind, why they'd chosen to stay in these mountains. At first, as she'd later tell Elizabeth, this had mystified her—she couldn't imagine why anyone not bound by family would choose the harsh climate. The dark, close-crowded trees, hemlock and cedar, spruce and pine, balsam fir with here and there the shocking light of a birch—how wild this place could seem! Snowshoe hares and deer and skunks, birds she'd never seen before and the slithering, weasel-like fishers and minks, which she despised although some of the men had first come to the mountains just for the pleasure of hunting them. Others, like Mr. Cameron, who'd taught astronomy in Connecticut before moving into Olive's house, came solely for the air. He'd been assured, Mr. Cameron said, that the pure air of these mountains was as dry and bracing and curative as the more famous air of a place called Davos.

The atmosphere was rich in ozone, a powerful disinfectant, while the trees themselves exhaled purifying balsamics. The frequent rain and snow of the Adirondacks Mr. Cameron claimed meant nothing; from his bed he lectured Nora in a stern voice, coughing between every sentence. The soil was so extremely porous and stony, he said, that no dampness could ever linger. This on an April day when the ground was soaked with melted snow, when for a week they'd woken to rain, seen the clouds rise a few feet above the rooftops only to descend again; when there was mist then rain then fog then sleet then wet snow then fog again. Shivering in a heavy sweater and a knitted hat, Mr. Cameron claimed stoutly that the air was actually dry.

Nora let him talk, she let all of them talk. She brought them herbal decoctions she'd made at the inn, and teas and salves and a syrup of horehound compounded with hyssop and licorice root. When the other women needed a hand, she aired the invalids' blankets and freshened their rooms and occasionally bathed those confined to bed. Sometimes—or so Elizabeth has envisioned from Nora's stories—when the snow was dry and the sun was bright and the air was perfectly still, Nora borrowed her brother's cutter and his gentle mare and took the men for drives or a lunchtime picnic.

If she were alive, she'd be eighty today—which no one, Elizabeth thinks, seems to remember. When she mentioned Nora's birthday, Dorrie, who as a girl had stood openmouthed before a microscope while Nora showed her pollen grains and the nettle's tiny stinging spines, had said only, "Is it?" Emeline didn't mention Nora at all and Andrew, who's working on the chimney in the nurse's room—Nora's old room—claims simply that the flue has been temperamental. How can he not feel Nora's presence? The room, despite having been occupied for eleven years by first Mrs. MacDonald and then Mrs. Temple, still speaks to Elizabeth most strongly of her dearest friend.

White walls, white ceilings, smooth, polished oaken floor, and a narrow bed with a white metal frame: Nora's, all Nora's. It had been Mrs. Temple, though, who several weeks ago complained about the draft.

"Is it the damper?" Elizabeth asks her husband now.

Andrew straightens, a chisel in hand. "It's almost fixed. When's the new nurse coming?"

"I haven't found anyone yet."

Andrew frowns. "You can't do everything yourself."

"I know," she says. "Especially not with Martin fading so fast."

"Martin needs to be outside more," Andrew says sharply. He reaches back into the flue and waggles something that makes a metallic sound. "I thought I'd take him for a drive to the dam tomorrow—he needs something to interest him. I hate to see him giving up."

Elizabeth stares at her husband. When did he last actually look at Martin? Martin weighs less than a hundred pounds and is coughing up chunks of his lungs.

Earlier, while Andrew was finishing his outside tasks, and while Livvie and Rosellen were filling glasses for the midmorning snack, each holding a raw egg garnished with salt and pepper and lemon juice, Elizabeth took a tray up to Martin. Some of the boarders will gulp down three eggs, swearing they taste like raw oysters. Martin might have swallowed two without any fuss and then gone back to sleep, but instead he'd raised a glass, taken an egg partway between his lips, and let it slip back, his face contorting horribly.

Months ago he'd told her this: that initially he hadn't felt sick, although a strange, almost liquid lassitude sometimes gave him wobbly legs. Often, he said, peculiarly often, it was true, he'd felt a need to clear his throat; and it was also true that he'd had a trifling but persistent cough: but these things were nothing. He hadn't suspected anything. He was at a family picnic when his cousin's three-year-old daughter ran out from behind the hedge crying, "Catch me! Catch me!" as she hurtled toward him. He'd swooped her up, over his head: a game a girl in a white blouse and a yellow pinafore had loved. As he lifted his Daisietta he'd had the strangest feeling in his chest, a warm, quivering, sickening feeling and then a flood of sweetness. His mouth had filled with blood as he set Daisietta down.

Dr. Davis, who will never say to a patient, *You are getting worse,* admits this about Martin: "You have not improved." Each week Martin loses weight; he sweats through two changes of sheets each night. His cough is ceaseless—she can hear him cough now—and he's had hemorrhage after hemorrhage. He's tired, he said an hour ago. So tired. She ran a cloth wrung out in witch hazel over his face and hands and neck.

"Martin needs to rest," Elizabeth says to Andrew. "He can't go anywhere. And I'm going to need your help with him, unless I find a new nurse in the next few days."

Andrew's face, usually so open and cheerful, sets, exasperating Elizabeth. It is only in this circumstance that they quarrel. When they have problems with the house itself, or with their guests—the ardent friendships that flare up so swiftly and later burn out in violent quarrels, the more secretive romances and renunciations, the jealousies and squabbles and the occasional slump into melancholia and withdrawal—they talk these over after they retreat to their own room at night. She rests her head on his shoulder while he agrees with her theories and diagnoses, or disagrees and proposes his own. Either way she counts on him completely.

But when someone is dying he disappears, clutching his own chest protectively, clearing his throat, tensing and flexing his arms and thighs as he wards off the years when he was sick himself. Convinced that he cured himself by an act of will, adhering rigorously to a regimen of exercise and nude sunbathing and frequent freshwater plunges regardless of the season, he's both horrified and disapproving when one of their boarders fails to recover. Especially when, as in Martin's case, they don't pack up before the end and return home to die.

Sometimes, despite her best efforts, Elizabeth thinks of Andrew's evasions as cowardice. Other times she's able to see how his constant optimism balances her own grimmer tendencies. When she and Nora first lost a boarder—Aaron Brown, whom she'd liked very much—she'd been ready to sell the house and find another occupation. Andrew hid in the woods through those terrible days, with a book and a jar of double-cream milk and a lump of cornbread. Half the time she'd been furious with him; the other half simply envied his ability not to see. If this was death, she'd said to Nora, if this was where we were all of us headed—then what was the point of anything?

"Everyone feels this way the first time," Nora had told her. "The first few times. As if we're the only ones to understand what really lies at the heart of the world. Until you get used to it, nothing can make you feel more alone."

What does it mean, to get used to it? That, after nearly twenty years of this work, Elizabeth can think, *Martin might have a week,* and still be able to plan calmly all she'll arrange for his comfort and consolation, and all she must also arrange to spare her other boarders during his last days. And that, although she's desperate with worry, and although Andrew has hidden his head inside the fireplace, his back muscles clenched with panic, she'll cook an excellent dinner and he'll sit at the head of the table, making pleasant conversation. He'll carve the roast mutton, she'll add potatoes to the plates. Upstairs Martin will cough and cough—he's coughing now, she'll bring him some syrup—and downstairs Livvie will pass through the swinging doors with dish after dish after dish.

"I can't talk about this," Elizabeth says to Andrew. "Not if you're going to be so stubborn."

Who will she find to move into this room? Dorrie spread her hands and said she didn't know of a single free nurse in town. Emeline shook her head and offered her a muffin and an advertisement for an electrified carpet sweeper. Elizabeth tries to imagine a stranger folding freshly laundered nightdresses and slipping them into the second drawer, where Nora kept hers. A stranger in Nora's armchair, reading by the afternoon light. Even with Andrew inserted into the fireplace, head and shoulders invisible and legs rising like andirons above the grate, she feels Nora's presence. But that feeling lasts only a minute, like so much else in her life: what presses her most is the ceaseless ticking of the clock. Breakfast, the ten o'clock trays, and then dinner—she should be cooking now. After dinner she'll have a tiny breathing space before the four o'clock snack: but then there's supper, almost right away, and later the bedtime trays. *For the consumptive invalid,* she hears Nora saying, *food is life.*

Andrew's voice comes from inside the chimney, muffled by the bricks and so distorted he might be speaking through the two stuffed pheasants splayed above the mantel. "Don't be angry at me," he says.

Is that what he says?

She backs out and closes the door behind her. Martin may have another month, but no more than that. For his sake, for Andrew's sake, she must find another nurse right away.

Andrew waits a minute, until he's sure she's gone. Then he slides his head and shoulders down, backs away from the chimney, and searches his workbox for the two smooth bits of metal he was about to seize when she appeared—magnets, one in the shape of a star, the other a disk, like the moon. Magnets may, he's read, shift the shape of the aura surrounding each person into a new and more healthful alignment. And a stream of heat carrying the magnetic waves—this part he's hypothesized for himself—might increase the benign effect. On its way to the roof this chimney runs between the outside wall of Martin's room and the inside wall of his porch. Ideally situated, Andrew thinks. When placed above the damper, on the brick ledge he's just chiseled clean, the magnets will exert a quiet, beneficial influence on Martin's health.

Back into the chimney he goes, his head and shoulders once more disappearing. He is his own boss, he thinks. Quite independent, capable of aiding Martin in his own way: not, whatever Elizabeth and her friends may think, simply Elizabeth's husband. All through the house, in fireplaces and windows and under the eaves, behind the boilers, beneath the compost heap, are hidden other objects that some—Dr. Davis among them—might scorn as superstitious and that his own wife might dismiss as useless.

But not Nora, he thinks. He's perfectly aware that today is Nora's birthday; he's placed the magnets in her honor. Nora, with her caches of herbs and bitter powders, her screens covered with drying leaves and flower heads, would have seen the possibilities in his metal shapes. The life she'd led, each of the places she'd called home sending unexpected shoots toward the next, had made her open to almost anything.

2

Nora Kynd was twenty-three when she reached Detroit in the summer of 1848: strong and active and eager, after a long journey down the St. Lawrence and over the lakes, to leave behind all that had happened to her in Quebec. At first she shared a dirty room and heels of bread with six other young women who, like her, were looking for employment. All she found was day-work, cleaning attics or windows; dismissed at nightfall to look again the next day.

One morning, discouraged after two weeks of this, she paused while wandering through the market in the Cadillac Square and stood staring greedily at the contents of a stall. Fancy game, food for the rich: quails and woodcock, venison and partridge. The quails lay on a pale plank, nested together as if they were sleeping, the soft speckled feathers of one supporting the claws of the next. She stood there drooling like a dog, until the stallkeeper scowled and told her to be on her way. She was stepping back when a hand touched her shoulder blade.

"Have you eaten today?" A woman with faded hair, gray eyes, a kind smile revealing a few missing teeth.

"Porridge," Nora said. "Not that it's anyone's business."

"What's your name?"

"Nora Kynd."

The woman bent in an odd little bow. "Pleased to meet you. I'm Fannie McCloud."

She drew Nora away from that stall and toward another, where she purchased an orange and shared the succulent pieces. Amid the pleasure of the segments she extracted, without Nora quite knowing how, an account of Nora's difficult first two weeks in Detroit. Then she convinced Nora to walk with her to Corktown, to the small house—she'd been a widow for years—that she'd once shared with her husband. As they wound through the narrow streets, she asked Nora why she'd chosen this place to settle and Nora offered the only facts she could bear to tell: that she'd left Ireland in the midst of the famine, after all her family but two of her younger brothers had died. What else could they do? she'd thought. Where else could they go? She had taken charge of her brothers, pretending more confidence than she felt—but on the passage over she'd taken sick and nearly died. On Grosse Isle, at the quarantine station not far from the city of Quebec, a kind doctor had kept her alive but had sent away the two little boys. While she was lying sick and unconscious, they'd been shuttled upriver with those still apparently healthy. By the time she could ask for them, they'd disappeared.

"Where were they sent?" Fannie asked.

Nora kept her eyes fixed on the gutters. "No one knows. I have asked everyone, everywhere." Were those pig tripes lying there, outside the butcher shop? "I've even had people put advertisements in the newspapers for me. But it's like a wind picked them up and blew them to the North Pole. Part of the reason I came to Detroit was because I heard some who traveled on the boats had made their way here. But so far I've not found a single trace of Denis or Ned."

Fannie shook her head and led Nora a few more blocks, to her house with its bright blue door. The spare room that she rented out, always to Irish girls, was free; the newly washed curtains, white with a soft green sprig, moved in the breeze. After Fannie asked what Nora was paying for her squalid shared lodgings, she said, "You may have the room for that. I'm an orphan myself, I know what it's like to be lost in a strange place."

Soon enough Nora learned that Fannie was a root-and-herb healer, with ways that reminded her of her own grandmother. In the kitchen she looked at the drying plants hung upside down and the bark rolled into crisp scrolls. Then she went to the woods with a flour sack and returned with curly dock and butternut, fleabane and witch hazel and pleurisy root, which she dropped at Fannie's feet.

"Wonderful," Fannie said, inspecting Nora's treasures. "We have this in common too."

How lucky they were, Nora soon thought, to have found each other. Because Fannie's patients could pay her only with eggs or a loaf of bread, occasionally a couple of coins, she couldn't pay Nora for her help. But she gave Nora that clean-curtained room and a kitchen where the two of them could dry their herbs together. There, using a book of Indian medicine as a first text, Fannie taught Nora to read. And within a few months, she'd found Nora work as a night-watcher: not in Corktown, but among prosperous Protestants in other parts of the city.

Nora moved from house to house then—a little girl with diphtheria, an old woman with cancer of the breast, a baby scalded by boiling water—spelling the families of the sick. She was with them until they were better or dead, she was often the last to see someone alive. Smells and sponges and chamber pots, hemorrhages and death; none of it frightened her. Every member of her own family, but for her two lost brothers, was dead.

In the mornings, after a stint of watching, she returned to her small neat room at Fannie's house and closed the curtains and slept. It suited her to work all night, until she could sleep without dreaming. She never dreamed about Ireland, or her grandmother, or the fields where they'd gathered herbs together; she never dreamed about her parents or her sisters or the rain. If she dreamed it was disaster, Grosse Isle come back to torment her again: the dank and crowded tents, thick with the gray mist of souls departing their anguished bodies. Why should she have to live that again? Or see, as if once were not enough, her brothers, her darling Denis and Ned, being lowered when she was too weak to save them down the side of the ship.

Better, surely, to give herself to her useful work and to enjoy her home, her friend, and the pleasure—still new to her—of books. Periodically Fannie would urge her to marry; her own marriage had, she claimed, been a happy one, and she didn't want Nora to miss those particular joys. But Nora had no desire to marry young, as their neighbors commonly did, and bear a dozen children only to watch half of them vanish before they took root in the world.

Her life was quiet, it had its satisfactions; and so she was surprised, after a dozen years had passed, to find herself suddenly longing for children of her own. At the market she had a favorite greengrocer, Francis MacEachern, who was kind and modest and had excellent vegetables. On a peculiarly warm late April day, when both of them were old enough— they were thirty-six—to smile at the sun's heat after the dank and freezing winter, Francis said, "You have very handsome eyes," and asked if he could take her out walking. They took a boat across the river to Windsor, where they walked along a path framed by enormous hedges. A flock of finches passed through one, streaming between the woven twigs on invisible and secret paths. A year later Nora and Francis were married.

For two years they lived in Francis's bungalow near the market. Nora helped him at the stall, spending each morning there even during the months she was carrying Michael. In the corner she'd taken for her own she spread the ginseng and wild ginger she gathered, the fresh soft elder leaves with their flowers and the roots of yellow dock. When the war came, no one expected Francis, a middle-aged man with a brand-new son, to volunteer. But the fighting went on and on, regiments were raised and mustered in and destroyed; one summer day a general stood in the square before a sullen crowd and begged yet again for more men. Francis and Nora left their stall and went out to listen. A man was calling, "Glory! Glory!" The crowd grumbled and called back, "Rich man's war!" Francis stroked Nora's hand and the copper-crowned head of the son they'd named for her dead father.

Their rent had gone up and Nora had not been able to help out as much as she wanted after Michael's birth. In August, despite Nora's fierce objections and her arguments that somehow they'd find a way out of debt, Francis took the bounty offered by a wealthy gunsmith and joined the Twenty-Fourth Infantry. Two months later, when the curtained room at Fannie's came free again, Nora went back to her old life.

Yet, as she'd later tell both Elizabeth and Andrew, everything about that life was different: because of Michael. She hadn't imagined, after losing Denis and Ned, that she'd ever again love a person like that. But now, when she was helping Fannie, she carried Michael in her arms or let him play at her feet. She wrote to Francis every week, describing Michael's progress: *He said Ma-ma, he stood by himself, we had to cut his hair.* For a while she got letters in return; then the letters stopped. She waited, and waited some more. When the bounty money ran out she went to the new hospital up the road, looking for work that might also bring her news of her husband.

She couldn't work as a ward nurse unless she lived in, and she couldn't live in because of Michael. Instead she signed on again as a night-watcher: one ward, nine at night to five in the morning; fifty cents plus one meal per shift. Scores of men poured in from hospitals in the east and south. Some were still recovering from injuries suffered at Gettysburg or Chickamauga; others had been hurt more recently. They had wound infections that refused to heal, or fevers they'd caught down South, or consumption that had flared up in the crowded camps and prisons. Nora asked them if they had news of Francis. Even among the soldiers she nursed from his own regiment, no one did.

Eight long, low wards, connected by a covered walk, flanked the hospital's two-story central building. From the pane of glass set into the wall of the small nurse's room, her own ward was visible all the way down to the walk: darkness turned the space into a tunnel. Twice each hour she walked the narrow lane between the two ranks of trim iron bedsteads. She didn't see the doctors making their rounds, nor the faces of the men removed to the operating room and returned later, minus an arm or a leg; those were events of the day. She didn't see the volunteer ladies, gaily dressed and bearing little hampers of fruit and jellies. The quarrels in the kitchen were not her problem, nor the difficulties in the dead-house, the continual failures of the laundry, the contract surgeon fired for drunkenness—all that was over when she came in and took, from the exhausted ward nurse, the day's summary of admissions and procedures. Her job was to comfort wherever she could, to ease the dying and cover the dead. Back home, she twined Michael's red hair around her hand and kissed his cheek and then slipped between her own sheets before she slept.

The beds filled, emptied out at the end of the war, refilled more slowly with invalid veterans transferred from all over Michigan; two of the hospital's wards—one Nora's—were designated a government Soldier's Home. The men she cared for then were missing an arm or leg or more; a few were blind and some broken down by injuries to their lungs or bowels; some had fevers that would not be cured and others were exhausted or starving or penniless. Some left by way of the dead-house. The stronger ones, taking shelter while they tried to ready themselves for the world outside, were restless at night. Nora read to them.

Not from the Bible, which the visiting clergymen pressed on them. Not from the improving tracts brought by the volunteer ladies. She read what the men were denied during the day: newspapers, magazines, books about faraway places. Letters, especially for those who'd been blinded. Those who couldn't read or write, but who still had eyes and hands, she taught as Fannie had once taught her. With scavenged books they worked beneath a list of regulations pinned near the door to the covered walk:

No lounging in the main hall.
No profanity.
No smoking.
No spitting.
No throwing anything on the ground below the windows.
No lights after nine p.m.
Do not damage or destroy the furniture.
Do not lie in bed with your clothes on.
Do not talk with each other about your diseases and afflictions.

Each time Nora looked at that list she thought: *Where is Francis?* Dead and unaccounted for, or lingering in a hospital hundreds of miles away? One of her patients, a man with a mountain twang to his voice, had no idea of his name or where he came from or who he'd loved.

After midnight, when the men finally slept, she sometimes tormented herself with those thoughts. Once she'd started, as she told Fannie, there was no stopping it. She'd end up thinking of Denis and Ned and how she'd never know what had happened to them. And how if they were dead, then Francis was also dead, as were her parents and the doctor who'd cared for her at the quarantine station on Grosse Isle. She'd taken Dr. Grant's notebook with her, hiding it in her carpetbag until she learned to decipher it. Later, after Fannie had taught her to read, she'd been afraid at first to open the pages.

When she finally inspected his account of those terrible days, she found not only his impressions of the emigrants, the conditions on the island, and the failures of the authorities to make any provisions for the sick, but also—shouldn't she have expected this?—his impressions of her. How eerie, to see herself through his eyes: *She sang me a song about a woman standing on a cliff in Ireland, waiting for a fishing boat to return. Untrained, uneducated, she has been of more use and shown more dedication than anyone except the Sisters. . . .*

That he'd thought of her at all was touching. But to be written about, to be seen from the outside like that: it made her own skin feel unfamiliar. And it was a shock too to learn that he'd been at least partly responsible for separating her from her brothers. *He—we, I—separate the sick from the healthy without regard for family ties; we have no choice.* He'd had no choice; he'd saved her life. Late at night, she sometimes looked around the ward—the stronger men helping her tend those worse off, one man reading aloud while others wrote or studied—and wondered if Dr. Grant would have approved of what she'd made from the life he'd returned to her.

———

Colm Larkin she met in the winter of 1868, when he made his way to the Soldier's Home after having been in and out of four different hospitals and, for a while, on the streets. His lungs were inflamed, he had pneumonia and perhaps something worse than that. The same wound that had left him mute—an exploding shell that scattered metal through his chest and throat, breaking ribs, which had never healed correctly, and shattering his voice box—also gave him a strangled, painful cough. The hole in his throat, where a field surgeon had pierced him with a reed and saved his life, still oozed.

Yet when his fever was down he was cheerful, and popular with the other men. At night he played checkers, always losing with a smile. When the others slept he often stayed up to read with Nora; and, using his slate, to make conversation. Tidy white letters, made with chalk: she learned where he'd come from, what had happened to him, which hospitals he'd been in. But only after seeing him identify his regiment and company to another patient did she think to ask if he might have known Francis. By then she'd stopped asking, she'd given up hope.

I knew Francis MacEachern, Colm wrote, as if this weren't astonishing news. *We didn't talk much, but I always knew where he was. You're his wife?*

"Or his widow—still I don't know. One of his commanding officers suggested that he might have lost his papers and perished in a prison camp without being identified. How can there be no trace of him?"

I don't know. It could be he just . . . left. Walked away. He wasn't himself after the Battle of Spotsylvania, he was weeping and he couldn't sleep. The rest of us thought he might be going mad. I lost track of him one morning, when a battle started up. Later I asked everyone if they'd seen what happened to him. No one saw him fall, or saw him wounded or captured. No one saw him walk away.

"Then where is he?"

No well man would leave you, he wrote gallantly. Nora was almost forty-five by then, while he was twenty-seven. *But if he's still alive, he may be sick in his mind. You've seen what happens to us.* She had, she thought, by then seen everything.

That June the weather was beautiful, so warm and soft that she let the men open the windows at night and move the table beneath them. The sky would still be gleaming with a bit of light when she got to work, and she'd find Colm at the windowsill, reading a book with a yellow oilcloth cover. One night she saw him busily taking notes, pausing to pull from a pocket inside the book's back cover a folded map marked "New York Wilderness."

"What are you studying?" she asked.

My future, he wrote. He pointed, smiling, to the first chapter heading of William Murray's *Adventures in the Wilderness:*

THE WILDERNESS. WHY I GO THERE,—
HOW I GET THERE,
—WHAT I DO THERE,—AND WHAT IT COSTS

That's where I'm going when I get better, he wrote. *A place where I can hunt and fish in peace, where no one will disturb me or care that I can't speak. Men grow healthy there. Look.*

He showed Nora a passage in which Murray described a consumptive young man, near death, who'd visited the Adirondack woods and, with the help of a guide, moved in a small wooden boat from one lake to the next, sleeping at night on boughs of balsam and pine, eating fish and venison. By the end of the summer he'd been entirely cured.

So will I be, Colm wrote. *Outside, away from everyone looking at me. I don't mean you, you've been nothing but help. But I'd be better off somewhere by myself.*

"It's a good idea," Nora told him. "A fine idea. But wait, maybe until next summer." Still he couldn't walk the length of the passage without gasping, and an abscess had opened along his ribs.

It's five years already, he wrote.

A week later she found his bed empty, his things gone, a folded note for her on the table along with the yellow book. He had no further need of it, he wrote. He would always remember her. And hoped she'd hear from Francis, and hoped she'd wish him well. She should read the book, which was entertaining and would help her imagine his new life.

She forgave him after a couple of days—she had work to do, and twenty-three other men who needed her attention. On a Friday night when the moon was full and a quiet drizzle fell, she opened Colm's gift and read:

> The Adirondack Wilderness, or the "North Woods," as it is sometimes called, lies between the Lakes George and Champlain on the east, and the river St. Lawrence on the north and west. It reaches northward as far as the Canada line, and southward to Booneville. Its area is about that of the state of Connecticut.

A place the size of a state, with no more than a handful of settlements: small clusters of people amid a thousand lakes and hundreds of peaks. The opposite of Ireland, she thought. How could there be so much empty land? She flipped through the pages, eyeing the chapter titles. In the back she found advertisements for fishing tackle and hunting rifles, recommendations for reliable guides, descriptions of the few modest inns. She read, uncomprehendingly at first—*You can't imagine it,* she later told Elizabeth, *you cannot imagine what this felt like*—these words:

THE NORTHVIEW INN
Boats, Guides, Provisions, etc furnished for
CAMPING PARTIES
Comfortable ROOMS
Hunting and Fishing Trophies PREPARED ON-SITE, as Desired
Terms per DAY or per WEEK
Innkeeper: Ned Kynd.

3

Dinner was lovely, the leg of mutton perfectly tender and the gravy smooth; everyone was pleased. But although Elizabeth brought a tray to Martin, and although mutton had always been his favorite, he didn't take a bite. She brought the tray down untouched and said nothing to Andrew, who as always presided buoyantly over the table.

Once dinner was over, though, once Andrew rose and headed, like the others, for the inevitable afternoon's rest in bed, Elizabeth put on her boots and her heavy cloak and left the house. Now she walks swiftly through the village—past the new hotel, past the lumber mill, past the boardinghouses rising nearby. Here, as everywhere else, there are far more patients than places for them. Despite the private sanatorium up on the hill, run by the famous doctor; despite the enormous, state-sponsored sanatorium for the destitute, and the one for sick foresters, and the one for children; despite the one that is really a prison, taking in consumptive inmates from all over the state; and despite the dozens of private rest-cure homes like her own, the hotel still bulges with invalids awaiting admission to a more permanent place. A newly built spur of the railway brings health-seekers right to the center of her adopted village: now a well-known center for the cure.

Around her are cure-porches, cure-chairs, the shops that build the chairs and the offices of the doctors who treat the patients lying on the chairs that line the porches. Dr. Davis, who calls on her boarders each week, displays his name on a bold brass plaque—befitting, he must think, the size of his practice. Yet so far he's been no help in finding a replacement for Mrs. Temple. She might have known better than to ask him. All his energy goes into lecturing his patients, which he does in a folksy tone she finds annoying.

Consumption, he likes to say, when he gathers her boarders together— but let us call it by its modern scientific name, *tuberculosis*—is caused by a germ, the tubercle bacillus. In our lungs the bacilli cause tiny dots of disease which the lung tries to wall off with scar tissue: these dots we call *tubercles,* little tubers. Your recovery depends on maintaining and strengthening this scar tissue, which is at first as delicate as a spider's web. Which is why you must rest. Why you must not exert yourselves or give in to anxiety or do anything, such as pick up an eager child—months ago he publicly, infuriatingly, chided Martin Sawyer—to cause a sudden deep breath or contract your chest muscles. Break the delicate scars and the germs escape, seeding disease in other parts of the lung. Build up your resistance; let the lungs make walls so perfect, so strong, that the germs are starved to death.

Some days, when his mood is particularly bouncy, he'll cast the germs as slow but sturdy hoplites undermining the lungs; the ones who break out as anomalous fleet-heeled messengers spreading deadly news. Stop the messengers! he barks at his invalids. Starve out the troops! It's almost touching, the faith he has in words. He passes out pamphlets, magazines, and his own private exhortations, which he prints on colored cards. Each of her boarders' rooms boasts an example of his latest:

REMEMBER!

If treatment is begun early most cases of tuberculosis can be cured, but it requires determination, perseverance, and often self-denial to accomplish it. There are no known specifics which will cure tuberculosis in the sense of directly affecting its exciting cause (the tubercle bacillus). The only known treatment is the indirect one of developing and maintaining a resistance to the toxemia of the infection—a method we call "the out-door life" or "the cure."

The four essentials of this treatment are—
  1)Follow your doctor's advice absolutely
  2)Breathe pure out-door air both night and day
  3)Take an abundance of nourishing food
  4)Rest, rest, rest

Most patients must devote their entire time to getting well.

Elizabeth might embrace his advice more wholeheartedly—here she rounds the bend in the river and passes the house that once belonged to Dr. Kopeckny—if she'd not already seen so much change. Every few years she's had to adapt her furnishings and her schedule to reflect the latest medical theories. Often she wishes she'd been present for the crucial early years, when Dorrie's mother first started taking in boarders and Nora was first visiting them. No one knew what caused consumption then, never mind what cured it. Nora, recollecting those times, once painted a picture for her of a typical February afternoon.

In six houses, on four different streets, eight men suffering from consumption are sitting out in the clear, cold air. Patient, bored, patiently bored, they're so muffled in blankets and coats as to be almost indistinguishable. The smallest happening, Nora said—three pigeons wheeling in concert across the sky, a squirrel skittering up a tree—is seized on as entertainment. What else is there to do? The village, in those years which Elizabeth can only imagine, consists of one store, two sawmills, five streets, a handful of houses. A small hotel, open only in summer, which looks across the river to a few farms dotting the valley and the lower slopes. The healthy residents have boats to build, land to till, livestock to tend, and game to shoot; houses and clothing and implements to make and repair: there is always work. The strangers sitting idly among them have only these long blank hours. The quiet is meant to cure them. The sweet freezing air, the constant, uplifting, improving sight of the stony mountains—*And us,* Nora said. *To help them, besides the air and the quiet, they had us.*

Sometimes, Elizabeth imagines now, the invalids must have gathered on a single porch, gossiping with each other; this would have helped. Sometimes they must have been cheered by the sight of Nora walking toward them along the river, a pack-basket on her back and her gray-striped hair blowing messily in the wind. Those who spent more than one winter here would learn tricks, which they'd pass to the new arrivals. Fur coats they found excellent, sheepskin and mink and raccoon. Best if the collar comes up over the ears and the pockets are big. Loose woolen mittens, worn inside deerskin mittens, are ideal. The hat—what about the hat? A wool cap, a knitted stocking cap, a fur hat with ear flaps. They trade among themselves as they see what works best.

Still they do this, Elizabeth thinks. Some parts of the cure never change, no matter what the doctors discover.

Then, as now, they wrote to their relatives with requests; then too the village residents adapted to the invalids' shifting tastes. Someone began to tan sheepskins for jackets. Someone else started making gloves, someone imported woolen sleeping bags and hot-water bottles. Now the livery caters to the sick, the builders specialize in storm enclosures. The hardware store sells sled robes and foot warmers while the drugstore sells cod-liver oil and pasteboard sputum boxes. The cobbler makes enormous sheepskin-lined moccasins and the carpenter makes coffins. Of which there are, Elizabeth belatedly realizes, two at the depot, awaiting a train—patients from one of the sanatoriums, returning home to their families.

So will Martin Sawyer travel, she thinks. This part has never changed either. As she rounds a corner, wishing that Martin might leave them some other way, the Northview Inn comes into sight. It too has hardly changed. Warped dock, sagging gutters, siding in need of paint. It's still the same modest size, with the same unimproved and slightly disheveled waterfront that she and Gillian and their mother, Clara, first saw one hazy, apparently unremarkable afternoon. Only the cottage has been added.

The cove is shining, not yet frozen but dotted with patches of water so still that by morning, if the wind doesn't rise, they'll have turned into floating islands of thinnest ice. The cove will appear to be open, but beyond the frozen rim birds will be standing far from shore, quite casually, on what still looks like water. Some will walk a few steps and then be swimming. *I wish*, Nora had once said, apologizing as soon as the words registered on Elizabeth's face, *I so wish that you and Andrew had been able to have children.*

4

Nora couldn't leave Detroit fast enough, once she knew one of her brothers was alive. She left Fannie, she left her job; she bundled up her bewildered son. On the train Michael wore a light jacket, which Fannie had made for him; a cloth cap that was his especial pride. The sheer novelty of travel entertained him for a while. But the train kept moving and moving; his soft red hair grew dark with sweat. This was July, and the weather was beastly all along the lake. Weary, unhappy, Michael glared at his mother and said, "I want to go home."

And still Nora pressed them on: to the steamboat dock on Lake Champlain; then into the enormous, strangely dressed crowd crushed onto the steamer and fighting for beds in Plattsburgh. She wiped Michael's face with a damp cloth and fed him tidbits from the hamper she'd packed, unable to explain to him all that had conspired to tear her family apart. Ireland was a word to him, England was another. Her days at Grosse Isle he knew nothing about, and she would never tell him. He clung to her hand as she tried to get seats on the stage and then gave in to an overcharging wagon driver. Who were these people, massed everywhere she wanted to be? Later she'd learn that the newspapers had given them a name: they—she and Michael included—were "Murray's Fools." Colm Larkin, as plenty of people would tell her, had not been the only one to read that cheerful yellow book and believe a stay in the Adirondacks would save his life.

Caught among the several thousand visitors swarming into a wilderness that had, in earlier seasons, welcomed no more than several hundred, Nora was shrill, her voice loud with desperation. *No one,* she'd later tell Elizabeth, *no one who hasn't lost a family can understand this.* When the driver dumped them off at the Northview Inn after hours of jolting along a corduroy road, she and Michael were two among a dozen. Nora's first sight of her brother, after twenty-two years, was this: a slim, pale, dark-haired man, still youthful-looking, but weary, standing on the porch of the inn with hands held out in a rueful gesture. The last time she'd seen him, he'd hardly been older than Michael. She might not have recognized him if he hadn't been speaking.

"We're full," he said. And there was his voice, still fresh and flavored with home. "We've been full for weeks." Now she could see that he'd grown to look rather like their father.

Michael leaned against her side, asleep on his feet. "Look up," she whispered. "That's your uncle."

There were lines around Ned's mouth, and the skin was gray beneath his eyes; she couldn't puzzle out what had happened to his nose. A small part of it seemed to have melted, as if the flesh were wax. Ten people rushed past her and swarmed him, crying that they must have a bed, they must have a meal, they had traveled for days; to each of them Ned spoke kindly. He had no beds, he repeated. But they were welcome to take their supper here, after which he'd make arrangements to carry them into the village. There they might find transport to another inn, to the rail station, or back to the ferry dock. Perhaps some of the villagers might have spare rooms to rent.

The crowd shuffled and grumbled and still Nora stood back, her arm around Michael. Finally Ned looked over the heads of the others to her.

"Ned?" she said. He gazed at her blankly. She'd grown very thin; her heavy black hair, striped with white, no longer hung loose but was braided and coiled in a careless knot. She had deep lines around her eyes and her hands were dry and cracked. "Ned?" she said again. "It's me. Nora."

What went through his mind then? Everything, everything. Around him the inn dissolved and the angry visitors disappeared. His sister had left him, she was dead. Since the morning when strangers had ferried her unconscious body away from him, he had lived an entire life: twenty-two years, during which he'd believed that in all the world he no longer had a single living relative. Those in Ireland had toppled all at once, like a village blown down by a windstorm. Over here Nora had vanished, then Denis; leaving him more alone than he'd thought a person could be.

For a minute, when he first saw Nora again, everything seemed to exist at once: both the toppled village of his childhood and his whole confusing life since then, which contained, on the one hand, this inn and its guests and his taxidermy shop, the mountains with their harsh and changeable weather, his beloved dogs moving swiftly through the brush—and, on the other, his essential solitude. Although he loved his hounds, and had companions among the guides, the life that moved within him was hidden from everyone. Denis and Nora had been the last to know him; Denis was dead. Where had his sister been? Her hair, once as thick and black as a horse's tail, was ruined. He opened his mouth, then shut it again. He would never be able to explain himself. He held out his arms and said, "Nora."

Why, during their first days together, did she ask so many questions? Her prying made him indignant. His reserve made her feel rejected. Both were bewildered by the way they jangled and clashed, despite the joy of being together: where was the ease of their childhood?

Ned tried to compress his life into stories that he could stand to tell and she could stand to hear, but this was like trying to convey, by the example of one perfectly stuffed rough-legged hawk, the essence not only of that single living creature, but of what it meant to be a hawk. In his taxidermy shop, where he hid after his worst failures with his sister, he stared at his recent work. Wings, splayed open in flight, conveyed nothing about their compact folded shape at rest. One bird said nothing about the others. His words—about, say, his years with the French-Canadian farmer who'd worked him so hard, or his first stay in these woods, at the lumber camp; about his winter with the consumptive lawyer who'd taught him to read, or his travels with the naturalists who'd trained him in taxidermy—were equally deceitful fragments of the truth.

"I don't understand," Nora said one day, after he'd started a sentence, faltered, and then snapped at her in exasperation. "Why is it so hard to explain what happened to you? I tell *you* as much as I can remember."

"I thought you were dead," he said. They were in the kitchen; she'd moved all his spoons. He moved them back. "Can't you imagine what that was like? I never thought of my life as something I'd want to tell you about someday. I wasn't trying to remember. Most of it I was trying to forget."

He kept to himself the harsher truth—that there were days, still, when he woke and forgot that she'd been returned to him. When, until he heard her speaking softly with Michael, he couldn't wholly resuscitate the corpse he'd once seen carried off a ship. For a few seconds each morning, until their great good fortune came clear in his mind again, she was a stranger to him.

"It's not that I didn't miss you," he added. "I thought of you every day."

That was the truth; the happiness that filled him when he looked out a window and saw Nora and Michael crossing the yard with their hands clasped, or when Michael leaned calmly against his shoulder, was also true. Yet still he flinched each time Nora dug into his past. The things he preferred not to think about—his sea voyage especially, his winter trapped in the arctic ice—attracted her most sharply. When she asked about his nose, he sighed and went into another room, then returned and explained that he'd once found work as a cook on a ship—not a whaling ship, nor a navy ship, but an arctic exploring ship, which had sailed farther north than she could imagine—and on that voyage had suffered from frostbite. He turned from her. "Do I look so different?"

"It's hardly noticeable," she replied. Which was true if she stood to his right; she tried not to stand to his left.

"At first I couldn't stand to have people looking at me," he said. "I still don't like it, I hate it when you stare."

"I'm not staring," she said. "I missed you, I like to look at you now that I can."

What she took from his hesitant explanations was that they'd been apart too long. They'd been through too much alone—this was no one's fault, it was their misfortune—and now they couldn't explain their lives to each other. Baffled, she watched the way Ned leapt into his work the instant he rose, as if he dreaded sharing a minute's idle conversation over their first cups of tea. He was glad to have her and Michael there, he said. More glad than he could say. Right now, though, he was very busy.

Forty guests filled the Northview Inn, spread between the two bottom floors of the main building and the low wing angled back from the lake. After a huge breakfast of eggs and muffins and chops and venison steaks, potatoes and coffee and more, the guests assembled on the porch: like children, Nora thought, waiting to be amused. Then the guides would slide up in their slim rowing boats and the guests would turn to Ned for advice. Who should go to Paul Smith's on St. Regis Lake and who to Bartlett's? Would the two gentlemen from Albany share a boat and guide between them or live like kings and hire two boats? And what about cartridges, and fishing lures, and the choice of guns and hatchets? If there were ladies among the guests—they were rare then—some would want to hire horses and others to climb a mountain.

All these decisions took time. At night, guests who'd been coming for several seasons would want Ned to play whist with them. They'd want advice about where to hunt; they'd want to make lists, with prices and shipping dates, of the trophies they'd ordered mounted. If the guests left Ned free for a minute, then Mrs. Yarrow, the housekeeper, would appear. What should she order, whom should she hire? She was used to having first claim on Ned's free time. Nora, not knowing how else to reach her brother, joined him in working long hours; through this, she thought, they would build a common life.

In September, when the flood of guests finally receded, Nora helped

Ned close off the guest bedrooms and bring in wood and seal the windows on the third floor of the main building, which formed the private apartment the three of them now shared. The sky grew dim, the snow fell and fell. She'd never seen anything like it. In the woods, between the massive dark trees, the snow lay three then four and then five feet deep. Michael adored Ned's brown and white spaniel-hounds, who crashed through the drifts and chased after snowshoe hares. Ned taught him to shoot and, when he saw that Michael wasn't squeamish, brought him to the shop out back, where he worked on the skins and heads his guests had left behind.

Even here, where Ned was most at home, he didn't open up. He welcomed Nora, she knew he loved her, as she knew he loved Michael. Although he seldom asked about her past life, he listened intently as she described her old room at Fannie's house, her friendship with Colm Larkin, the day when, with the sun deliciously baking the skin on their hands, Francis had asked her to marry him and she'd said yes. But when she asked questions of her own he answered only briefly, skipping great chunks of time. There'd been a friend, she gathered one evening, with whom he'd traveled through these woods, and who'd helped him find the site for this inn. Copernicus—what kind of a name was that? The brother, Ned said shortly, of the naturalist with whom he'd traveled north; the whole family had peculiar names.

Why did she keep asking questions? Because he volunteered so little, she would have said. He hid himself, he hid his life, he refused to let her know him. Her inquiries, he might have responded, were no different from the rude prying of his guests and clients. Over dinner or out on the porch, strangers asked the same blunt questions again and again, as if they were the first to think of them. Where was he from, when had he come from Ireland, did he have family there, or here? What had happened to his face?

For those people, who didn't matter, he made up stories. A she-bear had mauled him. A blizzard had caught him far from home. In Ireland he'd been scalded by a pan of boiling water.

But his own sister he couldn't lie to. Nor, at first, could he tell her the truth. His own sister, he thought, ought to have known what was crucial without asking.

During their second winter at the inn, Nora and Michael went with Ned to look at a litter of hunting dogs. In a sleigh heaped with blankets and fur robes they slipped through deep, unbroken snow, Ned's black horses working hard to break trail but the sleigh itself gliding noiselessly. Michael remarked on the hawks casting shadows on the slopes, the chickadees whisking past, and Ned pointed out lakes where he and Michael might fish through the ice. The sky, which had been clear and bright when they started out, was gray by the time they reached Alvah's cabin. While they drank coffee and chatted and played with the puppies—two were for Michael, Ned revealed then, Michael's own dogs, and so he should choose—the wind came up and the sky grew dark and more snow began to fall. It was very cold by the time they left. Before they were halfway home, a foot of fresh snow had fallen and the wind was already erasing their morning tracks.

"Are we lost?" Michael said, looking wide-eyed at the chaos. "Are we going to be lost?"

"I never get lost," Ned said calmly. By then both Nora and Michael knew this to be true; Ned's sense of direction was another reason the guides respected him. They steered around gigantic drifts, which the wind made in a minute and then revised: let's cover this bush here; no, this. A joke, if it had been warmer. The horses, who were not amused, stopped at the foot of a long, steep hill and refused to go farther.

The sleigh held puppies as well as people: Homer and Virgil—Alvah had named them—who wailed despite their distinguished names. The horses stood still, breathing heavily, glazed in their sweat.

"We'll rest for a while," Ned said, warming Michael's cheeks with his

hands after trying to coax the horses on. "We'll get warmed up while we
wait for the moon to rise. Then we'll ask the horses again."

"The dogs are cold," Michael said. "I am too."

Ned tossed him a shovel. "Help me," he said.

While Nora rubbed the horses down and covered them with blankets,
Ned and Michael dug a hollow into the lee side of a big drift. Inside
it Ned packed three bearskin robes, the puppies, and Michael. Nora
crawled in behind him, and Ned behind her. They huddled there while
the wind began to drop and the moon slowly lit the landscape. Michael
held Homer and Virgil inside his coat, one wrinkly-faced, half-mastiff,
half-greyhound puppy nestled in each armpit.

"Are you warm enough?" Ned asked.

"We're fine," said Nora. In the moonlight reflected from the snow she
could see him smiling. "You *like* this," she said. "How can you like this?"

More questions. He shrugged. "We're warm. We're safe. The storm
will lift, and until it does I'm with my family."

Then, not because Nora had asked, but because Michael looked frightened and pressed silently up to his side, Ned told them a little more
about his voyage north. On a wooden ship, in the company of fourteen
other men, he had sailed from Philadelphia. Past the mouth of the
St. Lawrence, past the same cliffs he and Nora had first seen on the
ship that brought them from Ireland; past Labrador and across Davis
Strait to the coast of Greenland. On the *Narwhal,* which was the name
of his ship, he'd crossed Baffin Bay just a few years after Nora had settled in Detroit, and then had sailed down long empty sounds, in and
out of ice-choked bays to a barren land where the expedition had met
Esquimaux and where they'd found traces of the lost English expedition they'd been looking for. The captain had been difficult. But two
friends had protected Ned: the ship's naturalist, Erasmus Wells, and the
surgeon, Dr. Boerhaave.

"They taught me the names of some animals and plants," Ned said to
Michael. Michael's face had relaxed; the puppies' heads peeped out from

his collar. While the wind howled Ned talked about those men, who had given him books and shown him how to prepare and mount animal skins. Later the ship had been frozen into the ice.

The doctor died, Nora learned; Michael was asleep by then. The one Ned had liked so much. The captain disappeared. In a little boat, not much larger than the guide boats here, the naturalist had led Ned and the remaining men out of the arctic.

"I was sick the whole way," Ned said. "We didn't have anything to eat, and I had a fever. A piece of my nose rotted off."

"How old were you then?" Nora asked.

"Twenty-one. Almost twenty-two."

"I was twenty-three when I got to Detroit," Nora said. "I missed you and Denis the way I'd miss my legs."

"What journeys we made," he said; while Nora thought, *How calm he is.* When they were young, when he was three and four and six and she was thirteen, fourteen, sixteen, she'd often known what he was about to do before he knew it himself. Time and again she'd reached for his collar before he fell into a stream, knocked a poisonous berry from his hand before he brought it to his mouth.

"After that," she said, "why would you settle here? If I'd been where you were, I would have wanted to move someplace with palm trees."

Ned spread his hands before him. "How can you explain these things? I love it here, it feels like home." With his left hand he stroked the robe protecting them from the icy drift. "I was so young when we left Ireland, I don't remember that place like you do. I know this doesn't look like home. But it *feels* right. In the winter it's like the arctic, except that I'm safe."

He stepped outside their cave to check on the horses, returning entirely cased in white. "The wind's down," he said. "The horses are rested, I think they're ready to try the hill again. We'll put Michael in the sleigh with his new friends and you and I can walk."

Because Ned always refused to raise the inn's modest rates, their summer earnings went largely to pay the staff and keep the buildings and boats in good repair. Everything else depended on what Ned made in the winter, when he went to work on the specimens he'd rough-cleaned earlier and stored in his shop.

Lumber, barrels of salt, heaps of tow and bales of straw, screws and bolts and wax and sperm oil. Behind Ned's workbench a half-finished pheasant was wired to a sawed-off branch; a varnished board supported four partial deer legs, the hooves bent up to form a line of coat hooks. An owl, wings half spread, pounced on a mouse near a moose head awaiting its eyes, which hung in turn above an opossum suspended from its tail. Ned was particularly proud of the infants clinging to the mother possum's fur, and of Mr. Hartley's cherished hunting dog, which sat obediently, as it had so seldom sat in life.

"Making the mounts look good, making them look *real*," he said to Nora, "—if I could, I'd keep them all here, instead of sending them off to some wealthy sportsman's parlor."

He smiled at Michael working beside him. Michael had shown a real talent for this and they spent long hours together, passing tow and hemp and scrapers and knives, hardly talking but both content.

"You don't like your customers?" Nora asked.

"Some are better than others." He wound another twist of twine around the excelsior padding the neck of a deer. "But I wouldn't work for most of them if we didn't need the money. They're too noisy. Too busy. Too rich."

From the tray of eyes Michael held out to him, round pupils with irises tinted shades of gold and brown, he chose a pair.

"Pretty," Nora said, plucking one from his palm and holding it up to the light.

"I need that," he said, taking it back.

Even when they annoyed each other, they shared their love for

Michael, as well as a sense of how much you could lose in a life and still survive. As they grew older they also agreed that they missed more and not less all the people they'd lost. Walking in the woods, Michael galloping far ahead of them after the hounds, Nora would recollect for Ned what their mother had looked like, stirring a pot of porridge with a baby on her lap and her hair folding over her face like a shawl. What their father had said when the first of the harvests failed.

"How do you remember those things?" Ned would ask.

"I had ten more years than you did," Nora said. "With all of them."

Ned pressed her hand but still couldn't explain how much he missed not only his family but also his friends: Dr. Boerhaave, who'd drowned beneath the ice, and Erasmus, who'd gone back to the arctic. Copernicus, who had simply disappeared. In the space where he might have spoken, Nora thought how much she missed Francis, still, and the men she'd watched over in the hospital—Colm Larkin, particularly—and Fannie. She'd left Fannie in such a rush, she'd hardly told her good-bye. The letters they'd exchanged since then were little comfort; Fannie's written words were terse and unrevealing, while Nora tended to run on too long, circling without ever quite reaching what she meant to say.

Trying to describe Fannie's strength and good sense, and the pleasure of the afternoons they'd spent collecting herbs and roots together, filled Nora with a longing to learn what grew in the woods of her new home. She found a little book, which helped her identify plants she hadn't known in either Ireland or Detroit. The guides taught her others. Luke and Asa and Charlie and Fiske, Daniel, Reuben, Hubert—the men who looked after the thick-set sports who came, with their guns and rods, to the inn—were Nora's first new friends. It pleased her to bring their dinners out to the table in the boathouse, where they ate separately, and to watch how kindly they treated Michael.

Moving among them, listening to their tales and watching them teach her son how to tie fishing lures, she'd sometimes think of the life she'd had so briefly with Francis. She was strong and healthy, her body alive although she was nearing fifty. No one touched her now but Michael and—a kiss on the cheek, a hand brushing her shoulder—Ned. Baffling to think how the rest had disappeared. Instead she had the respect of the guides, who noticed her cooking up poultices and began to come to her with their sprained wrists and smashed fingers and sore throats and boils. They saw her, she slowly realized, as she and the people in Corktown had once seen Fannie. After a while she grew so busy doctoring them and their families that she neglected her work at the inn.

The invalids beginning to winter in the village kept her even busier; Ned had to hire an extra girl to pick up what Nora could no longer do. She bought a notebook, two good pencils, a little satchel in which to carry her supplies. She kept track of the invalids' progress: *The young man on Harriet's porch, still at an early stage but sent here by his parents after both his sisters died, has a little fever, every night, which has been going on for months. A dry cough that comes and goes; sometimes a sore throat, sometimes pains in his chest.*

There were men who were worse, whose fevers seemed to be burning them up; and men who looked better, and coughed less, but who felt so tired and melancholy that they'd forgotten what it was like to anticipate something with pleasure. Once in a while someone hemorrhaged bright blood, foaming and terrifying. Then one of the women would come running with ice chips to suck and a cloth packed with snow, which would lie heavily on the sick man's chest: so cold.

Nora tried to explain her new work to Ned. "This is what I'm meant to *do*," she said—although the swiftness with which it came about had taken her by surprise. "It's what I learned while we were apart, it's how I make use of myself."

"As opposed to this, you mean?" He gestured ruefully at the room filled with mounted heads. "I won't argue, if it's what you want. But I wish . . ."

What did he wish? What she wished, perhaps: for the dead and vanished to return. Once, during a spring cleaning, she caught him staring out the window while holding a woman's walking boot in his hand.

"What is that?" she asked. It looked as old as she felt; the black calf was so worn it was almost limp, and one of the buttons was missing.

"Isn't it obvious?" He turned back to the window. "Erasmus left it with me," he added, as if to keep her from asking more questions. "For safekeeping, the last time I saw him."

By then she knew that, after their arctic trip, Erasmus Wells and a few other people had stayed for some months in the neighborhood of Ned's first cabin. Then they'd headed north again, leaving Ned behind. "His wife's?" she asked.

"His mother's," he said. He dropped the boot into her hand. "It got so damp over the winter, I thought I should set it outside to dry."

Mold had grown on the tongue, beneath the laces. "I can sponge this off," she said. "Does he want it back?"

"How would I know?" Ned said bitterly. "All I ever knew was that the mother's name was Lavinia, and that she died when the boys were young. But I said I'd keep this for Erasmus, and so I have."

"You've never heard from him?"

"Not from him, not from Copernicus. Not once in all these years."

It was with them, she thought, as it had been for her with Francis and then with Colm Larkin. Never a word. Where had all of them gone? Only she and Ned had returned to each other from the past.

5

Elizabeth enters the inn, as she always does, by way of the kitchen door. Through the empty room, past the draped chairs and appliances, the cold stove, the dim cabinets full of glassware; up the stairs to Ned's private apartment.

"Elizabeth," Ned says, stepping back to let her in. Still he holds himself quite straight, although he's shrunk several inches. Next to the stove in the front room is the armchair where he spends much of the winter months. She sits across from him, in what used to be Nora's chair.

"How are you feeling?" she asks.

"Very well." He'd say this, she knows, unless he were dying.

"Your hands?"

"Not too bad." He holds up the twisted joints for her inspection. "I worked all yesterday on a vixen for Mr. Claremont. And still they didn't hurt much last night."

"That's good," she says. She doesn't ask to see the stuffed fox; for the last few years, since Ned's vision began to fail and his arthritis has worsened, his mounts have been painfully shabby. The skins gape at the seams, the eyes don't always match. Michael praises them, thanks Ned for doing them, and then destroys them secretly, substituting specimens of his own.

As Ned continues to describe his projects, she nods, remembering the quiet celebrations they used to hold in this room on Nora's birthday. A ginger cake with lemon icing; mittens and a book as gifts. Surely Ned remembers these as well—but still he says nothing about his sister, talking instead about his new curved knife. When he pauses, she asks the question that has brought her here: where might she seek a replacement for Mrs. Temple?

"I don't know," he says. "No one is ever going to be Nora." Such a relief, the way he understands what she's actually asking.

"No one seems to know anyone suitable," she says. "And one of my boarders is failing, I'm going to need help soon."

"Who is it?"

"Martin," she says. "Martin Sawyer."

"Oh, what a shame." For a minute Ned stares past her. Then he says, "Why not look in New York again? You could have Clara do some preliminary interviewing for you, and send up the most promising, like she did with Mrs. MacDonald. That worked out fine."

"It did," Elizabeth says reluctantly. "But I hate to ask for her help unless I really need to. She gets so involved, and then she wears herself out."

"She likes to feel useful," Ned says. "When's the last time you wrote her?"

"October, I suppose. Maybe September. She wrote me back right away."

"Doesn't she always?"

Ned and her mother, Elizabeth knows, have been corresponding for almost twenty years. Both of them over seventy now, but still Ned sits down at least once a week and describes for Clara everything interesting that's happened at the inn, or at the cottage next door, or—when he's privy to it—within Elizabeth's boardinghouse. Clara responds, or so Ned claims, with reports of her daily life among what's left of her family in New York. Elizabeth has never been sure what lies behind this long exchange of letters. Simple affection, loneliness, some romantic urge?

"If Martin—" she begins to say, but Ned swiftly interrupts her.

"I can't believe things have gone so fast with him. We were fishing together in May."

"I remember that," Elizabeth says. Martin had been so proud of the new lures hung from his handsome vest. So delighted to present her with his pack-basket heavy with trout.

"I wish . . ." Ned says, before he falls silent. As he gazes out the window, Martin, in his room at Elizabeth's house, gives up all pretense of sleep and squirms against his pillows until his head and shoulders are raised and his knees sloped sufficiently to support his writing board. Next to him are several pencils and a tablet of paper. Although this is strictly forbidden—one is not to read during the afternoon rest hours, not to chat, not to write, not even to turn the pages of a magazine—Martin has decided to write a letter.

Dear Mother, he begins.

He will write, he thinks, about the departure of Mrs. Temple, whom he liked despite her lack of humor and a tendency to chatter. Her hands, when she rubbed his back and chest with liniment, were both gentle and strong. She never fussed when he coughed blood. She could change his bed without getting him up, rolling the sheets and blankets into slim flattened tubes along one flank, then gently easing him over the ridge and onto the clean linen. Elizabeth, so scrupulous about every aspect of her house, will surely hire someone equally skilled, but it won't matter to him.

Today, he writes.

Shouldn't he be writing the truth? What is really happening to him, what it feels like. He felt such comfort, as a boy, unfolding his secrets to his mother. And such isolation when, after his father died and he became sick himself, she stopped listening and insisted on his health.

He should say that, he could start with that. Or with the disturbing sound that is filtering up to him now, causing his pencil to pause— the sound of the lidded brass containers boiling on the kitchen stove. Stripped of their pasteboard liners, and of the bits of lung and life which he and his fellow boarders cough up, the nine apple-sized cuspidors clonk gently together. With the strange, upsetting acuity that has come to him in these last two weeks, he can hear them rolling, bumping each other, as he can hear the damp tea leaves falling from Livvie's hand onto the wooden floor, the soft *swish-swish* as she spreads them around, and the crisper noise of them being gathered, along with the dust that must not be allowed to rise, into neat piles by the broom.

He will write to his mother, he thinks, that the dull collisions of the cuspidors boiling reminds him of the eggs she boiled by the dozen, and tried to force him to eat, during the year before she finally let him come here. She would not believe he was sick; his father was dead, he could not be sick too. If he was sick he would lose his job, their new neighbors would despise them, they'd have to move yet again. If she didn't believe it, why did she keep showing up at his bedroom door with a bowl lined with strips of buttered toast, onto which she'd cracked the eggs?

He will write that he came here too late. That he is dying. Later she'll want to know that he knew the truth.

Everyone knows, he thinks. Maybe not Andrew, who shares his mother's ability to rebuff unpleasant facts—but certainly Elizabeth and Mrs. Temple, and probably his fellow boarders too. They know what will happen once he's gone. What's left of him will be sealed up, sent home on the train to his family; no concern to anyone here. But some of the boarders will flee the house on the day his room is cleaned and disinfected, spending hours walking briskly through the woods. Others will pace the hallways, both watching and trying not to watch as the walls and woodwork and floors and ceiling of his room are washed and painted with carbolic acid, as the curtains and bedclothes are taken away to be boiled and every smallest item that once was his is steamed or burned. He has himself, on similar occasions, both walked the halls and walked the woods.

Surely he should explain some of this to his mother. She kept him from coming here early, when he might still have recovered. As his aunt, who swooped down with her two loud sons and, on the pretext of comforting his mother, settled her family into his house, has kept him from returning home to die. Once she'd grasped the nature of his illness, she'd convinced his mother to urge him to stay in the mountains. Too much of a risk to her boys, she said; too awkward to explain his case to the neighbors. Better to wait until he was wholly cured. Together they have stranded him here, among strangers.

He might blame them, or forgive them. He might describe what it feels like inside his chest. Instead his hand writes, as it always does, *The weather continues to be fine, and I am feeling much improved.*

Ned, still thinking of the morning when he and Martin fished for trout, remembers something Clara wrote him recently and says, "Your father is headed to Alaska."

"Again?" Elizabeth says, wondering if this means he won't be back in time for a summer visit. When her parents come up they stay not with her—she seldom has a free room—but here at the inn, where Clara can be near the children.

"Right after Christmas," Ned continues. "Last week they went to the opera with some of your cousins. Iris and Hermione send their love."

Iris and Hermione, Julia and Otis—her cousins, her uncle George's children—grown now, with children of their own. As a girl she'd disliked all of them, along with the crowded, noisy, smelly city where everyone mocked her accent and where she knew no one. But her father had made connections in New York, and promptly found work that pleased him. Clara had been comforted to have her brother and his family next door during Max's chronic absences. This was home now, she'd told her daughters. And slowly England had disappeared, house and garden and landscape and birds, watery sky and secret hedgerows fading one by one.

Rising, Elizabeth says to Ned, "I appreciate your suggestion about the nurse." She puts the kettle on the stove and looks through the larder to make sure he has plenty of supplies. Tea and coffee and sugar and oats, a fresh loaf of bread, half a steak and kidney pie, preserved plums, and two kinds of jam—really there is nothing for her to do. Returning to Ned's side, she adds, "I'll wire my mother today."

As she leans over to kiss his cheek, he plucks from the table a small crimson book, which he hands to her. Poems, she sees. The work of a young woman who lived for eighteen months in the sanatorium on the hill. "Would you give this to Martin for me?" Ned says. "And tell him I'm thinking of him."

"He'll be glad to know that." She slips the book into her pocket and turns away.

"You might stop by the cottage on your way back," Ned says.

6

In the summer of 1882 a group of poplars stood, shivering their leaves, where the cottage next to the inn is now. Near them was the landing where the afternoon stage set down Clara Vigne's family, along with seven other guests anxious to settle into their rooms and start their holidays. Among them, only Clara hung back. Her stillness caught Ned's eye, and her air of being completely self-contained. Otherwise her looks—middling height, middling weight, smooth brown hair, and deep-set, grayish blue eyes—were not remarkable. Surrounded by her luggage and flanked by two young women, she stood calmly as Ned approached.

"Is your husband arriving separately?" he asked.

"He's in Borneo," Clara said, one hand tracing a serpentine path in the air. "Collecting plants."

"Then you must let my nephew help you with your things."

Even as he called Michael, Clara touched one hand to each daughter's arm and they said, simultaneously, "We don't need help." How could it be, Ned would wonder later, that their words made him long, paradoxically, to protect them?

They bent toward the bags as their mother introduced them. Gillian, whom Ned had assumed was older—she was taller by several inches, with sturdy shoulders and light brown hair and an easy, expansive manner—was actually younger than Elizabeth. Yet it was Elizabeth, gray-eyed like her mother, who yielded her bag to Michael with a smile. As it was Elizabeth, Nora saw later that afternoon, who stood by the edge of the beach, watching Michael from the unreliable shade of a pine.

He was standing over his boat, which was drawn up on shore. While he fiddled with an oarlock, Elizabeth pretended to examine the hills across the lake—as if her feet, hiding beneath her bell-shaped skirt, were not moving invisibly toward him. Flushed and narrow-chested, she was the opposite of Michael in everything but age; both were twenty-one that summer but Nora had, until that moment, still thought of her son as a boy. His friends were Ned and the guides and the dogs; she'd never seen him court anyone. Unless he was standing right before her she pictured him as he'd been years ago, galloping behind Homer and Virgil and chasing the wind in the grass.

The guides, who'd once made a pet of him, later made him their apprentice. By the time he was eighteen he worked alongside them as an equal. He dwarfed the men in Nora's family and resembled Francis only vaguely; he could carry a guide boat over his head and return for the guns and the oars and the packs while his clients were still catching their breath. With Homer and Virgil, who were ancient now, or with the new puppies, Helen and Dido, he joined his friends' hunting parties. Off-season, he worked in the shop with Ned, growing more skilled each winter. A vixen and her kits by their den, a family of ravens, twin fawns and their mother—whenever one of Ned's clients wanted not just a simple head or full-body mount but a lifelike tableau of several specimens, Ned proudly gave the project to Michael.

And so why, Nora chided herself that afternoon, did she persist in thinking of this competent person as a boy? Within a few days, she saw both that he was aware of Elizabeth's interest in him and lacked any feeling for her. Apparently unperturbed by this, he avoided her when he could. When he couldn't, he was careful to be polite but cool. Where had he learned that? Nora wondered. Briefly she felt sorry for the girl, whose frequent cough and occasional hectic flushes made her appear to be ill.

Mostly, though, Nora worried about her brother and the inn. That summer, for the first time she could remember, they weren't booked for the season. New hotels, expensive and spacious, were rising throughout the woods, and for much of July the Northview Inn had only fifteen guests. Nora and Ned spent hours fussing over the books and postponing payments to tradesmen. They printed new handbills; they paid for advertisements in the Syracuse and Albany papers. At dinnertime, she and Ned and sometimes Michael circulated among the three tables that now seated everyone: three, where they'd once had eight or ten.

Too often, Nora saw, Ned kept them sitting with the Vignes throughout the entire meal, asking Clara so many questions that Nora was embarrassed first for him and then for her own younger self. No wonder he'd evaded her, all those years ago. Clara sometimes answered him, sometimes ducked the questions politely. How was it, Nora wondered, that her brother, so reticent for so long, should turn not toward her but toward a guest who still spoke with an English accent?

She watched Clara closely, unable at first to see what had captured Ned's interest. It had something to do, she thought after a while, not just with the woman herself, but with her husband, Max. From Clara's reluctant responses, Nora gathered that they'd lived in England when they were young, and that Clara had raised their infant daughters alone while Max worked as a surveyor, and then as a botanist, in the Himalaya. Later they'd emigrated to the States so Clara could be near her oldest brother while Max continued to travel.

"Tell me again what he does?" Ned asked one night.

"He attaches himself to expeditions," Clara said. "Didn't I mention that? Government surveying expeditions, private exploring expeditions. Any kind of expedition you can imagine. There's always a need for someone who can collect and classify plants."

Nora watched her brother lean forward, utterly absorbed. In the arctic, she remembered, his companions had greedily collected both animals and plants. Perhaps this woman's stories reminded him of those lost friends. As he began to ask yet another question, Nora interrupted with one of her own.

"What kind of plants does your husband gather?" she asked.

"Oh . . . mosses from Tierra del Fuego," said Clara impatiently. "Orchids from the rain forests of Brazil. Tropicals from Java and Guinea and Tasmania—swamp palms, strange bamboos, all kinds of lilies and climbing vines, pitcher plants that eat live insects. The last time I heard from him, he'd found a new kind of pitcher plant, violet with a bright orange mouth."

She prodded a piece of meat with her fork. "Venison?" she asked. "It's delicious."

"Michael brought it in," Ned said. "He's an excellent shot. Does your husband have any interest in the mountain plants here?"

Clara shrugged. "I expect he wouldn't consider these real mountains. Not after where he's been."

Elizabeth, who'd been coughing quietly throughout dinner, coughed violently then. When she held a handkerchief to her lips and then hid the folds, Nora looked at her sharply and saw Clara reach for the handkerchief, before pulling her hand back to her own lap.

"I gather wild plants myself," Nora said, to fill the dreadful silence. "I know a bit about medicinal herbs and roots and I've treated our neighbors for years with them."

"Might you know something to ease Elizabeth's cough?" Clara said. For the first time she looked directly into Nora's eyes. "She's had it for months now."

Nora described some of the treatments she prepared for the invalids she visited during the winter. "Would you let me try a small experiment?" she asked, looking at both Clara and Elizabeth. "For persistent coughs, I've had good luck with a milk infusion of mullein leaves and a few other things, given warm, with honey."

"We'd be grateful," Clara said.

Restless herself, Nora blamed the unease she felt through the rest of that summer not just on the inn's peculiar half emptiness, but also on the three Vigne women, who seemed to unsettle themselves as well as everyone around them. Ned's interest in Clara continued; Elizabeth still seemed distracted and miserable even after the mullein syrup eased her cough. Gillian was never where she said she'd be. And Clara, who seemed to ignore Gillian's frequent absences, watched over Elizabeth with unnerving intensity. Yet who could blame her? Nora wondered. Max, who remained in Borneo, had been in Siberia the year before; Clara bore whatever happened to her daughters alone. Perhaps Max's absence also explained the way both sisters, although clearly devoted to their mother, seemed eager to escape on their own whenever they could. Turning a corner on the porch or entering the sitting room, Nora would glimpse their disappearing skirts. Sometimes she caught the sisters whispering intently. Or Ned and Clara, or Gillian and Michael . . . after a while, Nora tried simply to avoid them. They were guests; they need not be friends.

When that summer finally ended and the inn emptied out, Nora happily put the Vignes out of her mind. She didn't think about them again until she opened the workshop door one November day, after the first snow had fallen, and found Michael standing there in a white cloud so dense it seemed to be snowing inside. As she closed the door he brought his right arm down sharply, the thin switch in his hand whistling through the air before striking the bundle on the table. A terrible crack, again and again. He whipped at the form on the table as if he couldn't see her, white puffs rising into her nose and throat. She covered her mouth with her handkerchief and cried, "Michael!"

Whip, whip, whip.

"Michael!" she called again. Normally his movements were slow and meticulous, his workbench perfectly tidy.

At last he lowered the switch. His face was red, spattered with white. On the table was the skin of a loon, speckled black and white beneath the film of powder. Nora touched a feather and then examined her finger.

"Plaster of paris," Michael said. He was breathing hard. "It cleans the plumage. I shake off what I can, and beat out the rest. Three or four times and all the dirt and oil and blood are gone and the plaster falls out dry. Could you move?"

He held the skin by the neck feathers and beat it like a carpet, then picked up a finer switch, a thin supple twig, and bent close to the skin. Plaster clung to the sweat on his face and formed a white mask.

"What's the matter?" she asked.

"It's ruined if I don't get out every speck." He knocked the skin to the floor, picked it up, threw it back on the table, and leaned over.

"I've written her five times," he said. "She hasn't answered me once. Instead I get these ridiculous notes. . . ."

"From *who*?" Nora said.

"*Elizabeth*. About what she's reading, or some opera she's seen, or someplace interesting her father has been. . . ."

"You're writing to Elizabeth?"

"Not *her*," he said furiously. With a piece of wire he began flicking, fiercely yet precisely, at the webs of down clinging to the bases of the feathers. "Gillian. She never answers me. I don't even know if she gets my letters. I write her and instead of answers I get these foolish notes from *Elizabeth*. About concerts. The trees that grow in the park—what do I care about those things? What does she want with me?"

For a minute Nora was silent. "They'll probably be back next summer," she finally said. What else had she missed? "If Elizabeth's health doesn't improve."

He turned to look at her. "Really?" The film of plaster on his face was beginning to crack as it dried. "Gillian will be back?"

Nora shook her head and left Michael to go back to his work, back to his longing and confusion and his sense that neither his mother nor his uncle had the slightest sense of who he was or what he wanted. How could they pretend to know anything, when they didn't know the most important thing? In the woods, all through the closing weeks of summer, in a hollow lined with ferns and lycopodium, he and Gillian had secretly met when they were supposed to be separate and elsewhere.

Hands, tongues, bared flesh, lifted skirts and opened trousers: what he might have expected, except that he hadn't known what to expect. On the days it rained, they stood and wrestled in place. They lay down when it was dry. They hardly spoke, they had no words for what was going on between them. Their parents had told them nothing. Michael had heard things from the guides, but hadn't known whether to believe them. When Gillian put her hand inside his shirt and slipped her palm down his smooth white skin, the sky spun around his head and he saw every needle on every fir and hemlock. Why wouldn't she write to him?

When the Vignes returned the following summer, Gillian and Michael picked up not as if they'd been out of touch for nine months, but as if they'd been talking every day. Michael ignored Clara and Elizabeth when the wagon pulled up, holding his arms out for Gillian. She leaned into them and let him lift her over the side, while her pale hair, twined low on her neck, fluttered in small strands around his face.

After that it was Michael and Gillian on the porch together, or hunting or riding—she was a splendid horsewoman, an excellent shot—or training Helen and Dido. He turned down guiding jobs to spend time with her, and Clara did nothing to keep them apart; he was hired help to her, Nora saw, who'd be left behind come September. This was so annoying that Nora, who might have told Michael not to get involved with a guest, said nothing. She waited for the flirtation to burn itself out and watched Elizabeth, alone on the porch, pretending to read but always watching the pair and seeming to wait for the same thing.

Meanwhile Ned continued to seek Clara's company, although Nora, tired of the whole family, couldn't tell whether it was Clara herself or the tales she she told of Max's exploits that so fascinated him.

"I do love him," she heard Clara say one day, when she was sitting a few feet away from them on the porch. "Or I did—how can I know what I feel anymore, when we never see each other?"

Ned murmured something Nora couldn't hear and then there was yet more talk about Max. Max in Venezuela, on the slopes of Mt. Fuji, crossing the ice fields of Alberta. Clara's face, at first tight and drawn, softened as she supplied the details Ned asked for. Perhaps, Nora thought,

Clara thought he was safe to confide in because he knew no one from her circle in New York. Yet her manner toward him seemed genuinely friendly, and when Nora asked Ned what he liked in Clara, he answered promptly.

"It's a kind of courage," he said. "The way she waits, and takes care of his life for him. I admire that."

The mail, Nora saw, bound their friendship together. On mail days, Clara's lap would be heaped with letters. When they were younger, she said, Max had sometimes let months go by without a word. But now— she lifted the envelopes and let them tumble back onto her skirt.

"I've always let the girls read them," Clara told Ned. "But for myself—sometimes I've just skimmed them, to make sure he's all right. It's different now that you're so interested in his travels." She peered at the first three envelopes in the pile. "I wonder when he got to Japan."

"I wish I got letters like that," Ned said, as Nora wondered who from. Drawn into the conversation despite herself, she asked, "Do you write him back?"

"Once a week," Clara replied. "I used to be a great letter writer myself. But it's never enough. What could be?"

"My friend Copernicus," Ned said—here Nora turned toward him in surprise: already he'd mentioned that name to Clara?—"said he used to write his sister all the time. She stayed home and looked after the family house, so he was free to travel. He said he was grateful for that."

"Who *wouldn't* be grateful?" Clara said acidly.

Later Ned would tell Clara a little more—but not the dream, never the dream. Which was not a dream, exactly; he was often partly conscious when this came to him. Under a brilliant sky, he and Copernicus moved through the north woods again, everything they would ever need packed tidily into the guide boat. Hunting rifles, fishing rods, line, lures, leaders, a net, a cast-iron frying pan and some slabs of bacon, blankets to toss on the balsam tips they gathered each night. Wool socks, a spare shirt. Two good knives, pipes and tobacco; Copernicus's sketch-books and painting supplies.

In Ned's dream it never rained; the fish never stopped biting and the mosquitoes never bit. They never quarreled. They moved from lake to stream with the greatest of ease, never slogging through mud at the carries, never dropping the boat or the pack-baskets. Copernicus did not pull them, every week or so, toward any hamlet where he might find a girl. And Ned himself did not feel hurried, did not always sense that the six weeks they'd planned for their holiday were flying away. He had chosen the site for the Northview Inn because it was perfect, and not because their trip had ended here, near the spot where he'd spent his first Adirondack winters.

Once they'd set up camp by the lake, Copernicus set off for the nearest tavern, returning two days later only to say that he'd painted enough of these woods for now, it was time for him to head out West. Was Ned interested in joining him? To Ned's own surprise, something inside him had balked at moving any farther. He'd stayed behind, not sure what kept him, while Copernicus—like Erasmus, like everyone else—went off exploring and never returned.

Of course he was drawn to Clara, Ned thought. Tied to a wanderer, rooted herself.

7

What does it mean that Ned didn't acknowledge his sister's birthday? Perhaps, Elizabeth thinks, in his oddly delicate way he was trying to spare her feelings. Or perhaps his reminder that she visit the cottage was itself an oblique acknowledgment. The day as a kind of pilgrimage, each site that Nora knew revisited? The cottage holds all of Nora's descendants, every trace of her physical being. The rest, Elizabeth thinks, she carries inside herself.

As she drifts along the shore, what Ned notices from his third-floor window is the distracted sandpiper's track she leaves in the snow. She moves toward the water's edge and then away, back and forth as she's always moved between her desire to embrace her family and her fear of being engulfed. Never easy with any of them except Nora, who wasn't exactly Elizabeth's family; nothing has ever been simple for her but her work. Ned thinks this not judgmentally but fondly, his feelings for her neither natural nor spontaneous. He loves her because she's her mother's daughter, and because she gave purpose and shape and even joy to the last decade of his sister's life.

Back in his chair, his pen in hand, he continues his interrupted letter to Clara. *Elizabeth came to see me,* he writes. *She looks well, and sends her love. I think she has no idea of how much she now behaves like Nora—all the habits and attitudes she picked up.* He pauses, wondering if that last comment will wound Clara's feelings. Then he continues, knowing how truly Clara understands her daughter. *Even the way she speaks reminds me of Nora. She'd be glad to see her father, I think. Will he stop here on his way home from Alaska?*

Still, after all their meetings, Ned knows little of this solitary wanderer other than what Clara has conveyed to him. Lines quoted from Max's letters or repeated after a visit: from these, Ned's constructed a version of Max's life which resembles, he imagines, the unknown lives of Erasmus and Copernicus, his old companions. Or the life he could have led himself, if he'd had the strength and the desire. Instead he's stayed here, preserving animals and sheltering strangers, because this has been his nature. As it's been Clara's nature to build a private life for herself behind the shield of Max's absent presence.

You might meet him up here, he adds. *It would be wonderful to see you.* This letter, he sees, will be of the ordinary kind; most often they dwell on the family they now have in common. Only rarely will he mention the past to Clara, describing some long-ago incident—but when he does, she responds attentively, without pressing him. The odd result is that he hides far less from her than he hid from Nora.

He bites the top of his pen and adds, of his only sister and Clara's eldest daughter: *I have never really understood what either of them were thinking.* As he does, Elizabeth, chilled by the wind off the lake, moves more briskly toward the cottage.

At her own house, she thinks, everyone will be stirring. There each day resembles a week, the relentless rest periods chopping the days into miniature days—awake, asleep, awake, asleep—which pass in one sense with horrible swiftness (how can a person get anything done, always dressing or undressing, eating or sleeping, preparing to eat or sleep?) and, in another, with a devastating slowness. Each of her nine guest rooms forms the center of someone's life, her boarders caged behind the doors in their attitudes of loneliness and anxiety, boredom or melancholy or occasional elation. Logan wears his pajamas constantly, alone or under his oversized jacket and pants: the better, he declares, to nap or rise without missing a minute. With the time he saves, he means to write an epic poem celebrating his father's role in the Civil War. Farther down the hall Tillie lies flat, thinking optimistically of the children she'll have, the home she'll make, the man who'll find her when she recovers and for whose sake she's drenched herself in expensive wrinkle cream. On either side of her Niles and Celine, inseparable over the summer but now estranged, listen tensely for each other's footsteps but instead hear Meg, across from them—Meg, who speaks excellent French, but spends too much time in the bathroom she shares with Julie and Corinne. Below them Ezra reads illicitly: a long account of the Irish problem, which exactly as Dr. Davis warned has upset him. *This,* he thinks, closing the book, *is why we're forbidden to read during rest hours.* But who could rest with the noise upstairs, the footsteps tapping across the hall and the water running?

Martin, Elizabeth thinks, approaching the door of her sister's house. Let Martin be sleeping through these hours, dreaming of Daisietta. How she hopes he is still asleep.

Inside the cottage—too many bodies, too much noise; she loves every-one here, but the bustle still stuns her—she tries to respond with proper enthusiasm to her family's greetings. Her three tall, fleshy nieces, and the two nephews who tower even over Michael: a race of giants, amazing to her. One is musical, two are wickedly funny, all are as smart as their grandparents. She likes best the youngest, nine-year-old Eudora, the one grandchild Nora didn't live to see but whose expressions nonetheless often remind Elizabeth sharply of her dead friend.

"Look at my drawings," Eudora says, tugging at Elizabeth's hand. A blue bird, a yellow bird, three of the dogs curled up together, the front porch of the inn. "This is the best," she says, pushing forward her latest work: Dido asleep, one paw sheltering her gray nose.

"Very nice," says Elizabeth. She spends a few minutes examining Eudora's efforts and then admires her nephews' carved duck decoys and a dress her older niece is making. Finally her sister says, "Don't torment your aunt," and pulls Elizabeth into the kitchen.

"Don't these look good?" Gillian says proudly. "Would you like to take one back?"

On the counter are two more of the meat pies Elizabeth saw at Ned's, along with loaves of bread and trays of roasted squash and onions. "They smell delicious," Elizabeth says. "But everything's all planned for supper back at the house."

"Such a surprise," Gillian says, with affectionate mockery. Elizabeth returns her smile, thinking what a pair she and her sister are. Both of them so competent, such excellent cooks and household managers. When they were young, they'd thought themselves so different from each other.

"How did Ned seem to you?" Gillian asks.

"All right. A bit frail, the way he has been lately. And his hands are certainly no better."

For a few minutes they discuss their aging relative thoughtfully.

Although they've grown apart some over the years, they still have in common Ned, the details of keeping house for so many people, the children. And of course Michael. One of the children, Elizabeth knows, will already have skipped to the shed behind the cottage, where Michael runs the business that used to be Ned's. Michael will be setting down his draw-shave now, lifting his bulky body from the wooden stool, and moving calmly toward the kitchen. That noise at the back door is him, kicking the snow from his boots. One more thump and here he is. He clasps Elizabeth's hand and touches his massive cheek to hers.

"I just wanted to say hello," she says. If she could reach through his skin, she might find Nora inside. "And to see how the children are."

"In excellent shape," Michael says, stepping back to look over at his brood. "As you see." While a black and white cat with pearl-gray eyes twines among everyone's legs, he adds, "Won't you stay for supper?"

"I can't," Elizabeth says. "It's three-thirty, I need to hurry back."

The rigid schedule at the boardinghouse, Elizabeth's inflexible, invariable duties there, have never made an impression on Michael. What his mother did, he once said—not in the least meaning to be insulting—had been the practice of healing. Whereas what Elizabeth does is, in his eyes, no more than keeping house. How difficult can it be?

He has no idea, Elizabeth thinks, amazed again at what she'd once felt for him. He is nothing like Andrew, who, whatever his quirks, has always understood her devotion to the house and its constantly changing population. Andrew will be rising now, she thinks: stretching after his afternoon nap, ready to resume his duties. And in fact he's doing almost exactly what she envisions.

Two miles away, in the pleasant room at the back of their house, Andrew slips on a shirt, which he leaves unbuttoned, ignores the socks Elizabeth laid out for him, and then steps outside through the French doors and begins his afternoon exercises. Twenty deep knee bends, his arms straight out and his hamstrings burning. Windmills, touching right hand to left toe, left hand to right, straightening vigorously in between with a great whooshing exhalation. Sit-ups, jumping jacks, several minutes with the jump rope; he's breathing hard, his lungs strong and elastic and a healthy sweat, a useful sweat pouring down his temples—oh, the air is gorgeous today, the fragrance is like burying his face in a bed of balsam needles. Counting ONE and TWO and THREE and FOUR, he thinks of all the afternoons he's exercised in this handsome setting. And of the invisible line, a few feet to his right, that separates the bit of ground before his French doors from that in front of the doors to the nurse's room.

During Mrs. Temple's tenure, and also Mrs. MacDonald's, he was careful not to cross that line: he might have seen inside the room inadvertently, or they might have looked out at the birds and trees and been disturbed by the sight of his prancing. In this house, so packed with people, everyone's careful to guard each other's privacy. Yet Nora, so private in other ways, was the one who most often broke through his caution. She seemed to sense his movements, even when she couldn't see him; as he finished the last of his exercises she'd rise from her reading chair, tap on the glass, and wave as he stepped into view. Sometimes she'd ask him in for a minute, before they both returned to the duties of the day.

She might tell him, then, about a new remedy she was concocting. He might describe something interesting he'd seen, or confide some worry. Once he told her about a swimming companion who complained, weeks after they'd spent an afternoon splashing in an isolated stream, that he could hear frogs croaking in his stomach. They'd seen frog spawn, Andrew explained—he hadn't mentioned this to Elizabeth, for fear that she might laugh at him—floating in the brook. His friend believed that he'd swallowed some, which in his stomach had hatched and, after dining greedily on his own food, metamorphosed into frogs. "Can he get them out?" Andrew said.

Nora, listening attentively, asked a few more questions and then replied that in Ireland, where she'd grown up, people took it for granted that toads and frogs might live inside a person. "Once," she said, "I saw a man vomit a live toad after drinking one of my grandmother's herbal infusions. Wait here for a minute." While he sat gazing into the fire, she gathered leaves and powders from her stock in the attic and bound the mixture into a square of white muslin. Soon after Andrew gave this to his friend, the croakings vanished and he was cured.

The truth, Andrew thinks now, breathing hard and bending at the waist, is that they never saw the frogs expelled; perhaps they slipped out while his friend was asleep. But what matters is that his friend got better, not how Nora did it. So sharply does he miss those brief, private conversations, from which he always emerged restored, that he wonders how Elizabeth, whose friendship with Nora was both older and deeper, lives without her.

As Elizabeth, at the cottage on the lake, kisses Nora's grandchildren good-bye and accepts the pencil Eudora offers her, Andrew folds his jump rope and strides toward the trees, wanting a better view of Martin's porch. Why not, it suddenly strikes him—why not run a strand of wire around the entire frame? He could fix magnets to either end so the wind, blowing down from the hill past the stand of sugar maples and through the screen, would carry healing waves directly to Martin's bed. The magnetized chimney on one side of him, a magnetized porch frame on the other—perfect. He'll do this tomorrow.

He bounds back into his room and Elizabeth, eager to return to her duties, presses Gillian's hand and murmurs that she has to wire their mother later about some business, and will tell her the children are fine. Martin and Andrew are waiting for her, so is everyone else; she has to go.

8

Before Elizabeth had a house of her own, before Dr. Kopeckny arrived and changed the way they thought, Nora and her friends had their own ideas about the nature of consumption. Bessie had heard it was caused by perverted humors and hidden inflammations; Olive, that it ran in families and affected only those of a melancholy nature. Jane and Lillian had been taught by their mother that it rose directly from damp, cold air trapped inside a room crowded with people: a miasma, open the windows against a miasma. Their cousin thought, more straightforwardly, that dirt meant rot meant smells meant sickness: everything must be clean! Nora herself, as a girl in Ireland, had been told by her grandmother that consumption arose from putrid phlegm, draining into the chest from the head. If you lit a dried cow patty and let it smoke, and then inhaled the smoke through a reed, you'd be cured. Or if you ate the cooked and powdered lungs of a fox, or the blood of a goat. The forequarter of a dog that had drowned, claimed one of her grandmother's friends, would if boiled and made into a stew cure the sickest patient.

One of Ned's guests, a Dr. Fuller from Baltimore, ridiculed everyone's theories but his own. Hearing that Nora nursed invalids wintering in the village, he sniffed and said, "What do you know about phthisis? It takes a good solid classical education and medical school and some years in a hospital after that before you can even think of understanding this disease. What can you do for those men?"

Nora explained the diets she and her friends had devised, the arrangements they made so the invalids could rest, as their doctors back home had ordered. The astringent teas she made and the soothing syrups. Another guest leaned forward and said, "But don't you worry you might catch it from them?"

Dr. Fuller thrust out his chin. "It isn't contagious," he said. "It's inherited, the result of constitutional peculiarities inflamed by indulging in unhealthy living and excessive emotions." Just then Elizabeth—this was during their second summer—coughed.

"The mountain air seems clearly helpful," Clara said nervously. Around the table everyone was suddenly embarrassed. "Our Elizabeth has suffered from bronchitis, and still has a bit of a cough. Summers here seem to help her. Perhaps the winter air is even more beneficial to Nora's friends."

"I was taught that cold and stormy weather was the worst possible thing for the consumptive patient," Dr. Fuller said. "That a warm and sunny climate was essential and that staying in a place like this through the winter was tantamount to suicide. Yet now there are fashionable doctors claiming quite the contrary." Frowning, he turned to Michael and started a conversation about his spaniels.

Another doctor, Jacob Kopeckny, offered a different perspective. Two hemorrhages, less than a month apart, had brought this even-tempered young man to the mountains; a summer at an inn on another lake, where he regained much of his strength, had convinced him to close his practice in Rhode Island and settle in the woods. He'd built a small house near the river, between the village and the lake. Each time Nora passed his porch on her way to the village he called out a greeting to her.

Soon she began to stop so they could talk at more length. He had clear brown eyes, a gray streak in his beard, and a wife at whom he gazed with obvious affection. They'd known each other, he confessed with a laugh one day, since they were ten. When Nora asked him if he felt bitter at having his life and career so disrupted by illness, he shrugged and gestured toward his wife. "This place has its own charms," he said. "And wherever I am, I'm lucky enough to live with the person I've loved since I was a boy. How many people can say that?"

Not many, Nora thought. They spoke so easily together that after a while it seemed natural to welcome him when he asked if he might join her on her rounds. The invalids were delighted to see him, particularly as he charged no fees: he was still too sick himself, he said, to actually practice. He was simply getting acquainted with his fellow sufferers. With Nora's permission he also joined her friends for their occasional gatherings, answering questions and demonstrating his stethoscope. Only Nora had seen one before.

During his second winter in the village, once he'd gotten to know all the women who took in sick boarders, Dr. Kopeckny invited them to visit the room off his kitchen he referred to, somewhat fancifully, as his laboratory. There, after his wife served scones and jam and the women gave him news of the invalids, he said that he had something astonishing to show them.

In Germany, he said, a doctor named Robert Koch had discovered what caused consumption and had proved how it was transmitted. The culprit was a germ, he said. A little plant, although it wasn't green and wasn't shaped like a plant: it was invisible except under a microscope. Inside the lungs these germs made deadly poisons.

One by one the women bent to the eyepiece and peered through the metal tube. A smear of gray mist, the broken fragments of a decaying lung. Between these fragments were brilliant blue rods—so slim, Nora thought. The blue of wild gentian, or iris, or lobelia. Astonishing blue. Nothing like the tattered, dark red bits she'd seen her invalids cough up. The peculiar color, Dr. Kopeckny said, came from the blue dye with which he'd stained them, to make them visible.

That first time, the shock of that first sight: Sophie put on her cloak and left, taking Jane with her. Phoebe, who shuddered and said her flesh was crawling, stayed but withdrew to the kitchen with Mrs. Kopeckny. Nora stared and stared. She'd looked in books over the years, whatever books she'd been lucky enough to find; she'd seen drawings of lungs and stomachs and hearts and she knew how blood and lymph moved through a body, and food and air and water. But this—"Where do you find them?" she asked. "Are they everywhere?"

"In the sputum," Dr. Kopeckny said. "And in the spray a patient coughs out, and inside the airways and the lungs."

"Can you kill them?" Bessie asked.

"Not yet," he said. "But the things you give your patients, rest and good food and clean air, make the body more able to fight off the infection. Sometimes the bacilli can disappear entirely."

"All the bedding I've changed," Olive said quietly. "The laundry I've carried and washed, the dishes I've handled. The handkerchiefs, the nightshirts, all the times I've been coughed at and sneezed at . . ."

She looked at her friends. "It's not that simple," Dr. Kopeckny said. "I didn't show you this to scare you—don't you think you'd already have it, if you were going to get it?"

"Eight years," Bessie said. "Since I took in the first one. Everyone told me it wasn't contagious."

"In a big city almost *everyone* is exposed to the bacillus. But most of them don't get sick, any more than you have."

"That's true," Bessie said. "Not one of us has, nor our families. No one native to the village."

"Then are the bacilli the cause or not?" Nora asked. "How do you know the bacilli aren't just *there* in a person's sputum, the way . . ." She looked at her friends and at her own arm, which she held out. "The way these freckles are here on my skin, but not on Bessie's. They don't mean anything, they don't mean I'm sick or she's not sick. They're just here."

"That," said Dr. Kopeckny approvingly, "is a very good observation."

"Then why do you think the blue plants cause the disease?"

There were experiments, Dr. Kopeckny said, which Koch had done with mice and rats and rabbits. He tried to explain these and then frowned and tapped the microscope. Later, when he acquired a newer, more powerful instrument, he'd give this one to Nora. "Without the germ there's no tuberculosis—no one has found a sick person who didn't carry the bacilli. But you don't always have the disease just because you carry the germ. If you think of the germ as the plant, perhaps we're like the soil. Uncongenial soil and the plant doesn't grow. The plant might be fussy. Or delicate—maybe it dies easily when it's outside the body, and maybe the care you take to keep things clean in your houses is enough to keep it at bay."

The women left his kitchen in a clump, talking furiously among themselves and delegating Nora to learn, as quickly as she could, whatever else Dr. Kopeckny was willing to teach her. As the cold deepened and the snow kept falling, Nora visited his house repeatedly. He talked to her, he thought out loud in her presence, he gave her things to read. Some of the articles startled her. Criminals condemned to death might well be experimented on, one doctor wrote. There is nothing cruel nor revolting about this idea; for a certain period prior to the execution, the criminal should be exposed to the dried sputum of one known to be sick. After execution a careful necropsy would show if tubercles had developed. Thus might useful results be secured.

She stared at the pages, thinking about her days, so long ago, at Grosse Isle. If Dr. Grant hadn't been there, what else might have happened to her? We must be scientific, the paper said. The white plague puts all of us at risk. But meanwhile another doctor claimed that the presence of the bacillus in the sick might be only a harmless concomitant, useful perhaps as a diagnostic sign but in no way a convincing demonstration of the germ theory.

"What does he mean by 'germ theory'?" Nora asked.

"I shouldn't have assumed you knew that," Dr. Kopeckny replied. As simply and swiftly as he could, he told her about Pasteur, in France, who'd proved that all life came from earlier life, and that putrefaction and decay were not spontaneous but were caused by living germs. He'd found germs that fell from the air or lived in the soil, that made wine go bad or killed cows and sheep. Under the microscope Dr. Kopeckny showed Nora the creatures swarming inside spoiled meat and then those that lived in her own saliva: brethren to the brilliantly blue sticks.

For weeks she looked in that eyepiece, always seeing something new. On her way home the world would seem utterly different to her, every surface quivering with a thin secret film. There was life on the leaves and in the rivers, on the food she ate, and on her clothes; it was wonderful, it was horrifying, some days she couldn't eat and she wanted to boil her hands. The world was alive in a way beyond the way she knew. What did that mean?

Nora went back to her friends and together they worked through the implications of what she'd learned. The bacilli come into the lungs, Dr. Kopeckny had said, attached to dust particles in the air. Infected dust might be spread about by the swish of a skirt or a vigorous broom; the worst things they could do were to raise any dust or allow infected material to dry before it was disinfected. Most of their habits still made sense in the light of this new information. They'd never used carpets or curtains in the invalids' rooms; they'd always damp-mopped the floors instead of sweeping, and wiped down the walls and woodwork frequently, simply to keep the rooms tidy and fresh. But now they figured out, together, that the invalids' laundry might best be kept dampened until it could be washed. That scraps of torn paper, used only once, might be better than handkerchiefs, and that the papers should be burned.

For a while, some of the women kept more than their usual distance from their guests. But after the initial fright they relaxed, partly from habit—they'd been doing this work for years, it was hard to think about it differently—and partly because they realized that what Bessie had said was true. Not a single person in the village, not even those who cared directly for the invalids, had ever gotten sick.

To Nora's surprise, it was not people in the village but guests from the cities who first began to shun the sick. The following summer, a wealthy widow objected to sharing a table with Elizabeth, whose cough had grown much worse. She had not paid good money, the widow said, to be in contact with the same germs the filthy immigrants assaulted her with in Boston.

Ned moved the woman to a distant corner of the dining room, and later took Nora aside. People were getting ideas, he said. From articles in the paper, from conversation with doctors. After all the years when people might share a bed with a consumptive family member, sleep in the same room, share dishes and food, suddenly they were being told about invisible, lurking germs that leapt from person to person. It might be better, Ned said, if Elizabeth took her meals separately for a while, and if Nora didn't talk about her work. A few guests, he said, had left simply after hearing what she did in the winter months.

"You didn't tell me that."

"I didn't want to upset you," he said. "But if you could do something about Elizabeth . . ."

"She might have bronchitis," Nora said. "Or hay fever—she coughs more when there's a breeze and when the weather changes. I'm not sure what's wrong with her."

But she brought Elizabeth her meals on a tray for the next few days, unsure how to comfort this frail, unhappy stranger. *Do you think I don't know?* she might have said. *Do you think I haven't seen you looking at Michael?* She'd been lucky enough, herself, to have Francis, if only briefly, and to have her son and her brother. But she thought she knew what it felt like to be the one who always stood outside, watching the others settle in contented pairs. Still she felt trapped when, just before the Vignes were due to go home, Elizabeth looked up at dinner and asked her mother if she could stay in the Adirondacks for the winter.

"Nora would keep an eye on me, I know," Elizabeth said.

"I would not ask her for such a favor," Clara said, avoiding Nora's eyes.

Stubbornly, Elizabeth continued, "It would help me so much, I know it would. I could stay at one of the houses in the village, like the people Nora goes to visit."

"Olive has a free room," Nora said reluctantly. Did Elizabeth think that, if she were around, and Gillian were not, Michael would somehow change his mind? "At least I think it's still free."

"You'll stay here," Ned said firmly, looking not at Elizabeth but at Clara. "No need for you to stay in the village. Our guest rooms aren't warm enough for the winter months but we have room in our own apartment. You'll stay with us."

Nora seldom went alone to the village that winter. Visiting the invalids, or meeting with the women, almost always she had Elizabeth at her side. Together they looked at the three new houses Bessie's cousin had built in the meadow, each now rented to someone who wanted to take in invalid boarders.

"Smart women," Elizabeth said approvingly. "They should do well here."

Nora turned to her with surprise. "You have a head for business?"

"Gillian and my mother do too," Elizabeth said. "How else would we have managed?"

Her strength and energy were surprising, Nora thought, after her frailty during the summer, but week by week she seemed healthier. She helped Nora order new snowshoes for the invalids, listened carefully when Nora gave Olive advice about washing dishes—a rinse in boiling water: all the dishes, every time—and seemed to absorb every word and sight when Nora stopped at Dr. Kopeckny's to ask a question or peer once more into the microscope that soon would become her own.

Elizabeth read what Nora read, she learned what Nora learned. Around the invalids she was clumsy at first but she knew enough to sit back and watch and listen. Soon she began to seem comfortable. Almost, Nora thought, to flirt gently with them. Was she flirting? At the inn, where Elizabeth cramped the family quarters, Nora still sometimes caught her gazing at Michael. Yet her voice at dinner was low and calm and her attention to Ned's stories apparently genuine.

One March day, after they'd found one of Bessie's guests coughing frothy blood, Nora asked Elizabeth how her own health was.

"I'm fine," Elizabeth said. "Don't you know that?"

Nora stopped on the street and stared at her. "I know no such thing," she said. "When you first came here I thought you might be in real trouble. Why else would you—"

"I had bronchitis the winter before our first visit," Elizabeth said. "But nothing worse than that—I pretended I wasn't better so we could get out of the city for the summer. You have no idea how annoying it is to always be under my uncle's thumb."

"You were *faking?*"

"I suppose."

"Then why did you keep coming back?"

Elizabeth rolled her eyes.

Michael, Nora thought. "What did you think would happen this winter?"

"I don't know," Elizabeth said. She bent down and packed a handful of snow into a ball. "It doesn't matter anymore. It's done, it's like I had an abscessed tooth and then I pulled it. Michael and Gillian are perfect for each other, I'm glad for them." Her gaze, Nora saw, was quite steady. "I'm glad I stayed, though," Elizabeth continued. "I like being here. And I like helping you. Can't I stay?"

"I didn't ask you to go."

She watched Elizabeth stretch her arm back over her head, heave the snowball, and then bend and make another. Just the idea made her shoulders ache. Sixty years old, she thought. How did I get to be sixty? Michael no longer needed her, Ned managed perfectly well on his own. If he wasn't working in the shop—he and Michael had an enormous number of commissions that winter—he was scribbling letters to Clara about Michael and Gillian's impending wedding, or sending plans of the cottage he planned to build for the new couple. Next summer, Nora thought, the guests would come and go, the wedding would happen and then be over, Elizabeth would leave with her mother and everyone else. And then there would be, come wintertime, only her and Ned.

There is so much left to me, Nora thought. *So much left that I want to do. How am I to do it?*

Some weeks later she begged Elizabeth for a sputum sample. By then Dr. Kopeckny had tested all the invalids in the village, and found the bacilli in every one. He'd tested Nora, Bessie, Olive, and Jane—the others would not permit him—and found none. He'd found them in himself, although he was presently feeling well. And in his wife, although she had no symptoms and appeared radiantly healthy. He and another doctor who'd recently arrived were making a map of the village, showing every house and listing every person: who had consumption and who did not, which houses took boarders and which had healthy occupants who worked with the sick. Where should he include Elizabeth?

Where you want, Elizabeth said. She refused him and Nora, and refused again. By then she'd become so useful that Nora gave up pressing her. She was not a child, she could not be forced. At the bedside of one of Nora's favorite patients, she stanched a hemorrhage without flinching. How had this girl, Nora thought—this skinny, obdurate, interesting girl—become such a large part of her life?

9

Snow begins to fall as Elizabeth walks back along the river. A light snow, dry and airy, carried by the wind; who could object to this? Exactly this harmless confection decorates the cover of the pamphlet promoting their village as a health resort. Piles of these pamphlets, she knows, lie in faraway libraries and dispensaries, churches and city offices. The message they trumpet resembles William Murray's advice of half a century ago: *Come to the woods and let the pure air cure you!* But the popularity of the pamphlet seems ominous. Orders pour in from Boston and Baltimore, New York and Detroit—who is reading all these copies?

The heads of large companies, Elizabeth thinks. The directors of each city's Board of Health. For the moment, a tubercular patient may still choose whether to stay home or seek treatment at a sanatorium. But now that most general hospitals will no longer admit such patients, and most resorts turn them away; now that phthisiophobia is, in some cities, so prevalent that a coughing and feverish person may be dismissed from his employment or turned out of her lodgings, the insistent pressing of this pamphlet into the hands of the sick means something different than it would have in Nora's day.

As the snow picks up, Elizabeth quickens her pace; it is ten past four. Martin will already be awake, patiently waiting for her—inexcusable to let him fret for a moment over something she can fix. She takes comfort in the knowledge that everything else, despite her absence, will be running smoothly back at the house. The parlor will be warm, the lamps lit, and the center table spread with tea and cakes; she's trained Livvie and Rosellen well, while Andrew knows exactly what to do. Livvie will be pouring tea for some, glasses of frothy rich milk for others. Rosellen will be circulating through the rooms upstairs, bringing milk or eggs to the few who remain in bed. Andrew will be making conversation, concealing his mild irritation that she's failed to join him for their nap. Late afternoons are his favorite time to approach her, when the sun streams through the long windows, over the clean white sheets and mounded pillows—over her, he says, with a certain smile. This part of her marriage, which she feels absurdly lucky to have, and thinks of as secret, is in fact perfectly obvious to everyone who has ever stayed in the house. But even if Andrew plans to reproach her later, for now he'll be tending to the guests. One of them, Corinne, may in her new exuberance and strength have offered to help him.

Last week, while Elizabeth was preparing the grocery order, Corinne ran down the stairs so quickly, calling out so breathlessly, that Elizabeth rose from her desk in alarm: nothing but a hemorrhage usually generated such noise. Corinne cried, "I'm bleeding, I'm bleeding!" but this was triumph, not dismay—she'd not had her monthlies for more than two years, they'd stopped even before she knew she was sick. Almost all the female boarders, as well as Elizabeth herself, are similarly afflicted. But Corinne, after months observing every rule of the cure, has been rewarded.

"It's such a good sign!" she said to Elizabeth. "You know what Dr.

Davis says, he says it is a *splendid* sign for one's monthlies to return, it means my system is restored. . . ."

Elizabeth made a special cake. Corinne proudly blew out the candles and, without embarrassment, told the other boarders what they celebrated. Where else but in this village could such a scene take place? In this village, in this house, which is Elizabeth's place. The minute she slips inside the door, she'll feel like herself again. Her house holds her as a shell holds an egg, giving form and structure to a substance that is worthy in its own right, useful and nourishing, but which would otherwise drain away into nothing.

Again she passes the train station—the coffins have disappeared—and the hotel, the cobbler, the greengrocer, Phoebe's house, where she met Andrew, and Bessie's. How fortunate she has been with her own house. At Gillian's wedding, which was held here, and not in New York, because that was what Gillian wanted, she could not have anticipated any of this.

That day she sat in the dining room of the Northview Inn, a room crowded not with her own relatives but with guides and their families, including all the women she'd gotten to know; with Dr. Kopeckny and his family and his patients; with guests who'd been visiting the inn for years. Gillian had looked beautiful. Nora had looked old. Clara had cried, and clung to Max's arm—Max, who'd arrived not the week before, as he'd promised, not even the night before, but the very morning of the wedding.

Elizabeth watched Michael and Gillian stand side by side, speak words she couldn't hear, turn to face each other. She saw this through a haze of shimmering color, as if it were taking place on a slide, below the lens of Nora's microscope: distant bits of protoplasm darting and flaring and colliding. By then she no longer wanted Michael for herself; already it was hard to remember what she'd seen in him. But as Gillian turned toward him, and as Clara, despite Max's presence, dropped his arm to seize Elizabeth's, Elizabeth felt a baffled sense of failure. If she fit nowhere, if her only work was to keep her mother company . . .

A few weeks after the wedding, pale and quiet and coughing into a handkerchief, Elizabeth convinced Clara that she needed to leave their stuffy house in New York and return to the Adirondacks for the winter. This time the village felt like home as soon as she arrived, and within days she was working side by side with Nora, living among the invalids as one of three boarders in Phoebe's pleasant house. It was there that she met Andrew, who despite being sick was amusing and kind and even-tempered.

On his good days Andrew took her snowshoeing, guiding her along a creek to a frozen waterfall glinting in the sun. They walked, they skated on the lake, they ate picnic lunches on sheltered mountain ledges. When he had a relapse, Elizabeth nursed him; he thanked her with pots of hyacinths he forced after he'd recovered. Ten months after their meeting they married outside, in a grove of white pines on a hill that would, a decade later, be covered with new houses.

By their second summer together—Andrew's health was much improved, but his money was running out—they too began building a house, one ample enough that Elizabeth could take in boarders. A different kind of house, she said, when she approached Nora. A house that would take sicker patients than did the regular boardinghouses, a house in which there'd be a resident nurse: "You'd live here," Elizabeth said. "With us. I'll manage the business end, and do the cooking, and hire whatever other help we need; and you'll supervise the health of the invalids."

Nora's face lit up and her eyes glowed; she seized Elizabeth's hands in both of hers and said, "*Really?*" As if Elizabeth, in offering her hard work and a daily acquaintance with sickness and death, were giving her an enormous present. As if, Elizabeth thinks now, it hadn't been Nora who'd given her everything. For seven years they worked together, building a reputation that extended far beyond the village. For seven years, while Andrew took care of the house itself, they shared the care of the boarders, the surprises of their lives, and, occasionally, their deaths. When Nora finally sickened—"It is my *heart*," she said, with peculiar pleasure. "My *heart*, not tuberculosis"—she chose to spend her last days in her room at the house. Michael and Ned came daily; often Gillian appeared with the children; Andrew spent hours with her. But it was Elizabeth who was with her through the nights.

The disjointed, delicate, fragmentary conversations they held then, a phrase dropped one night, picked up the next, Elizabeth has never repeated, not even to Andrew. During the nights she spent in Nora's room she felt her friend's life sliding through her body. Separate stories, different aspects of her journey lay adjacent one moment, passed through each other and merged the next—a ship filled with fever, a hedge filled with finches, a hospital filled with broken men. The astonishing sight, after so many years, of Ned; or the no less surprising discovery, under Fannie's patient guidance, of her own gift.

During the hours when Nora couldn't talk, Elizabeth told stories of her own. She kept back only this, which still no one but Andrew knows: although she's never let Dr. Kopeckny test her, she's always been sure, despite what she told Nora, that in fact she's mildly tubercular herself. She can feel it, she can read the signs she conceals. She's never worried about catching it from her boarders because she's already infected: an excellent thing, she thinks, it has made her fearless in certain respects, stripped concern for herself from her acts. To be fearless in other respects—to give her heart, as she did with Nora, and has with Martin—is another story. Again and again, she pays for that. Still, there's nothing she'd change. Long ago she decided to keep her house always open to the sick.

Recently she saw, in a magazine read by the invalids, an article about a window tent. The illustration showed a grotesque structure meant to offer, to the poor trapped in city tenements, a version of the out-door life. On a narrow cot, in a shabby room, an anonymous man's legs and lower torso were outlined beneath heavy blankets. Head and shoulders and chest were enclosed in a tent that formed a quarter circle: one edge sealed to the cot, the other clamped, like a lamprey's mouth, to the open window. Fresh air blew in, the caption claimed. And foul air out. In this way, the article noted, the patient may benefit without protruding his cot through the window. Such a sight, viewed by the neighbors, might result in the unfortunate sufferer being obliged to seek other quarters.

That stifling, useless tent, or her own large, airy rooms with their private porches: no choice at all. Had she stayed in the city, had she not met Nora, she might be sleeping in such a tent herself. What difference does it make that she will always be an outsider here? So was Nora, so are half the residents.

For a minute, Elizabeth misses her friend so sharply that she grows dizzy. She stops, she draws a deep breath, she thinks again of the faceless man trapped beneath the window tent and then of Martin, still waiting for her in his room, trusting that she'll replace Mrs. Temple with just the right person and, during the coming weeks, know exactly what he needs at each stage. She bends to the ground, grasps what has caught her eye, and then straightens, slipping the speckled feather between the pages of Ned's crimson book. The poetess died before she finished her work, before she saw it printed; yet the poems exist. Martin, Elizabeth thinks, will take the book and its page marker gladly, knowing it came from both her and Ned. Not knowing that what they'd most like to give him is Nora.

The new nurse, she thinks, should be someone younger. Someone vigorous, warm, and good-humored, who can cheer Martin's last days and counteract her own increasing tendency to worry. Nora grew more relaxed as she aged, gentler, more accepting; she herself is growing fussier, more and more anxious. The tasks that Nora and her friends approached with curiosity, friendship, even joy, have in her, she has thought recently, had a tendency to turn to duties.

Author's Note

Although the main characters and situations in these stories are invented, all grew from a foundation in fact. Among the historical characters in the fringes are William Bartram, Charles Darwin, Henry Godwin-Austen, Asa Gray, Joseph Hooker, James Hutton, Charles Lesueur, William Maclure, William Murray, Robert Owen, Rembrandt Peale, Thomas Say, Johann Scheuchzer, John Cleves Symmes, Godfrey Vigne, and William Wells. Excellent guides, every one.

I'm grateful as well to those who guided me to crucial sources and showed me various wonderful stones and bones: Carol Spawn, Ted Daeschler, and Elana Benamy at the Academy of Natural Sciences in Philadelphia, Gary Mason at the Providence Athenaeum, Martha Kelly and Chris Rozzi at Gutenberg Books in Rochester, and Roderic Long of the Sedgwick Museum at the University of Cambridge; also to Philip Gwyn Jones, who brought me to Cambridge and Wales and shared my pleasure in the fossils, Cecile Pickart, who taught me about ubiquitin, Sarah Stone, who gave me the antique *Manual of Geography* that inspired "Theories of Rain," and my husband, Barry Goldstein, who introduced me to the Adirondack Mountains and helped me over the glaciers of three countries. The Rochester Public Library, the New York Public Library, and the New York Academy of Medicine provided inspiration as well as information.

The errors and infelicities here are mine, but the book would be much less than it is without the wonderfully insightful readings and helpful comments of my editor, Carol Houck Smith, my agent, Wendy Weil, and my friends and readers, Thomas Mallon and—always, essentially— Margot Livesey.

THE FAMILIES

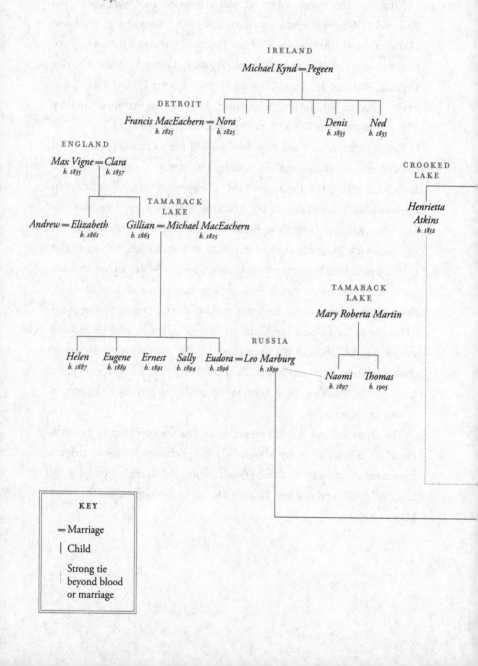

IRELAND

Michael Kynd = *Pegeen*

DETROIT

Francis MacEachern = *Nora*
b. 1825   b. 1825

Denis   *Ned*
b. 1833   b. 1835

ENGLAND

Max Vigne = *Clara*
b. 1835   b. 1837

CROOKED
LAKE

*Henrietta
Atkins*
b. 1852

TAMARACK
LAKE

Andrew = *Elizabeth*   *Gillian* = *Michael MacEachern*
b. 1861   b. 1863   b. 1825

TAMARACK
LAKE

Mary Roberta Martin

RUSSIA

Helen   *Eugene*   *Ernest*   *Sally*   *Eudora* = *Leo Marburg*
b. 1887   b. 1889   b. 1891   b. 1894   b. 1896   b. 1890

Naomi   *Thomas*
b. 1897   b. 1903

KEY

= Marriage

| Child

⋮ Strong tie
beyond blood
or marriage

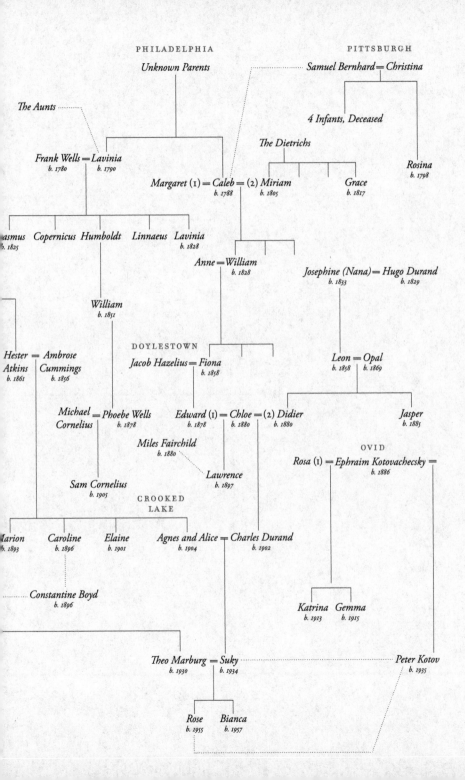

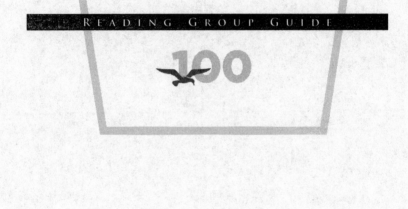

SERVANTS OF
THE MAP

Andrea Barrett

100

SERVANTS OF THE MAP

Andrea Barrett

The six stories gathered in *Servants of the Map* range across time from the beginning of the nineteenth century to the end of the twentieth century, and across space from the western Himalayas to an Adirondack village. Some stories are short while several are novella-length, but all, regardless of size or setting, share Andrea Barrett's characteristic curiosity about science and history, and about the conflicting desires of people drawn to explore the natural world. Although each richly layered tale stands alone, readers who are already fans of Barrett's work will discover subtle links to characters in her last two books, *Ship Fever* and *The Voyage of the Narwhal*.

"As I wrote these," Barrett says, "I was thinking about the physical relics that pass down through families—books, letters, clothing, collections of stones and bones—and also about some other, less palpable links: what is inherited and what is learned, what is hardwired into us and what can be taught. And I was thinking about the *fluidity* of families during the eighteenth and nineteenth centuries, when disaster was a part of daily life and parents routinely lost their young children, even as children were routinely orphaned.

"So many people were handed over to the care of relatives and friends, to grow up in the homes of those not their natural parents. It's hard not to be curious about both the enormous kindness that implies, and the potential difficulties. Or not to wonder if this isn't one of those places where science intersects with personal history. A child wondering, 'How do I know who I am?' may later wonder, 'How do we know anything we know?'—that passionate curiosity about identity becoming the seed of scientific inquiry.

"The truth is that, like an overprotective parent, I have a lot of trouble letting go of characters after I've created them—their lives seem to continue without me long after I've sent the books out into the world. What started these new stories was the continuing evolution, in my imagination, of Rose and Bianca Marburg, who first appeared in 'The Marburg Sisters' in *Ship Fever*. No sooner had that book been published than the sisters were clamoring for more stories: from that impulse grew 'The Mysteries of Ubiquitin' and 'The Forest.'

"While writing 'The Mysteries of Ubiquitin' I became aware of Max Vigne, whose letters Suky Marburg had hoarded without fully understanding how they'd come to her. As Max's life unfolded in 'Servants of the Map,' the oddest thing happened: it was as if Max, walking out of some other realm and toward me, had left the door open behind him. Beyond the door lay the history of *all* the ancestors of the Marburg sisters, however distant they might be in time or space or even blood relationship.

"As the new stories emerged, I began to see a family tree that not only tied together these characters, but also revealed their relationships to characters from *Ship Fever* and *The Voyage of the Narwhal*. Through the Marburg sisters I found the story of the young Lavinia Wells (from 'Theories of Rain'), who had existed in *The Voyage of the Narwhal* only as Erasmus's dead mother. Lavinia led me to her lost brother, Caleb Bernhard (from 'Two Rivers'). Similarly, once I realized that Ned Kynd, who appeared very briefly as a boy in *Ship Fever*, and then turned up as a crucial minor character in *The Voyage of the Narwhal*, was the person to who Erasmus had entrusted the relics of his mother, and through whom these had passed down to the Marburg family, it became possible to imagine the story called 'The Cure.'

"Finally I could see what had happened to Nora Kynd as a result of the early experiences that lie at the heart of 'Ship Fever'; finally I could see how, through one of her granddaughters, she was connected to the Marburg family. That she also turned out to be intimately involved in the life of Elizabeth Vigne, Max's eldest daughter—well, who can account for these things? They are a mystery even to me, even after all these years.

"The truth is that you don't need to know any of this for the stories to make sense—they exist on their own, and none depend in a factual way on each other or on the preceding books. But the stories' internal relationships were for me the central inspiration.

I wrote them beneath a big sheet of white paper tacked to the wall above my desk: a physical representation of that family tree, which still continues to grow.

DISCUSSION QUESTIONS

1. Letters—from Clara to Max and Max to Clara; from Max to his brother and to Dr. Joseph Hooker—are at the center of "Servants of the Map." Of these, perhaps, the most unusual are the ones Clara writes to Max before he even leaves home. She's addressing these in a sense, to a Max who doesn't yet exist, living a life that exists only in her imagination, and in the future. What does this say to you about Clara? How do you think emails and texting—which are instantaneous, and encourage impulsive comments—have changed the relationship of people who might formerly have sustained an important relationship primarily by letters? Consider the difference between Max and Clara Vigne's experience, and that of the climber recently lost on Mt. Everest, who was able to reach his wife in America by cellphone during his last minutes.

2. In "The Forest," sections of the story alternate between the points of view of Bianca and of Krzysztof Wojciechowicz. How does this influence your perception of their developing relationship? How do they view each other at the beginning of the story, and at the end? Who's been changed more by their time together?

3. How would you characterize the relationship, in "Theories of Rain," between Lavinia and the aged botanist William Bartram? What does he see in her when she is playing with his crow? Do you think his tacit approval of her helps make possible the question Frank asks at the end of the story? And what about her answer—has her passionate scientific curiosity helped her see Frank's actual strengths, in contrast to her fantasies of James?

4. "Two Rivers" opens with a letter from Miriam, writing in 1853 to Stuart, her "dead husband's dearest friend." You might expect, then, that the story would be largely about Miriam at this point in her life, or about her relationship with Stuart— but in fact, after that opening section, the story is concerned primarily with Caleb Bernhard's early years. Only midway through the story does his life intersect with Miriam and her younger sister, Grace—and only at the end does the story return to middle-aged and now-widowed Miriam. Why do you think the author might have chosen to keep shifting the perspective of the story in this fashion, and to keep you guessing—until the end—about the story's "real" center? What is conveyed about how, in our own lives, our perspective shifts as to what the "real" or "important" events of our lives have turned out to be?

5. When did you realize that Caleb Bernhard's lost sister was the Lavinia of "Theories of Rain"? In light of this, how do you think Caleb's longing for Lavinia colors his feelings for Grace? Miriam, so devoted to Grace, might seem to some people to have sacrificed her own desires on behalf of her sister; what do you think her married years with Caleb were like?

6. In "The Mysteries of Ubiquitin," Rose is upset when Peter explains, at a dinner party, that her research into ubiquitin and his on beetles, is similar in that "both break large dead things into smaller bits, so new things can be made" (p. 190). Why do you think she finds this analogy between their work upsetting? What does this suggest about her memory of her mother, and about the way it may be shifting under the influence of Peter?

7. Elizabeth Vigne, one of the two central characters in "The Cure," chooses to stay in the Adirondacks after a youth disrupted by her father's travels and adventures. Why do you think she felt so drawn to Nora, and to Nora's work, that she would establish a boarding house for people with disabilities (who, in the nineteenth and twentieth centuries, were commonly referred to as invalids)? What role do you think Andrew played in her decision to do that, and how do you think he comforts and supports her?

8. If you're familiar with "Ship Fever," then you might remember Nora Kynd, who appeared in that novella as a young woman, newly emigrated from Ireland and desperately ill at the quarantine station on Grosse isle. What is it like to encounter this character again, later in her life? Were you satisfied with the way the rest of her life unfolded?

9. Story collections are always ordered intentionally, with the hope of evoking, by rhythm and contrast, certain responses in a reader. That's especially true for a collection like *Servants of the Map*, in which the stories are linked to one another and speak to one another. Why do you think the stories are presented in this particular order?

Meghan Kenny	*The Driest Season*
Nicole Krauss	*The History of Love*
Don Lee	*The Collective*
Amy Liptrot	*The Outrun: A Memoir*
Donna M. Lucey	*Sargent's Women*
Bernard MacLaverty	*Midwinter Break*
Maaza Mengiste	*Beneath the Lion's Gaze*
Claire Messud	*The Burning Girl*
	When the World Was Steady
Liz Moore	*Heft*
	The Unseen World
Neel Mukherjee	*The Lives of Others*
	A State of Freedom
Janice P. Nimura	*Daughters of the Samurai*
Rachel Pearson	*No Apparent Distress*
Richard Powers	*Orfeo*
Kirstin Valdez Quade	*Night at the Fiestas*
Jean Rhys	*Wide Sargasso Sea*
Mary Roach	*Packing for Mars*
Somini Sengupta	*The End of Karma*
Akhil Sharma	*Family Life*
	A Life of Adventure and Delight
Joan Silber	*Fools*
Johanna Skibsrud	*Quartet for the End of Time*
Mark Slouka	*Brewster*
Kate Southwood	*Evensong*
Manil Suri	*The City of Devi*
	The Age of Shiva
Madeleine Thien	*Do Not Say We Have Nothing*
	Dogs at the Perimeter
Vu Tran	*Dragonfish*
Rose Tremain	*The American Lover*
	The Gustav Sonata
Brady Udall	*The Lonely Polygamist*
Brad Watson	*Miss Jane*
Constance Fenimore Woolson	*Miss Grief and Other Stories*

Don't miss other titles by National Book Award–winning author

ANDREA BARRETT

ANDREA-BARRETT.COM

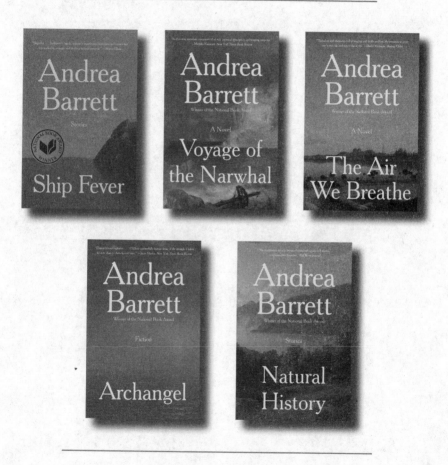